# Wonderful Weddings and Deadly Divorces

Patricia Fisher Mystery Adventures

Book 10

Steve Higgs

Text Copyright © 2021 Steven J Higgs

Publisher: Steve Higgs

The right of Steve Higgs to be identified as author of the Work has been asserted by him in accordance with the Copyright, Designs and Patents Act 1988

All rights reserved.

The book is copyright material and must not be copied, reproduced, transferred, distributed, leased, licensed or publicly performed or used in any way except as specifically permitted in writing by the publishers, as allowed under the terms and conditions under which it was purchased or as strictly permitted by applicable copyright law. Any unauthorised distribution or use of this text may be a direct infringement of the author's and publisher's rights and those responsible may be liable in law accordingly.

'Wonderful Weddings and Deadly Divorces' is a work of fiction. Names, characters, businesses, organisations, places, events and incidents either are the product of the author's imagination or are used fictitiously. Any resemblance to actual persons, living or dead, events or locations is entirely coincidental.

**Dedication**

To Stephen Halstead

A champion among men who bravely struck out on a quest to buy a Bakewell pudding.

And by George he succeeded!

Table of Contents:

- Rehearsal Dinner Revenge – A Felicity Philips Investigates short story
- The Poisoned Chef
- My Family and Other Animals
- Steadying the Ship
- Wrong Fungus
- Private Investigator
- Chief Inspector Quinn
- Mrs Howard-Box
- Situation Saved
- Imposter
- Extreme Parkour
- Not Patricia Fisher
- Worrying Clues
- Reason to Kill
- Enter the Real Sleuth
- Author's notes
- My Curious Streak
- Fair Warning
- Inadvertent Eavesdropping
- Missing Persons
- After Midnight Excursion
- M.I.L.F.
- The Cake
- Back on Track
- Collision Course
- First Body of the Weekend

Not as Dead as I Thought

The Body in the Bog

Charlie

The Ex-Girlfriend

Sasha's Lies

Footprints in the Mud

BFF Barnstormer

Dire Panic

The Door to Nowhere

What's in Bobbie's Closet?

Coercing Vince

Assembling the Pieces

In the Library with a Knife

Surprises

Getting Married

Concerned Friends

Getting Divorced

Gin and Tonic

Author's notes

What's next for Patricia Fisher?

A FREE Rex and Albert Story

More Cozy Mystery by Steve Higgs

More Books by Steve Higgs

Free Books and More

Rehearsal Dinner Revenge – A Felicity Philips Investigates short story

## The Poisoned Chef

'What do you mean Chef Olafson has been poisoned?' I had to ask Bridgette to repeat her statement because it defied belief.

A few feet away, a pair of ears overheard what she said. The mouth they were connected to gasped in horror. *'Not Chef Olafson! He was the best.'*

Ignoring the comment, I focused on my phone conversation. 'Just that,' replied Bridgette, Chef Olafson's sous chef and second in command. 'There's an ambulance on its way here now. He's in ever so much pain, he says. Stomach cramps and the like. He thinks it might be the mushrooms.'

Her statement made my heart thump in my chest. I knew how deadly some mushrooms could be. 'Is he going to be all right?' I asked cautiously, though why I thought Bridgette might be able to answer my question, I had no idea.

'I don't know,' she wailed.

'Did anyone else eat them?' I wanted to know. I'd been working alongside Chef Olafson for nearly a decade and I considered him to be a close friend. He came to my husband, Archie's, funeral and was one of the people I looked to for support in those dark days. That he could die by his own hand, eating poisonous mushrooms that he prepared, was unthinkable.

Bridgette stammered, 'No, I don't think so.'

The news was a relief if only a small one. 'Can you continue?' I asked. The wedding of the year was tomorrow with the wedding party holding a rehearsal supper this evening at Loxton Hall. They expected dinner for a hundred at eight o'clock this evening. That gave me three hours and it was already clear the first course was off. There were many things I needed to do quickly, and one of those was to steady the boat.

I heard a huff of breath from the other end of the phone – Bridgette, now in charge of the kitchen, was going to have to rally the troops and get the job done without their leader.

Sensing a wavering will, I said, 'You can do this, Bridgette. Chef Olafson knew that. It's why he asked you to be his sous chef.'

'Yes, but I've never led the kitchen before. Not for a full banquet. I've only ever ...'

I cut her off. 'You can do this, Bridgette. I am leaving now, okay? I will be there in half an hour and I'll have the caterer meet me at the venue. The mushrooms can be replaced. Just get everyone back to what they should be doing. That is what Chef would want. Am I right?'

Somewhat reluctantly, Bridgette said, 'I guess.'

The soft beeping noise of an incoming call sounded in my ear. I lifted the phone away from my head to see the screen, but I already knew who it was going to be and thus it came as no surprise when I saw my client's name displayed.

'I have to go,' I told Bridgette. 'I have Mrs Howard-Box waiting.'

The voice at the other end snorted a laugh; the message clear – rather you than me. At least Bridgette could see that things could always get worse.

With one call ended and a swirl of thoughts spinning around my head, I took a breath and answered the call waiting. 'Mrs Howard-Box, I assume you are calling about my chef.'

'Your chef?' snapped Angelica Howard-Box. 'Your chef? I should think that he was my chef given the price I am paying, wouldn't you?'

'He is … was in my employment, Mrs Howard-Box. I've no wish to split hairs though.' Actually, I wanted to point out that she wasn't paying. Her millionaire footballer son was picking up the tab.

I thought I might be able to start a conversation with her and foolishly expected that she might be reasonable. Apparently, though, my client had done quite enough listening already. 'Well, I want a new one,' she snapped. 'I want a new one right now, do you hear? What good is hiring the best wedding planner in the county if your chef up and drops dead before he can serve the first course at the rehearsal dinner the night before the ceremony, eh? What good is that? The next one had better be in rude health.'

Feeling my knuckles tighten on my phone, I did my best to defuse my client without resorting to saying what I thought. 'Chef Olafson is not dead, Mrs Howard-Box, he is merely feeling unwell. His team are experienced and professional. There is no reason to believe any interruption to your plans might arise. Please rest assured, my highest priority at this time is to make sure the wedding goes ahead without any hiccups. My Master of Ceremonies, Justin Cutler, is at Loxton Hall. You have nothing to worry about. Please give this matter no further thought.'

There was silence coming from the other end as Angelica tried to work out if she had just been spoken back to or not. In the end, she settled on, 'Yes, well, just make sure there are no further chefs dropping dead. That's not what I am paying for.'

The call ended, leaving me wondering if this particular contract had been worth taking. Sure, it was going to be in all the glossy magazines, a young rising star Premier League footballer marrying a sweetheart internet star. However, though they were picking up the bill, the planning, all the meetings, and the individual arrangements had been left to the mother of the groom.

Mrs Angelica Howard-Box was something else.

I am already at the top of my game and in constant demand by the county's richest and most famous. I could ... in retrospect, should have turned Mrs Howard-Box down when I first met her, but despite the client's loathsomeness, the bride and groom were lovely and my name in all the top magazines would help me in my bid to get the most coveted ticket – the anticipated royal wedding.

The young prince, now twelfth in line to the throne was never going to be King, and unlike his elder brothers, he was rarely in the limelight. However, he'd been dating his girlfriend, a successful lawyer, for two years and I had it on good authority he had recently purchased a rather expensive diamond solitaire ring.

When I say good authority, I mean directly from the mouth of the jeweller who sold it. I've made some friends along the way. A few enemies too, unfortunately. Anyway, getting my name in all the glossy magazines just when a certain member of the royal household might be thinking about tying the knot was a deliberate move on my part. If I had to smile and tolerate the ignorant, infuriating Mrs Howard-Box, then so be it.

With a huff of breath, I pushed myself up and onto my feet, placed my still warm but empty coffee cup into the dishwasher and went to the front door. I always stay at the venue for any of my weddings. I visit beforehand to make sure everything is right and to discuss my needs for the event with venue management. Then my team arrive two days in advance to get things ready and I make sure to be there the day before the event itself. It was precautionary more than it was necessary – Justin Cutler ran the event and chivvied the staff here and there as required. I operated in the background and did not need to attend, but I found myself nervous and fretting if I were anywhere else. Staying at the venue, I was better placed to react to any minor issue that might arise.

Like the chef poisoning himself the afternoon before the big day.

My bags were already in the car where I loaded them earlier. I needed only my handbag and a coat before leaving the house. Plus Buster, of course.

Buster is a pedigree English Bulldog. He looks a lot like an overstuffed footstool with a head at one end and an odd little stump of a tail at the other. His coat is a milky white and tan brown, like a chestnut in September fresh from its spiky outer case. The canines of his lower jaw protrude out at an angle to give him a fearsome face, though he is as gentle as a lamb, unless you happen to be a sock or a cushion. Hmmm, or a pair of my knickers accidentally dropped on the carpet next to the laundry hamper, or the mail, or ... Buster likes to chew things. I'll leave it at that.

When my Archie died three years ago, I was lost. Feeling like I was folding in on myself, I went to the local RSPCA home hoping to find a pet that would fill the bottomless hole in my heart. Unable to decide between getting a cat or a dog, I ended up with both. Amber, a drop-dead-gorgeous ragdoll cat with blue eyes like backlit sapphires, and a puppy called Buster.

Buster had been abandoned on Upnor beach and was shivering and alone when he was found by a pair of canoeists heading for the water. He was roughly twelve weeks old at the time. With the puppy under one arm and Amber in a crate with a handle on top hanging from my other hand, I returned home from the RSPCA centre and gave them all my love.

Unfortunately, that was where the problems started. I'll explain what I mean by that shortly.

Amber, being a cat, could stay at the house while I was away. She had a cat flap and a machine that dispensed food on a timer. Like all cats, she was entirely self-sufficient. I tried the same machine with Buster once.

Only once.

He reduced the machine to a mangled mess and ate the entire supply of food inside. I was only gone for four hours.

Waving goodbye to Amber, and getting a flick of disinterested tail in response, I secured Buster on the passenger seat of my Mercedes SL convertible sports car and hit the road. I didn't need satellite navigation – I knew where I was going.

From the car, I used the voice-activated phone to call my caterer. I call Chef Olafson my chef and refer to the caterer as my caterer, but they are nothing of the sort. I prefer not to employ too many people. It causes all manner of additional work with the taxman and I would have to manage holidays and sick pay and such. Almost everyone I work with is a contractor. They run their own businesses and I pull them together to create a singular total wedding offering. Everything from the wedding car to the cake, through hair and makeup, outfits for the groomsmen, photography, venue ... well, I'm sure you get the picture.

The point is, they all do very well out of me, and the caterer was going to have to jump through some hoops if the mushrooms he'd supplied were indeed poisonous.

'Felicity,' boomed a deep voice over the speaker system in my car. 'My favourite customer. You have the Howard-Box wedding this weekend. Calling to get more champagne?'

'You supplied me with poisonous mushrooms,' I got straight to the point.

Met by silence from the other end, I thought I was going to have to confirm if he'd heard me when he asked, 'Is anyone dead?'

It struck me as an odd question to ask and his relief was clear when I said, 'No. Well, not yet anyway. Has this happened before?'

'Goodness, no, Felicity. Heaven forbid. I'm just checking your order now.' There was a pause before he spoke again. 'Twelve boxes of chanterelles. I cannot see how the mushrooms can be the wrong kind. We buy them from a speciality grower; the same one I have used for years.'

'Well, Chef Olafson is on his way to hospital with severe stomach cramps and he thinks it's the mushrooms.' Again, my heart thumped with worry for my friend.

The caterer, a short, rotund man called Barry Bateman wasn't bothering to bluff me or hide his own concern. 'I'll have someone there to collect the mushrooms within the hour, Felicity. You can count on that.'

'Good enough,' I replied. We exchanged a few words about Chef Olafson, and I ended the call.

## My Family and Other Animals

You probably worked out already that my name is Felicity. My last name is Philips. I'm fifty-five years old, widowed ... well, that's about it really. That's how I tend to think of myself anyway. I was happily married and then the disease came along and suddenly Archie wasn't there. The space on the other side of the bed still feels empty three years later.

If you want a better description, I can tell you that I have naturally wavy jet-black hair from Italian heritage way back in my family's past. I'm five feet and five inches tall and as a child had high hopes to be a ballerina. I am what some might call stick thin, though I don't see myself that way and I am heavier now than I have ever been in my life. I'm a size four though, so I guess when compared to the national average, I am classed as petite.

I never let being smaller than average hold me back in life. When the ballerina thing didn't pan out, I went into catering, working in a kitchen for someone else until I realised what a drag that was. In a moment of clarity, a chance conversation got me my first shot at organising a wedding.

A woman I knew through a friend was getting married – a cheap affair with few frills – and she was looking for someone cost sensitive to do the catering. It wasn't much more than sandwiches and cakes, but when I met her, we got talking and before I knew it, I was volunteering to organise the whole event.

It wasn't big and sumptuous, but I earned more from that small wedding than I had the previous month working for someone else and ... well, I never looked back.

The memory of that first wedding three decades ago and the phone call I received from the bride just last weekend, played through my head as I approached Loxton Hall. Patricia Fisher, a name I remembered but had not heard spoken aloud until earlier this year when she was suddenly all over the news, called me out of the blue and begged for my help.

How could I even entertain the idea of saying no?

Obviously I didn't, and now I had the biggest wedding of the year to manage this weekend plus a small, yet elegant affair on the side.

From the seat next to me, where he sat with a seat belt around his belly, Buster said, '*Are we nearly there yet*?'

I suppose I need to explain about the dog as well, don't I?

The talking to animals thing started when I was very small. Small enough, in fact, that I cannot remember a time when I didn't do it. Of course, as a child I thought it was normal and natural and could not understand why my parents thought my antics were funny. Only when I got bigger and continued to do it while claiming adamantly that I could hear what the family dog and two cats were saying, did I begin to worry them.

My elder sister, Ginny, was cruel about it. Always trying to score points and calling me a weirdo. Ginny made out like I pretended to talk to the family pets because I had no friends. It wasn't true, but it was intended to be hurtful and so it hurt.

Angry that no one believed me, I got the dog to listen to conversations my parents had while I was in bed or at school, and then relayed them to my horrified mother and father later. In hindsight, regaling them with the one about whether mummy was a naughty girl who needed a good spanking, probably tipped the balance. It got me a trip to a special doctor who asked me lots of questions.

He even brought a cat into one of the sessions to see if I could talk to it. He wanted me to get it to do something it would not normally do, because that would help me to demonstrate that my claims were not just fanciful lies. I couldn't, of course, that being the point, but my tearful insistence that it was because I only heard the voices of the pets in our house, and only they responded to my words, got me nowhere.

Basically, even my parents thought I was nuts, and my attempts to prove that I was not backfired because unable to make me stop *pretending*, mum and dad took more drastic action and got rid of the dog and both cats while I was at school one day.

I cried for a week.

By and by, I forgot about my special ability and it faded to become an almost memory - something I half remembered like a dream but could not be sure had ever been real. Maybe I was just making it up like they all said. No other animals ever talked to me, just those three I lived with when I was little.

Then, about a week after getting Buster, the dog cocked his head to one side and clear as anything, a voice appeared in my head. 'Biscuit?'

I dropped my coffee cup and fainted on the spot.

When I came around, the dog was licking my face while saying, 'Wake up, wake up, wake up,' over and over again.

Fighting to get the dog away though he had done a good job of cleaning my teeth, I sat up to find the cat looking at me with barely concealed contempt. *'Humans are so weird,'* she said, with an annoyed twitch of her tail.

Despite the coffee staining my white jeans where I rolled in the puddle the broken cup created, I levered myself off the floor and onto a breakfast bar stool where a three-way conversation ensued. Whatever was broken in my head, it allowed me to hear what the animals were thinking, and they could understand me when I spoke.

Three years on, I still couldn't decide if it was a curse or a gift, but I had found a few uses for it.

To answer Buster's question, I said, 'Yes, Buster. We are nearly there.'

He licked his nose, a habit that sounded like an octopus eating a banana. *'When you say nearly there, is that like really nearly? Or the kind of nearly that requires me to go back to sleep for an hour first?'*

'The first one,' I promised him.

He licked his nose again and shifted in his seat. *'Good because I need to go.'*

My foot applied a tad more pressure to the accelerator.

*'You might want to open a window,'* he volunteered.

I needed no further warning, but was ill-prepared for the drastic change in temperature the chilly late autumn air delivered.

It was dark out and already bordering on being evening rather than afternoon. As such, and aided by clear skies, the temperature was plummeting. As if to accentuate my thoughts, a gritting truck went by on the other side of the road, showering my car in bits of grit, several of which came through my open window.

I shut it again and held my breath.

'*Are we going on an adventure?*' Buster asked, sitting up to look out the window.

I hitched an eyebrow. 'I'm not sure what you are asking.'

'*Like are we just going for a drive to a park, or do we have to fight people when we get wherever we are going?*'

'Fight people? Why would we have to fight people?' My forehead had creased in confusion.

'*I'm an adventurous sort,*' Buster bragged. '*I get into scrapes because of my naturally inquisitive nature and my need to test the boundaries of my canine limitations. Also, I feel that fighting crime falls within my remit.*'

Shaking my head in amused surprise, I said, 'You get into scrapes because you chase squirrels, and they gang up on you.'

'*I might need a cape,*' he murmured as if he hadn't heard me. I didn't think a reply was required. Silence ruled for a few minutes until he said, '*I love these trips away.*'

Still holding my breath, I gave him a tight-lipped smile.

'*Just you and me without that horrible cat.*'

Getting both pets at the same time from the same place, I'd foolishly told myself they would get on. They didn't. I think Amber gave the dog a small amount of leeway when he was still a small puppy, but long before he was fully grown, she was playing tricks on him.

In her opinion, he was one step above horse manure. That Buster thought horse manure was a nutritious snack didn't help matters.

He got his own back by eating her food, eating her bed, eating her cat toys, and sometimes attempting to eat her.

Conversationally, Buster asked, *'Do you think she would be happier living elsewhere?'*

'Like where?' I enquired as I flicked my indicator on.

Buster considered his options. *'City dump? Or the beach,'* he suggested. *'Not one nearby, obviously. We wouldn't want her finding her way back. Stick her in the back of a van heading overseas, that could work, or maybe just chuck her into a burning building.'*

Shaking my head, I said, 'Buster you seem to forget that I quite like Amber. She is a nice cat.'

*'She's pure evil and has brainwashed you into believing you are safe to be around her. That cat will bring a plague upon our house.'*

I turned the steering wheel, taking the car off the road and up the driveway toward Loxton Hall, which filled the horizon from side to side ahead of me.

'A plague of what?' I wanted to hear, entertained by the dog's desperate need to be rid of his feline housemate.

I got a quizzical look in response. *'Of cat, obviously. You only need one cat to have a plague. We are already infested.'* He fell silent for a moment before repeating, *'I really need to go.'*

'Less than a minute,' I reassured him.

I was wrong though, for the next thing I knew we joined a queue of cars. The police were checking everyone in and out. There had been a number of threats against the bride – she was rich and famous and thus attracted nutters – and I could see they were being cautious.

I suggested Loxton Hall to Mrs Howard-Box because I know it has a solid wall going all the way around it. That wouldn't keep a person out for long, but it made access harder and gave security a defined perimeter to patrol and control. It's surprising the things a person picks up as a wedding planner.

I'd spotted tents along the grass verge on the way in but only now did it occur to me they must belong to fans hoping to catch a glimpse of the two stars. The bride is vastly more famous than the groom when looked at from a global perspective, but a premiership footballer is next to God in some circles in England.

The identification check held me up for only a couple of minutes, but it was long enough for Buster to start whining his discomfort.

Pulling the car into a parking space, the first person I saw, or rather, the first person to see my car heading up the long winding driveway and make a beeline to head me off, was my young assistant/wedding planner in training, Mindy. At nineteen, Mindy has neither the patience, the mindset, the education, nor the interest to be a wedding planner, but she is my niece and my big sister, Ginny, guilted me into giving Mindy a job.

Now I was stuck with her.

'*Mindy!*' barked Buster, catching sight of her as I pulled to a stop on the gravel. He was always glad to see anyone he knew, and anyone he thought might have food for him. Mindy generally fell into both categories.

'Aunt Flicka!' Mindy started, excitement bubbling over before I could even get my car door open. I held up a finger to cut my young charge off.

'We are working, Mindy. You need to address me as Mrs Philips. We have been over this before, several times …' Whatever I had planned to say next got lost as I stared open-mouthed at my niece's outfit.

'Yes, Auntie,' Mindy replied, nodding her head vigorously in agreement and understanding while failing to actually comply.

'*Let me out, let me out, let me out!*' resounded in my head because I was yet to open Buster's door.

From the corner of my eye, I could see Buster trying to work the inner door handle with one stumpy front paw. With my jaw still hanging slack, I let him out.

'*Yay!*' barked Buster, instantly climbing Mindy's left leg.

Forcing myself to take a breath, I asked, 'Mindy, what are you wearing?'

Mindy looked down at her outfit. 'Working clothes, Aunt Fl … I mean Mrs Philips.'

My eyes flared wide. 'Working where?' Mindy wore a lot of black in general and that was especially true today. Her hair was naturally blonde, but had a bubblegum pink dye through most of it, which was then lowlighted with black underneath and cut so half an inch of the black hung below the pink. Some days she would pull it into bunches like she was five years old, but today it hung loose. The hair wasn't great, but I could live with it. It was the clothes that were making my left eye twitch.

Though it could be described as leggings and a stretchy top, such a description would be stretching things a little too far. Each garment was tight to Mindy's gymnast figure and looked to be made from the kind of fabric that would stop a bullet. It was combat clothing crossed with gym gear. The top had a hood that came around the front as well to gather under her chin. It was more snood than hood and reminded me of clothing worn in the sort of films Archie liked to watch where there would be black-clad ninja's leaping from roof to roof.

'They are easy to move in, Mrs Philips,' Mindy supplied dutifully. 'I've been getting a lot done, just as you suggested, mixing in with all the different people to learn something of everything. Justin has had me flower arranging, and passing things to the hairdressers and makeup girls. I say girls, but there's one boy working with them called James and he is ever so pretty. Do you think he might be gay?'

It was another trait of my niece that she was easily distracted. By herself as often as not. There would be a time to address the many and varied issues I had with my niece's outfit, but now was not it. I needed to find Bridgette in the kitchen and make sure we were on course for dinner at eight.

'Ah, Mrs Philips,' said a voice from my left. 'Your room is ready. Can I have your things taken up?'

The speaker was the venue undermanager, Kevin Falstaff. He had a large hook nose and almost no chin. Combined with a hairline that beat a hasty retreat many years ago, it made him look very upper class.

I stepped forward to shake the man's hand. 'Thank you, Kevin. Yes, please. I'm really rather keen to get to the kitchen though. I'm sure you are aware my chef has been taken ill.'

He nodded his head just once. 'Yes, Mrs Philips. I heard that he was poisoned. Your event manager, Mr Cutler was good enough to inform us before the ambulance arrived.'

That sounded like Justin. I used to be the one running the event, micromanaging the staff, and coordinating every step of each element on the wedding day. Not long after hiring Justin to assist me, I discovered he was better at it than I was. Not only that, leaving him to get on with it allowed me to move in the background, heading off minor issues before they arose.

'What shall I do?' asked Mindy.

Kevin was already walking, leading me where I wanted to go. Following on behind, I checked on Buster. He gave me a face that required no translation.

'Can you take Buster for a walk, please?'

Mindy curled her lip in disgust, 'What if Buster goes number two?'

'There are baggies in a holder on his lead,' I pointed out.

The lip curled back a little further. 'Ewww.'

Leaving her to it as a pair of porters came for my bags, I followed the venue undermanager into Loxton Hall.

Normally upon arrival, I would enter the same way I expected the bridal party and guests would. Doing so always gave me the opportunity to see what they would see. Not so today, for I was too keen to get to the kitchen.

'I'll take you straight there, Mrs Philips,' said Kevin, leading me through a side door and along winding passages. This was my twenty-third wedding at Loxton Hall, making it my third most frequented venue, but I could still easily get lost in the back rooms.

Loxton Hall was originally built for Viscount Loxton in 1783. A member of the peerage, his family made their money in tobacco brought back from America. Later, family heads proved to be less astute businessmen, and the house was sold in the mid-twentieth century, changing hands twice before falling to a billionaire property baron who specialised in creating wedding venues for which he could charge the Earth.

Possessing more than one hundred rooms and surrounded on all sides by lush gardens, it had been adapted to allow multiple functions simultaneously. There were also multiple kitchens, because there is no quicker way to create a war than to have two chefs battling for the same space and facilities.

Kevin escorted me to the kitchen, where I could see Chef Olafson's team working.

'If you please, Mrs Philips, I really must get back. I have a surprising number of trivial matters to which I must attend, not least of which is a chef with a stolen uniform.'

With his excuses made, he departed, leaving me to find out what trivial problems I might need to address.

## Steadying the Ship

Coming into the kitchen no one spotted me, and I kept quiet, watching the dynamic interplay as chefs literally ran from point to point. Chef Olafson ran an efficient kitchen that operated as a close-knit team. No one ever shouted at anyone but in just a few seconds, I heard curse words and insults when two chefs reached for the same knife, and Chef Olafson's usual number two growled a warning about something burning.

It was time to steady the ship, a phrase I'd employed in my head many times since hearing the news about Chef Olafson.

'Everyone,' I called, raising my voice so it would be heard. At five feet five inches, I was the shortest person in the room, but my voice ruled, nevertheless. Heads turned my way, faces bobbing up or down to peer around obstacles to see who was shouting. 'Everyone, please stop what you are doing, kill the flames under your pans, and gather around.'

No one grumbled but there were a few questioning comments as the chefs in their white tunics complied.

The sous chef, Bridgette, Chef Olafson's immediate next in charge came rushing forward. 'Mrs Philips. Oh, goodness it's so good to see you.' Then she burst into tears.

Bridgette Young was a very English, white skinned, pear-shape bottomed woman in her early thirties. All the chefs, faces I recognised from working with them over several years, came to gather around where I stood now hugging her.

The sous chef's body was shaking as sobs escaped her. At nearly six foot and a good deal broader than me, I felt swamped, but held on to provide a much-needed shoulder to cry on. In the absence of their leader, Bridgette had rallied the troops and battled on with the task of getting ready for the evening meal. They had a hundred guests to serve at the rehearsal dinner, a very American practice which I was only too happy to adopt when clients began asking for it a decade ago. It meant I got to charge almost twice as much for a wedding – good for everyone on the team.

Looking around Bridgette's arm, I spotted one of the older chefs, a man called Winston Teach. Of him, I asked, 'Where is Chef Olafson now?'

'He went in the ambulance about forty minutes ago, Mrs Philips,' he replied with a shrug.

Bridgette, hearing the question and answer, gathered herself and pushed her frame back to upright. 'Carmel found him,' she murmured between snivels. Taking a break to blow her nose, she said, 'He was in the larder, curled into a ball and moaning.' The larder she referred to would be the refrigerated one Chef Olafson's team travelled with.

'He was sure it was the mushrooms?' I asked. Then cautiously, 'Does anyone know what they are?'

'They look like chanterelles to me,' said a nervous fidget of a man called Davis Larue. Then, because it was his nature, he whined, 'We're to serve a chanterelle mushroom soup in less than two hours. We're short on time and don't have any mushrooms. How are we going to serve dinner at eight?'

I was more concerned about Chef Olafson's health than serving dinner on time, but I knew the chef had been a stickler for such things so it came as no surprise that his staff were all fixated on being ready.

'He wouldn't have wanted us to be late,' sniffed Bridgette. 'He was never late.'

I nodded my head, then set out to get them all back on course. 'I spoke with the caterer already. He has a new supply of mushrooms en route to us as we speak.' That one statement seemed to provide a sense of relief. 'We all want to do our best for Chef Olafson and we all wish him a speedy recovery from whatever it is that ails him. I hope that it is not poisoning by mushrooms, but I am certain that while he would want us all to do our best, he would not wish for you to stress unduly about serving dinner on time. Were it any one of you taken ill, Chef's first priority would not be correctly seasoning the potato dauphinoise.' I paused for a second, looking around to make sure I had their attention. 'Unless it was you, Davis,' I added, getting a laugh from the team.

The laughter died away after a few seconds; it was never going to change the underlying mood.

Bridgette shot me a sorry look. 'Mrs Howard-Box has already been down here shouting about how she expects us to serve dinner on time.'

It came as no surprise – the woman was a natural bully. 'As the wedding planner who hired Chef Olafson for this event, I will overrule. Dinner will be served at eight thirty plus we'll add a palette-cleansing fruit course after the starters to draw things out a little longer.' A rippling of approval went around. 'That should give you the additional time you need to get the soup ready once the mushrooms arrive. I will deal with Mrs Howard-Box.'

'Hello,' said a voice from behind me. Most everyone was looking at me so could see whoever had just entered the room. I had to turn through a full one hundred and eighty degrees to see what they were seeing.

A tall, attractive woman in her late twenties hung half in and half out of the door.

'I'm looking for Felicity Philips,' she announced. As my eyebrow rose, she added, 'Barry Bateman sent me. Something to do with mushrooms.'

## Wrong Fungus

The woman's name was Chablis Chimera. She was Barry's local representative/salesperson. 'When I got the call from Barry, I dropped what I was doing and came straight here,' she revealed.

'I hope you didn't have far to come,' I replied.

'I was with a customer in Hastings, but the meeting was over. I was looking for a reason to escape, actually. The customer kept asking me to stay and have dinner with him. He's a bit creepy.'

This was far more information than I needed. 'Mushrooms,' I said to focus her attention.

'Yes,' she pulled an oops face. 'Barry said I needed to check what you have here. I think he is worried they might be Jack O Lantern instead.'

'That's a poisonous one?' I hedged.

Chablis nodded vigorously, but it was Bridgette who answered.

With a horrified hand to her mouth, her voice came out as a gasp. 'Those can be deadly!'

I couldn't come up with anything to say. To pray was the only response I could find.

Breaking the tense silence that filled the seconds after Bridgette's gasp, Chablis said, 'I think we had better take a look.'

The mushrooms were stacked in boxes inside a walk-in refrigerator. The door to it was just inside the back door that led outside to the loading area. The boxes all had a porous film over the top to seal the contents inside and just one had been broken, most likely by Chef Olafson.

'He insists on trying everything,' Bridgette told us. 'I think he made his soup recipe to try for lunch at around two o'clock. He was sick by three.'

Chablis took the open box of mushrooms to a countertop where she removed the film completely.

Chewing on her lower lip, she said, 'These look like chanterelles.' She produced her phone from a back pocket, opened the screen, and let her thumbs fly around the keypad like only a young person can. A beat later she had an image on her screen showing a chanterelle mushroom and its poisonous imitator the Jack O Lantern side by side.

I couldn't tell the difference.

Taking the phone away again, she read, 'It says here the Jack O Lantern is slightly more yellow than orange and has false gills, not true ones.'

I knew enough about mushrooms to understand what she was saying. Using the tip of a pen, Chablis was poking a mushroom about.

'I think these are all chanterelles,' announced Chablis. She sounded confident, yet still a little cautious as if testing our opinion. 'Barry said he was rushing a fresh supply here, but I doubt you need them. These are clearly the right thing.'

'If the mushrooms are okay,' started Bridgette, 'what poisoned Chef Olafson?'

Blowing out a hard breath of disappointment, I said, 'We need to wait for the new supply to arrive. We cannot risk poisoning people.'

'But these *are* Chanterelles,' Chablis protested.

I met her eyes. 'Barry can charge me the cost of the replacements and the rush charge to get them here.'

'You're not going to use them?' she asked.

Making it my final word on the matter, I said, 'We cannot risk it.'

Bridgette looked panicked. 'So what do we do instead?'

I grabbed her arm, steering her back toward the kitchen, leaving Barry's salesrep in the fridge with the dubious mushrooms. 'Barry has never let me down before. The mushrooms will be here soon.' I checked my watch. 'He said an hour and that was almost an hour ago now. You can get the team on with everything else and get the base for the soup ready. You might have to adapt Chef Olafson's original recipe ...'

When her eyes went even wider, I grabbed her other arm as well, turning her so she faced me. Looking into her eyes and doing my best to impart calm, I said, 'You can do this, Bridgette. You were born to be the chef.'

In a quiet voice, Bridgette managed to say, 'Thank you, Mrs Philips.'

'I think we should get a couple of your staff working on some canapes to keep the guests going now that dinner will be later than they expected. How about Carmel and Lacey?' I suggested, blurting the first two names I knew at random so the emotional sous chef, now finding herself in charge of the kitchen, didn't have to think.

Taking my prompt, Bridgette shouted, 'Carmel?'

'Yes, Chef?' came back immediately.

'Grab AJ and meet me in the larder outside. You're being promoted to head of canapes.'

Breathing a sigh of relief that she was forging ahead and seemed to have her mind back on track, I took a step backward. There were many other things to which I now needed to attend, not least of which was speaking with Mrs Howard-Box to break the news about dinner. That it would not go over well was a foregone conclusion.

## Private Investigator

Heading away from the kitchens and trying not to lose my bearings, I was looking for the front of the stately home. From there I could navigate to the palatial suites on the upper floors where I would find Mrs Howard-Box.

Still discombobulated, I bumped into Mindy. She was being towed along by Buster, exuberant as ever in his desire to arrive wherever they were going.

'*I smell food!*'

'Oh, hi, Auntie, I mean, Mrs Philips. What shall I do with him now?' she asked, reeling the dog in.

Looking down at Buster still straining to get somewhere, I commanded, 'Sit.'

Obediently, Buster's backend hit the carpet, his tongue hanging between his canines at the front like a welcome carpet rolled down a short flight of stairs. '*Sure thing,*' the bulldog replied.

I acted as if I hadn't heard the dog since I knew Mindy hadn't. 'I'll take him,' I offered, reaching for the lead. 'You should head to the kitchen. They will need every bit of help they can get.'

Mindy pulled a worried face. 'I'm not much of a cook. I can make a mean Pot Noodle ...'

Pinching the bridge of my nose between thumb and forefinger and wondering why my sister allowed Mindy to grow up with such limited life skills, I said, 'Just report to Bridgette and tell her you are there to do whatever she needs but not to trust you with anything unsupervised.'

Mindy grinned as if it were the perfect answer. 'Okay, Auntie.'

As the teenager sped away, I looked down at my dog. 'I need your nose, Buster.'

Buster bounced back onto all four paws. *'Righto! What for?'* he gave me a questioning look.

I sighed to myself and checked about to see if anyone was watching. Once satisfied I could see and hear no one, I crouched to make eye contact with my dog at close to his level.

'You remember how that evil cow Primrose Green sabotaged the flowers at the Kennedy wedding, and put up a sign outside Itchester Cathedral to send everyone to the wrong venue? Well, I'm rather worried she might be up to something again here.' Primrose would not go so far as to murder Chef Olafson, but I wouldn't put it past her to set something up that backfired and poisoned him by accident. She was another wedding planner, a good one, I reluctantly admitted, but I was recognised as the best and she didn't like it.

While I happily paid no attention to what she was doing, I knew she was watching me like a hawk. She wanted the number one spot and would resort to dirty tricks if she thought they would help her get what she wanted.

*'Got it,'* said Buster. Then he tilted his head to one side slightly. *'Soooo ... what is it you want me to do?'*

Wishing I'd found a brighter dog staring up at me through the bars of his cage with mournful, yearning eyes, I said, 'I need you to sniff around and let me know if you smell that god-awful perfume Primrose insists on wearing.'

Buster raised his nose to the air and sniffed deeply, his tail wagging spasmodically from side to side.

'Are you talking to your dog?' asked a voice that made me jump and Buster bark.

Spinning around, I found a man in an expensive suit looking at me with a curious curl at the edge of his mouth. I scowled at him. 'Do you often sneak up on people?'

The man sniggered, 'Yes, actually. That's my job. I'm a private investigator and security specialist.' From an inner pocket of his expertly tailored jacket, he produced a business card in what looked like a practiced move. 'Vince Slater,' he introduced himself.

Looking at the card, I idly noticed Vince was tall, broad shouldered, and handsome. He had a tanned face and hands like he'd recently spent time in the sun or was a frequenter of those ghastly suntanning places. His hair was turning silver above his ears where it was cut short, possibly to hide the change in colour, and he had thin lines around his eyes to betray his age which had to be at least mid-fifties.

'I'm Felicity Philips,' I replied, dropping the card into my handbag. 'Are you here working?'

Again, he gave a little chuckle. 'I know who you are, Mrs Philips. That's why I am here. Mrs Howard-Box hired me. She has a few concerns about ... well, about somebody attempting to interrupt the imminent nuptials and wanted a team to run security here. But professionally and invisibly if you get what I am saying, unlike the police who are here mob-handed to manage the crowds.'

I shook my head, confused about what he was trying to tell me and how it was that he knew me on sight when I'd never seen him before.

'No. What are you saying?' I asked.

Adopting a straight face for the first time, he said, 'It's my job to know who you are, Mrs Philips. I doubt there is anything to Mrs Howard-Box's concerns, but she hired me and my team to make sure nothing happened here to derail or upset her son's wedding. Now your chef is in hospital as I understand it, and that makes me nervous.' He finished speaking and fixed me with a questioning look.

'Chef Olafson accidentally ingested a poisonous mushroom. At least, I believe that to be the case. There is no need for you to be nervous. Or even concerned.'

'Yet it is my job to be concerned, Mrs Philips.' His cheeky grin returned. 'Was it an accident, like you say? There is a lot of interest in this wedding. Could it be that someone was attempting to poison the wedding party?'

I couldn't prevent the horror I felt making its way to my face when a vision of a career-halting newspaper headline wormed its way into my head.

Vince pursed his lips. 'I think we should investigate.'

'We?'

He started moving, walking backward away from me so I could see his face when he spoke. 'Yes, Felicity. You are invested in finding out if someone is attempting to sabotage this wedding, are you not? Plus, there are a lot of people here in your employment and if I am right about you ...' he paused to offer me the knowing grin again, 'then you know all the guests too.'

I didn't like that he had me pegged. Yes, I could spot and identify almost everyone on the guest list of over three-hundred people. It was a skill I picked up long ago – know everyone and surprise them by addressing them by name. It made them feel special, like they were someone worthy of being known, and that in turn made me memorable. Guests went away from one of my weddings with nothing but praise for the organiser. As the person aiming at the rich and famous, that was all the advertising I needed.

Vince wasn't done talking. 'There's a rather suspicious party who arrived a short while ago. A very eclectic bunch. They are yet to attempt to make contact with anyone from the Howard-Box party and that makes me very suspicious.'

'Why?' I asked with a frown.

He shot me a surprised look. 'Because there is only one wedding here this weekend. I checked to make sure of that just a few days ago. If they are not here with them, I want to know why they are here. I have two of my men watching them now.'

'Ah,' I said, my cheeks colouring a shade as my conversation with Patricia flashed through my head. She didn't want anyone to know she was here. It was her one express desire, because she was not the one getting married, and the happy couple deserved a peaceful ceremony without the press invading merely because they discovered super-sleuth, Patricia Fisher, was in town.

I started to say, 'I have other things to do,' but the words never made it past my lips because he was leaving me behind.

He turned around, waving for me to follow. 'Come along, Mrs Philips. This will be fun.'

In truth, I was truly curious to see if the accidental poisoning of Chef Olafson was anything of the sort and if it wasn't, then what was it?

Primrose Green was exactly the sort of person who would sabotage my plans for this wedding. I'd let her meddling go the first few times, and then hadn't been able to prove it was her the next few. But Primrose Green was determined to knock me off my throne, and would sooner employ unfair methods to bring my reputation down than to work hard on her own business to build it up.

Was she behind this?

To my great surprise, I followed the private investigator. 'Where are we going?'

## Chief Inspector Quinn

'*He's got beef jerky in his pocket,*' said Buster. '*I can smell it.*' He wagged his tail and sniffed, pulling at his lead to get closer to the man walking ahead of them.

Cutting my eyes at the dog, I hissed, 'Shush.'

Vince turned his head, one eyebrow hiked to his hairline. 'Did you say something?'

I put a hand to my neck. 'Just a tickle in my throat.' Buster looked around and up at me, consequently walking into a large flowerpot with a thump, two steps later. Glaring at the dog, I flared my eyes, telling Buster to remember that I couldn't talk to him while other people were around.

My phone rang, shrill in the quiet of the stately home. Every call can be important in my business, and to be honest, I was glad to have a reason to ignore Vince Slater who continued to observe me with an amused grin.

'Felicity Philips,' I announced without first checking to see who was calling.

'It's Barry,' Barry's voice assured me. 'Are the mushroom's there yet?'

I frowned. 'I hear subtext in that question, Barry. Why are you asking me where they are when you should already know their location?'

He muttered something under his breath. 'There's a problem on the road, okay. I'm sorry. They are coming. I'll call the firm again to check the driver's location. It's late on a Friday. I only just caught them before they shut for the weekend, but they are on their way, I promise.'

'What problem on the road?' I asked, having sailed down the motorway to get here.

Barry made a frustrated noise. 'An accident on the main A road out of Rye. The whole road is closed off but late on a Friday that means everyone trying to get home took different roads and now every road is clogged up in every direction.'

My frown got deeper. 'I thought the mushrooms were coming from you.' Barry and his warehouse were both near Rochester in the opposite direction.

'No, Felicity. They're coming direct from the grower. Only the freshest for my number one customer, Felicity. You know that.'

What I knew was that Barry would argue the price down to the nearest halfpenny, but his goods were the best I'd ever found, and Chef Olafson trusted him.

'Very good, Barry. Please keep me informed. I need those mushrooms, or I need to know they are not coming.' If I'd known they were going to be even later than the original hour, I would have told Bridgette to come up with a plan B first course.

'Don't worry, Mrs P. They'll be there any minute.'

Feeling entirely unconvinced since his promises would have no impact on road conditions, I slid my phone back into its little slot in my handbag.

Still walking, Vince asked. 'Do you want to speak to the police first, or Mrs Howard-Box?'

A twitch in my stomach told me that I never really wanted to speak to Mrs Howard-Box again as long as I lived, but I knew I was going to have to get over that. My interest, however, was piqued by the mention of the police. I'd seen them on the way in; they were checking identification as one might expect with such a well-publicised celebrity wedding. I'd sailed through, yet could not help but notice the crowds already gathering with a hope to see some of the many celebrities attending the ceremony.

Turning his head and twisting his body slightly, Vince walked like a crab for a few paces, waiting for me to answer.

'Why would we want to speak to the police?' I asked, truly curious. Did I genuinely suspect that Primrose might have someone here messing with the food for the wedding? Surely not. It was too far and too risky. What if Chef Olafson or someone else died?

Vince stopped; his change of pace so sudden Buster bumped into his leg.

My dog looked up at the new person. *'How about you start handing over the beef jerky and I won't need to get extra friendly with your leg?'* he offered.

Vince looked down, saw Buster eyeing up his left leg, and took a pace back just as I hauled on the lead to drag his paws back a foot in my direction. I knew what 'extra friendly' meant and had no desire to see it in action.

'The police are here in numbers, Felicity,' Vince explained. 'I need to see them anyway, as I have a private security firm operating inside the same area. But they may also prove helpful if you are right and there is someone trying to sabotage the wedding.'

'What! I never said anything about that!' What on Earth was he talking about? It felt like he'd been reading my thoughts.

'Sure you did,' Vince argued. 'It was all over your face when I first suggested it. You think someone might have messed with your supply of mushrooms. Is there anyone new to the crew of chefs? Someone as successful as you must have rivals.'

I puffed out my cheeks, wondering how to respond. Not wishing to slander Primrose when I had no proof, I chose my words carefully. 'I suppose sabotage cannot be ruled out. Let's go to see the police, shall we?'

The police had a mobile command centre set up around the back of Loxton Hall where it was invisible to guests arriving at the front. Long whip-like antennae reached for the sky amid satellite dishes and other communications paraphernalia. Approaching it I began to feel nervous, though I could not work out if that was a natural reaction to being close to the police, or because I believed there might be something sinister going on.

A low barrier fence, the clip-together kind, created a funnel around the command centre and vehicles parked near it. At the mouth stood a uniformed police officer, looking bored and grumpy. Seeing his expression, my feet wanted to turn themselves around.

'*I can smell bacon sandwiches*,' came a voice from near my feet. I could not, though I had no reason to disbelieve Buster's opinion on the subject.

'He does not look like he is going to let us through,' I commented nervously as the officer's posture shifted. He'd seen us approaching and was moving to block our path.

The cheeky grin back in place, Vince turned his head slightly to tell me, 'This is called the name drop bluff.' Quickening his pace to arrive just ahead of me, Vince walked confidently up to the police officer, reaching into his jacket for something as he slowed.

'Vince Slater, Chief Inspector Quinn is expecting me.'

The cop paused, not saying anything for a heartbeat as he flipped a mental coin. Vince paid the man no attention, checking his phone as if he needed to get moving but not acting overtly impatient. After no more than a couple of seconds, the officer stepped aside without questioning Vince's claim.

'He's inside the command hub,' the officer let us know, turning his head away as we passed.

I tugged at Buster's lead to get his attention. 'Best behaviour, please, Buster,' I begged.

The dog offered me a confused look. '*Whatever can you mean?*' He sniffed the air as we advanced.

'The trick,' Vince revealed, 'is to make it obvious that you belong where you want to be. In my experience, people rarely challenge those who are confident and calm.'

I filed his advice away, doubting I would ever have reason to test his theory, and followed him to the steps of the command hub. Mounted in the back of a big-rig trailer, the kind that an articulated truck pulls, it had sides that were extended outward to make it wider when parked than it could be in motion. Inside, their feet at our head height, we caught sight of more police officers. Vince raised a hand and called, 'Chief Inspector Quinn.'

Clearly, he knew who that was, though I had no idea, but a man in his mid-forties with a thin, but fit figure turned his head our way. Upon seeing Vince, he closed his eyes and audibly groaned.

'Mr Slater what are you doing here?' the senior police officer wanted to know. 'You know this is off limits to you.'

'Same as always, Chief Inspector. I'm working security. You are aware, of course, that a man was poisoned this afternoon.'

'I am aware,' the chief inspector replied with impatience. 'I am led to understand it was due to accidental ingestion of a harmful fungus. Are you here to tell me something different?'

Vince did not answer the question. Whether that was deliberate on his part or not, I could not tell, because the next thing he did was put me on the spot. 'This is Felicity Philips, Chief Inspector. Felicity has organised the chaos you see around you. The poisoned chef was one of her employees.'

My cheeks warmed as all eyes swung my way.

'He was your employee?' Chief Inspector Quinn wished to confirm.

'A contractor,' I clarified. 'He worked for whomever he wished, but mostly it was on my projects. I'm managing the Howard-Box wedding this weekend.'

'I see,' CI Quinn replied, still looking down at me from his elevated position inside the trailer. 'Is there a reason I should be taking an interest, Mrs Philips? Do you wish to reveal a complex conspiracy theory that will require my officers to run around looking for clues, only to have you reveal the criminal yourself at the end?'

I swear I heard the man behind him mutter the name Patricia Fisher with an expletive as a prefix and suffix.

'Um, no,' I managed to stutter. He was talking down to me, both literally and figuratively. Belittling me to make me go away, and I was handing him the right to do it by not fighting back. Flicking my hair to get it out of my face, I fixed him with a new expression. 'It is entirely possible, is it not, given the media frenzy around this event and the number of devoted followers Miss Allstar has amassed globally, that someone might wish to ... mess with the proceedings?'

Quinn flicked an amused expression at his fellow officers. 'And that would start with poisoning your chef?'

I found a sudden desire to let Buster do his business in the man's shoes. 'It might start by poisoning the entire wedding party.' I countered. 'Chef Olafson is dedicated enough to test out his recipes before anyone is served them. Had he not done so, the dish might have been tasted only moments before being served to a hundred guests, and they would all miss the wedding tomorrow.'

I got a dismissive nod from the chief inspector as he turned his face away to go back to what he was doing before we arrived. He replied though. 'That is all very cloak and dagger, Mrs Philips, but I believe we have things in hand. I have fifty additional officers committed to control the crowds of fans. Sasha Allstar has quite the following as you just highlighted, but they will not be able to interrupt her nuptials.'

The chief inspector referred to the bride, Sasha Allstar, known to her army of fans as Sashatastic. Bursting onto the global stage when her small filmed-at-home real life of a teenager internet show was picked up by a huge media conglomerate, she lived on the internet, live-streaming every moment of her life for more than six years. Merchandise followed, and by twenty-one she was a billionaire. Now twenty-eight, I had no idea what her net worth might be, but if rumours were true, it had a lot of zeroes in it.

Sasha was famous for many things, among which was the Sasha hairstyle and outfit. Her legion of followers all wore wigs, dresses, and boots to match. I thought it odd that she was rarely seen in public wearing anything else. I had only met her briefly at the Howard-Box family home when she and Bobbie arrived there during one of my meetings with Angelica. This is unusual as the wedding planner more normally spends a vast amount of time with the bride. Coming to understand each bride's express desires is what has made me so successful. However, Sasha was far too busy for that and did everything by proxy. I had to send a dress maker to her, not the other way around.

Chief Inspector Quinn appeared to have finished with me, but just as my feelings of discomfort ratcheted up another notch and my feet demanded I go somewhere else, he asked another question. 'Was there anything suspicious about Chef Olafson's poisoning?'

Instantly on the spot and feeling flustered, I fumbled for words as my cheeks began to glow. 'Well ... Not as such.'

'There you have it then, Mrs Philips.' He'd walked me into a trap. Now it was sprung, he stopped what he was doing to face me again, boring into my eyes with his. 'I have enough determined amateurs on site already. Please leave the investigation of crimes and the pursuit of criminals to the professionals.' He jinked his head to glare at Vince. 'That goes for you too, Mr Slater.'

I felt an almost overwhelming urge to tell him about Primrose Green yet managed to keep my mouth shut. Like a naughty schoolgirl, I had been admonished by the headmaster and was now expected to slink away with my tail between my legs.

I wanted to have the last word, however Vince got there first. 'Tell me, Chief Inspector, how will you frame your apology to Mrs Philips when she's proven right, and someone does manage to ruin the wedding?'

I thought we were going to wait to see how CI Quinn responded, but Vince had my elbow and was wheeling me around already. If the chief inspector had a comeback, he didn't bother to use it as we let ourselves back out through their barrier.

Escaping from a situation that proved more awkward than I expected, I then realised I still had to speak with Mrs Howard-Box.

## Mrs Howard-Box

Outside the Clairmont Suite where I knew I would find my client, two of Vince's security guards were stationed.

'Any bother?' Vince asked as he came to the door.

Both men looked like ex-military or something. They were relaxed, yet also ramrod straight, with short, functional hair styles and curly wires snaking over their left ears to a device fitted inside. Were they carrying weapons? The question surfaced, and though I was sure they would not be allowed to have guns, their suit jackets could easily hide something.

The man on the left as we approached said, 'No. No bother. All quiet outside and in.'

The door opened without Vince needing to knock because he'd already spoken to someone via his own curly wire. It connected to a radio hidden in his sleeve.

Just inside the door, a third man stood upright but at ease just like the men positioned outside. The suite contained multiple rooms and an entrance lobby which is where we now found ourselves. I paused to observe the huge bouquet of flowers arranged ornately in a vase opposite the door.

They were fragrant and exactly as Mrs Howard-Box insisted they should be in all rooms.

'The principal is in the living area, sir,' the security guard informed Vince once the door was closed again.

The sense of discomfort rose in my middle again but this time I shoved it down, refusing to allow one demanding mother of the groom to make me feel off balance. With that done, I strode ahead of Vince to find her with Buster pulling me along.

'*I can smell beer,*' he declared. '*I'm parched, I am.*'

'You are not having any beer, Buster,' I scolded quietly. 'It makes you act silly and you will get fat.'

Buster jinked his head around to fix me with an incredulous stare. '*I'm a bulldog. Fat is sexy.*'

'Ah, Angelica,' I addressed her by first name as if we were old friends. 'I see you have settled in. This must be exciting for you.'

Angelica was sitting in a chair in front of a large mirror while two of the ladies from *Transformations Wedding Hair and Makeup* did their thing to her face and hair. At the sound of my voice, she twitched her eyes to catch sight of me in the mirror and raised a hand to ward off the two women putting the final touches to her unhappy face. They both backed away a pace.

Her son, the groom, looked comfortable and relaxed on a couch. He had a football match on the television and a football in his hands. The beer Buster could smell was almost finished, a condensation coated glass resting on a coaster on a coffee table at arm's reach. He glanced my way, but only for a second before a roar from the crowd drew his attention back to the game.

Buster snorted, sampling the air because it smelled of things he wanted to eat. The noise drew Bobbie's attention again.

'Hey, cute dog,' he commented.

Buster scowled at me.

'I am not cute,' he grumped. 'I am the embodiment of danger and a purveyor of peril.' I shrugged one shoulder to acknowledge that he might be perilous to a doughnut. 'Cute indeed,' Buster continued to moan. 'I told you I needed a cape.'

Across the room, Mrs Howard-Box was scowling. She did it a lot. So much so, in fact, that it shocked me whenever I saw any other expression displayed.

'Is everything back on track for tonight's meal?' she snapped.

'Indeed,' I replied. 'There was a question regarding the mushrooms, so I have had the entire supply replaced. Guests can meet for dinner as expected where they will be served canapes and champagne. Dinner will be served at eight thirty.'

Angelica froze, her eyes seeming to burn like embers in her head.

Just behind me, Vince whispered, 'Boom! And the volcano blows its top.'

'Dinner is to be served at eight,' Angelica insisted, her voice a low growl.

She wanted to be the bully and I suspected it was a tactic that had worked for her throughout her life. However, this was not my first rodeo. 'That is no longer possible, Angelica. Losing the chef in charge has created unavoidable delays. Were it not for the diligence and resolve of the sous chef, dinner might ...'

'I don't care about your excuses, woman,' the mother of the groom raged.

Honestly, I could not remember the last time a person addressed me as 'woman'. Or addressed me with such disdain.

'You are being impolite,' I pointed out, calmly.

'That is due to you being disgracefully inept at your job,' Angelica shouted in response.

'Calm down, mother,' Bobbie begged without looking away from the television.

Angelica kept her eyes locked on me when she demanded, 'Stay out of this, Bobbie. This does not concern you.'

Bobbie snorted. 'Silly me. I thought this was my wedding.'

Ignoring him, Angelica poked a finger rudely in my direction. 'Dinner will be served at eight o'clock sharp.' It was an order.

'That will not be possible,' I countered. I wasn't even sure the replacement mushrooms had arrived yet.

'You will make it possible,' Angelica growled as if repeating her orders would make time work differently. 'Who ever heard of dinner being served at eight-thirty?' she wanted to know. 'It's ridiculous. I will be the laughingstock of the community.'

Sounding bored, Bobbie begged, 'Let it go, mother. No one will even notice.'

'You do not understand how these things work, dear,' she argued, softening her voice as if talking to a child.

It proved to be the final straw. Bouncing athletically to his feet, Bobbie Howard-Box crossed the room to get between me and his mother. His attention was all on me, his back to Angelica as he reached out to shake my hand.

'Mrs Philips, isn't it?'

'Yes. It's a pleasure to meet you properly, Bobbie. I assure you everything this weekend will go according to plan.'

He waved me into silence. 'I have no doubt. You came highly recommended. We both hope your chef makes a full recovery. A half hour delay is a minor hiccup that no one will notice. It is of no concern, is it mother?'

Angelica's face was a mask of barely suppressed rage. 'I would hardly call a sick chef ...'

'IS IT, MOTHER?' repeated Bobbie, making his point by raising his own voice, something he undoubtedly learned from his mother. Focussing back on me, and with the calm tones returned, he said. 'Thank you for all you are doing. Sasha and I are most grateful.'

I waited a second to see if Angelica had anything more to say on the subject, but I appeared to have achieved my aim. Dinner would be served half an hour later than originally planned which would give the kitchen the time they needed to get the first course ready. Now I just needed to make sure the mushrooms were actually here.

Quite what I would say to Mrs Howard-Box if they were not, I had no idea.

## Situation Saved

Vince followed me back through the suite and into the corridor outside where the security guards still stood like automatons.

Guessing there was something he wanted, I said, 'I'm going back to the kitchen, Mr Slater. I need to check on their progress and then I need to head to the banquet room to make sure everything is set up. Is there something you need?'

'No, Felicity.' A broad smile broke out on Vince's face.

I narrowed my eyes at him. 'What is it, Mr Slater? You grin at me far too often.'

We were five feet apart one moment but then less than that the next as he moved in close enough for me to smell his aftershave. 'You feel a need to tell me where you are going to be so I will be able to find you, don't you, Felicity?'

'What?' He thought I was flirting with him. 'No, Mr Slater I ...'

'It's okay, I get it,' he came back toward me with both hands held up in surrender. 'I have this effect on women of a certain age.'

Now my ire was rising.

*'Are we going to see the chefs?'* asked Buster, still tugging at his lead. *'It's been ages since I ate something.'*

'Women of a certain age?' I growled, my forehead narrowing into a glare that dared him to expand on his statement.

If I expected him to signal a verbal retreat, which I did, I was to be sorely mistaken for he laughed at me. 'Yes, Felicity. Neither of us are spring chickens. I will be fifty-eight on my next birthday and that makes me prime candy for women in their fifties.'

My jaw dropped open.

He wasn't done though. 'There is no way a beauty like you can have broached the sixty mark,' I almost choked at the suggestion. 'But you possess the grace and dignity that comes from any woman over the age of fifty.'

I could hardly argue with his assessment – I would be fifty-six in a few months. Nevertheless, I was hopping mad. 'I do not find you to be prime candy, Mr Slater,' I all but snarled. 'Or any other kind of candy for that matter.' He was trim and fit looking, like someone who went to the gym most days, and he was both handsome and well-groomed without being pretty or vain. Except he was vain. Terribly so. 'Perhaps you should return to Mrs Howard-Box. Though I don't see how there will be room for her in that suite once your massive ego gets inside.'

The insult never even registered on his face. 'It's a pretty big room,' he joked. 'I think we can both fit.'

I started walking away. 'Good day, Mr Slater.' As I left him behind, telling myself to not look over my shoulder to see if he was following, I heard him making appreciative sounds as if he were ogling my bottom. Then I realised that was probably exactly what he was doing!

Buster led me to the kitchen, following his nose while giving commentary on what he could smell.

'*Carrots, fresh cream, venison loin ...*' it was a long list, his nose easily able to pick out individual smells as if he'd been born in a kitchen and raised by a cook.

Spotting Bridgette, I called to her and got the attention of almost everyone in the room. 'Have the mushrooms turned up?'

Bridgette's head swung my way, but I didn't need her to say anything for me to know the answer, it was written all over her face.

A lump like a bowling ball formed in my gut. The wedding of the year and things were going wrong. Things did not go wrong with my weddings. Well, except when Primrose Green meddled with my arrangements, that is.

Sucking in a deep breath as I rallied my brain to supply a solution, the brief deathly silence of the kitchen allowed us all to hear the fast clip-clopping sound of a woman running in heels.

'Got them!' shouted Chablis, bursting through the back door with six boxes of mushrooms wedged under her chin.

Bridgette gasped a loud sigh of relief. 'I've been calling around everyone to get a fresh supply of chanterelles – no one had any they could get here in time.'

She cut her eyes across the room. 'Mike, Jake, quick get … Hey!' she snapped. 'Quit trying to chat up Teagan and go get the mushrooms!' I had to duck my head a little to look under the hotplates. Across the room, two men in their twenties were looking abashed.

They were moving away from a very pretty young woman who they probably had been chatting up. Her chef's whites were different to those everyone else was wearing, though I had no idea why. As the two men hurried by me on their way to collect the fungi, Bridgette shouted after them, 'Get the mushrooms and get on with preparing them.' Then she jabbed a finger at two more of her chefs. 'Gail, finish what you are doing, then take Bernadette and help the boys.'

At the back door, Chablis handed over the new supply of mushrooms. 'Take these,' I'll go back for the rest.'

'Dave, go help her,' Brigette instructed.

Dashing back out the door, Chablis paused half in, half out. 'No need. I won't be a second.'

With the relief of the mushrooms arriving, I made a show of wiping my brow. Looking at Bridgette, I could see the strain showing on her face. 'How are you holding up?' I asked, taking her to one side so we could speak quietly.

I got a sad smile in reply. 'I feel like a fraud. They are all looking to me to lead, but this is Chef Olafson's team, not mine. I don't know what I am doing, and the new girl is causing such a distraction, not that it's her fault.'

'New girl?' I asked.

Bridgette nodded her head toward the pretty woman. 'Teagan showed up a couple of hours ago. Sent by an agency to bolster our numbers. I didn't know Chef had asked for extra hands. She's not very good, truth be told, and the men won't stop finding a reason to wander over to help her.'

'She is rather pretty,' I observed.

Bridgette pursed her lips. 'Yes. Annoyingly so. She doesn't even have any makeup on.'

Chablis reappeared with the last of the mushrooms. Her elegant salesperson's trouser suit had marks on it from carting the mushrooms around but like everyone else, she understood the urgency in the room and was doing her best to help. 'They are definitely different to the ones you had before,' Chablis assured us. 'I took those away already. They'll go back to the supplier with Barry's big boot attached, I expect.' Handing the boxes over as Mike and Jake jogged back to get them, she held up two mushrooms to show us. 'I took a couple out and checked them on my phone to be one hundred percent certain.'

She broke one into two pieces and popped half into her mouth. It was quite the demonstration of faith on her part.

Bridgette took the other half when offered, eating it as if to doubly prove the point.

I made a point of shaking her hand. 'Thank you, Chablis. I will call Barry shortly to thank him and will be sure to let him know how responsive you were to our needs.'

She made an embarrassed face. 'Well, Barry makes it clear the customer is to come first. I'm just glad no one else ate the other mushrooms.'

'I should get on,' said Bridgette, making her excuse as she departed.

By my feet, Buster made a grumpy noise. *'Why is it that all the people are eating but the poor dog has to go hungry? I'm wasting away here.'*

He was anything but.

'I should go too,' said Chablis. 'Traffic will be terrible if I stay here much longer.'

I thanked her again for her diligence and turned my attention inward. What did I need to do now?

Before I got a chance to give the question any thought, my niece appeared, her pink hair stuffed into a chef's hat. 'Hey, Aunt Flicka. Do I stay here? Or do you need me to do something else?' I could tell by her tone that my teenage apprentice was already bored in the kitchen.

'I started in the kitchen,' I told her. 'Getting the food right is the key to any wedding. Hungry people or those disappointed by their food are always the first to complain. Alcohol can be used to mollify them, remember that, but years after the event, guests will remember the food more than anything else.'

Mindy listened to what I had to say, her boundless energy making her almost vibrate with a need to do something else. 'Yeah, so what do you need me to do now?' she asked again, my attempt at infusing knowledge utterly wasted.

'Bridgette?' I called to get the sous chef's attention. 'Do you still need Mindy?'

The tall woman running the kitchen shrugged. 'What I need is qualified chefs I don't need to watch. That's not Mindy's fault any more than it is Teagan's. There's no point to Mindy staying though.'

Reading between the lines, I said, 'Do you want more staff for tomorrow?' I got an unsure look in return. 'I'll call the agency and get them to send me a couple of top-drawer chefs. I'll pick up the bill,' I assured her. Since Chef Olafson was working to a contracted value, any additional expense came out of his profit. I was quite prepared to lower my own take rather than run the risk of anything going wrong. Not now we looked to have overcome the hurdles thrown at us by the mushrooms.

Bridgette's look turned hopeful. 'It might make things easier,' she admitted.

I nodded. 'Consider it done.' Spinning on one heel, I made my way from the kitchen. 'Come along, Mindy. We need to catch up with Justin. He'll have other tasks for you.'

Yanking off her chef's hat and tugging at her apron, I heard her mumble something that sounded like, 'Thank goodness,' but let the comment pass because the number for the catering staff agency was already ringing.

## Imposter

'That's what I am telling you,' repeated the woman at the agency for the third time. I'd made it as far as the door to the banquet hall and could see ahead of me that the tables were made up and looking splendid. If there was one thing I could always count on, it was Justin's ability to get things done just the way they should be.

To the woman at the other end of the phone, I said, 'You need to be absolutely sure about this.'

Beginning to sound bored repeating herself, she tried again. 'I can assure you, Mrs Philips, my agency has not sent anyone to work with Chef Olafson today. He did not call here asking for additional staff. If you have someone there claiming that we sent them, they are an imposter.'

My heart hammered in my chest as I started to retrace my steps. Mindy shot me a confused look as I ran past her in the corridor. She was back in her tight-fitting fight wear, or whatever the heck the name for the style might be, and bewildered about where she was supposed to be going now that I was heading the other way.

'Auntie?' she called after me, her voice getting lost as I rounded a corner.

'Can you supply chefs tomorrow?' I asked, wanting to finish the call but also needing to deal with the reason I dialled their number in the first place. 'Good ones. Not someone straight from college who can do eggs on toast. I want people who trained in Paris. No, scratch that. I want people from Paris who have Michelin stars to their name.' I was being demanding, so when I heard her draw breath to respond, I added, 'I am unconcerned what their daily rate is.'

Her tone changed instantly, 'Well that's different then, Mrs Philips. How many do you need?'

'Send me five,' I requested. I knew that was going to be expensive, but … well, I won't tell you what my fee is for events such as this one, but let's just say I wasn't concerned about the bill for five extra chefs. 'Please ensure they are top-drawer,' I repeated to drive the point home.

Mindy caught up to me, jogging along by my side, but making it look effortless while I was beginning to wheeze from the effort.

Buster didn't do a lot of running. His natural centre of gravity demanded he spend most of his life lying on his back where his jowls fell back to cover his eyes, but right now he thought we were having a great game and was thrusting along the carpet with his stumpy little legs.

I passed his lead to Mindy, ended the call, and stopped before I threw up from the stitch now digging into my side.

'Ere, are you all right, Auntie?' Mindy asked.

'Got to get to the kitchen,' I wheezed.

It was just around the next corner, so with a couple of deep breaths to get some air back into my lungs, I pushed off again.

I landed flat on my face, driving the air from my lungs, and stinging my face as my chin hit the carpet.

Buster licked my ear. *'You're on the floor,'* he observed as I twisted to try to slap him away. *'I am going to kiss you, kiss you kiss you,'* he sang at me. *'Because I love you so much.'* It was not the kind of love I could truly get behind.

'Yes, Buster, thank you. I tripped on your lead.' I didn't waste time explaining that I tripped on his lead, because he darted forward and got under my feet just as I started moving.

Mindy gave me a hand up, demonstrating surprising strength as she pulled me effortlessly from the floor. I started running again, this time making sure there was nothing to fall over.

Bursting through the kitchen doors, which slammed back on their stops, all heads shot around to see the crazy woman heaving for breath and looking demented.

'Where is she?' I demanded. 'Where's Teagan?'

## Extreme Parkour

Breathing heavily, my legs feeling weak as I mentally berated myself for not keeping up my Pilates class, I scanned around the room. Twenty faces stared silently back at me and no one was moving. The lights suspended from the hotplates made some of the faces hard to see, but when a figure backed away a pace, it drew my eyes.

It was Teagan and her face had panic etched into it.

Mike and Jake were either side of her, doubtless chatting her up again. The kitchen was filled with incredible smells, steam rising from various pots and sizzling noises came from pans as the team assembled the components that would feed the hungry wedding party soon. To one side, a platter of canapes were in the final stages, two chefs staring at me with their hands halfway through carefully arranging the delicate morsels.

'What's happening?' asked Bridgette, appearing from an office in the far corner of the kitchen. She looked utterly miserable and there were tears flowing down her face.

My heart sunk, though I told myself guessing the cause of her tears was jumping to conclusions.

As the people in the room swung their attention from me to her, she sobbed, 'It's Chef.' Her shoulders started shaking and her eyes closed as her face crumbled. 'He's dead!'

Somehow I knew she was going to say it, but the news still hit me like a cannonball to the belly. My friend, Chef Gustav Olafson, was dead. Dead at the hand of whoever switched out the mushrooms, but it wasn't a someone anymore. It was an imposter, posing as a chef to get inside the kitchen.

Anger propelled me across the room. 'Why?' I shouted, my eyes locked on Teagan's. Her pretty face might turn the boys' heads and confuse them, but it wasn't going to have any effect on me. 'Why did you do it?' My voice became a scream that demanded an answer.

Teagan had been backing away from me as I advanced, but when her backside bumped into a counter, she had nowhere else to go. Tears were flowing freely from my eyes, the counter emotions of rage and misery both fighting for control as my hands began to shake.

'What?' stuttered Teagan. 'What did I do?'

I wanted to scream at her. I wanted to throw things, but the sane rational part of my brain caught up with the rest of me and took the steering wheel just before I did something I would regret.

Trying to keep my voice from wavering, I asked, 'Mindy, would you please fetch the police?'

Mindy, unhelpful as ever, asked, 'Um, why? What's going on?'

'Teagan is not from the agency,' I announced loud enough that everyone could hear. 'She switched the mushrooms. Didn't you, Teagan,' I accused through gritted teeth.

'No!' Teagan protested. 'I never touched the mushrooms. I swear!'

'What was the plan? Poison the wedding party? Kill some celebrities? Did Sasha Allstar not sign your autograph? Or does Bobbie Howard-Box play for a team you don't like?'

'I would never hurt, Bobbie,' Teagan wailed. 'I love him.'

Her words caught me off guard. It was not only that it wasn't what I expected to hear, but also the emotion behind the words.

No one in the kitchen was moving. They were all caught up in the drama unfolding before their eyes. Then a shout and several expletives arose because a pan caught fire, the contents ruined because the chef minding it had been watching Teagan instead.

'Perhaps I can shed some light here,' offered a new voice. New to the room, that is. Not new to me. I swivelled around to find Vince strolling into the kitchen.

The scene around me was like a frozen plateau. Eyes were wide, mouths were gawping, and all the food was going to ruin if they didn't snap out of it soon. Bridgette needed a shoulder to cry on and everyone else needed her to take charge again.

Huffing out another frustrated breath, I grabbed Mindy's arm. 'Get Bridgette into a chair and make her a cup of tea. You can do that, can't you?'

'Yes, Auntie,' Mindy rolled her eyes.

'Good. Do that and make sure she stays off her feet until I get there.' The last thing I needed was Bridgette fainting and bashing her head on her way to the floor.

Behind me, now that my eyes were off her, Teagan made a run for it. Nimble and light, I was never going to catch her, and Vince was the wrong side of the room as she fled toward the back doors and the gardens.

'Stop her!' Vince and I shouted at the same time.

Jolted into action, half a dozen of Chef Olafson's team stepped into Teagan's path.

'No! Let me through!' she cried, running straight at them. Determined to get away, she snatched up a pan from a lit gas ring, the contents bubbling and boiling. The threat was clear, and I believed she meant to use it.

The chefs forming the barrier did too, bumping into each other in their haste to get out of her way once more. There were squeals of fright from both men and women while I looked on helplessly. No matter what, I could not move fast enough to stop her. No one could.

Which is why what happened next came as such a surprise.

Believing Mindy was on her way to the office to settle Bridgette and get her a cup of tea, my eyes did a double take as she shot by me running across the kitchen counters. It was like an extreme Parkour course where the organisers chose to include flames and boiling liquids as additional hazards.

Demonstrating agility I had no idea she possessed, Mindy cut a diagonal path across the kitchen as if she were lighter than air and didn't need to bother with trivia like gravity. Honestly, if she had next chosen to run along a wall, my surprise would not have been any greater.

Teagen was past the temporary barrier of chefs where they had scattered to leave her a path, and would be at the doors in seconds. Sure, the police would catch Teagen later, but as Mindy reached the last counter, I could see she was going to save them a job.

With legs made of springs, Mindy launched into the air, flipped in a somersault while pulling something from behind her back with both hands.

Landing in front of Teagan, Mindy, my niece I had to remind myself, dropped into a crouch and looked up at the woman running toward her with a glare so intense it might melt steel. In her hands she held two foot-long black batons. They were out and away from her body, her arms spread wide, but there was no question about the threat they signified.

Teagan screeched to a stop, her shoes struggling to find traction as she tried to reverse her direction. The pan, now almost devoid of the hot liquid it once held, fell from her grip to clang noisily on the floor.

*'If it's on the floor, it's the dog's!'* barked Buster, barrelling through the chefs behind Teagan to get to the spill.

Her forward motion arrested, and her weapon discarded, Teagan's chance of escape was gone. Vince placed a heavy hand on her shoulder.

'Miss, I think you had better come with me.'

## Not Patricia Fisher

Teagan Clancy was a former model who had dated Bobbie Howard-Box for almost a year. We found that out in the first thirty seconds when Vince said, 'Tell me what your connection to Bobbie Howard-Box is,' and she started spilling the beans.

Apparently, Vince already knew that part. When I returned to the kitchen, he started poking into the staff here for the wedding with a focus on those working in the kitchen because of Chef Olafson. It didn't take him long to discover the former girlfriend who failed to turn up for her barmaid job today.

She'd taken a job at Loxton Hall the moment she heard the wedding announcement. Working as bar staff, she was able to pass through this weekend's additional security with ease but once on site today she stole a Loxton Hall chef's uniform and reported to the kitchen instead.

The why of it was obvious. She had intended to poison the wedding party. She would have achieved it too had Chef Olafson not tried the mushrooms far enough in advance for their poison to take effect. That he paid with his life would secure Teagan's fate.

To get her away from the chefs whose boss she'd killed, Vince took Teagan to the office in the corner. Bridgette was no longer there, expressing a need to be somewhere else. No one argued.

Thankfully, Winston, one of the older chefs and respected by the team, stepped up to fill in where Bridgette left off. I didn't think any of the team felt like continuing but his wise words and Dunkirk spirit would get them through the next couple of hours.

Once this meal was served and finished, we could take a breath and work out how to tackle the bigger day tomorrow.

Chief Inspector Quinn appeared just as Mindy returned from the bar with a double gin and tonic for me – I needed something to settle my nerves.

'Mrs Philips,' he acknowledged me with a nod just as I took a glug of the clear liquid. I made him wait while I savoured it.

I was sitting on a plastic chair outside the corner office, feeling like it had been a long day. Tomorrow would be even longer, and for once I felt like I was facing it alone. It's my business. My name is a successful firm all by itself, but without Archie with me to share the experience, I sometimes found myself questioning why I did it.

Pausing to speak with me, Chief Inspector Quinn looked over my head and through the office windows where his junior officers were already taking over from Vince. 'I understand you discovered an imposter among the ranks. You believe she poisoned Gustav Olafson?'

I nodded, feeling tired. 'Yes, Chief Inspector. I believe she intended to get her own back on the Howard-Box family. Perhaps she also carried a grudge against Sasha Allstar for being the one Bobbie chose to marry. It would seem Bobbie's mother split the couple up when she discovered Teagan had posed for some … racy pictures in her early career.' I overheard her yelling obscenities about Angelica, and the world in general, while she explained her presence here, and so had everyone else in the kitchen. It would have been impossible not to overhear her ranting at Vince while he made her wait for the police. Refusing to crumble, she continued to deny any involvement in the mushroom confusion. I couldn't decide if I was relieved or disappointed that my arch-rival Primrose Green wasn't to blame after all, but I was glad I hadn't shared my suspicion with anyone but Buster.

'And you believe she intended to poison the whole wedding party?'

I sipped my drink, letting the alcohol seep into my body and feeling my tension ease just a little. 'Had the mushrooms been served, it's likely she would have poisoned everyone here tonight, along with several of the chefs who would have tasted the soup as they seasoned it.'

The chief inspector nodded his head again. 'How very Lucrezia Borgia,' he murmured, referring to the historic character famous for allegedly poisoning guests at parties in Renaissance Italy. 'Well done, Mrs Philips. I believe you averted a terrible crime this evening.'

I looked up at him to find his eyes looking at something invisible in his head that only he could see. 'Don't worry, Chief Inspector. I do not plan to make a habit of foiling criminals' attempts to kill people. I am not Patricia Fisher.'

The mere mention of her name refocused his eyes, both swinging down to look at me with an unspoken question on his lips.

'You referenced her earlier I believe, though you did not name her. She is here somewhere, isn't she?'

'You know her?' he asked.

I started to lever myself from my chair; I needed to get on with things because the canapes were going out in a few minutes and the guests would start arriving in the banquet hall soon. I still hadn't had the chance to speak to Justin and soon he would be swept up in running the rehearsal dinner.

'I organised her wedding,' I revealed. 'It was my first.'

I got another nod as he absorbed the information. 'Very good, Mrs Philips. I must leave you now. My officers are arresting the suspect. I trust the rest of the wedding will proceed as planned.'

I hoped so too.

I looked around for Mindy, finding her chatting with one of the younger men working in the kitchen. They were all impressed by her display of athleticism earlier, though personally I thought it ought to make a man want to run the other way.

She had Buster sitting by her feet, staring up and praying for food to fall into his mouth.

Hooking her elbow on my way by, I said, 'Come along Bruce Lee, we have work to do.'

A final glance across the room allowed me to see a tearful Teagan being led away in cuffs by the police. She was sandwiched between the two junior officers Chief Inspector Quinn arrived with, and held by her shoulders.

Vince was heading my way, but if he wanted me specifically, he was going to have to catch up because I really did need to be somewhere else.

Outside the kitchen, I took Buster's lead back from Mindy and sent her to get changed. It was evening now, and she had formal attire to wear which included a wig to cover her pink hair.

'Do I have to wear the wig, Auntie?' she moaned.

'Only if you want to work for me,' I quipped in reply. 'And …'

'I know,' she raised her hands as she backed away. 'I have to call you Mrs Philips.'

'Yes,' I agreed, 'but that is not what I was going to say.'

Her mouth formed an O of question.

'I wanted to see the weapons you are carrying and ask how on Earth all the ninja stuff happened? When did you learn all that?'

Her cheeks coloured. 'You know mum always sent me to gymnastics class with dad?'

'Yes,' I wondered where this was going. 'You're a county champion on the asymmetrical bars.'

'Yeahhhh,' she drawled. 'Not really. I hated gymnastics, but mum insisted I had to go, so dad found a freestyle martial arts club that was on at the same time.'

'How long has that been going on?'

Her cheeks coloured a shade darker. 'Since I was five.'

'What? All this time … what about the county championships? I've seen the certificates and trophies.'

'Fake,' Mindy shrugged. 'Dad had them made. He said we needed to maintain the lie, and since mum never cared to come to any of the supposed competitions, she was never going to find out.' As a new thought occurred to her, Mindy's eyes widened, and she gasped. 'You can't tell her. Mum would go nuts.'

At last, something to laugh about. 'I don't think you need to worry, Mindy. Your mother and I were never ones for sharing secrets. Now get changed and find Justin in the banquet hall. I'll meet you there.'

As she dashed away, I led Buster through the quiet corridors of Loxton Hall. A quiet buzz of conversation drifted out through the doors of the banquet hall where two elegant young men in tails stood either side to greet the guests and announce them. They were more of my people, all drafted in for the weekend and all tried and tested through many previous events. These two were Damian and Stefan, twins with very Germanic features. The exact replication of their hair and features made them look like bookends either side of the door – attention to detail was what made my weddings so special.

I stood aside as more guests approached, this time a British rap star and his girlfriend who wore a dress so sheer and so small that it was basically underwear. I probably had more thread in my pocket than they used to make her entire outfit.

When they passed through with Damian leading them inside, I lowered my voice to ask Stefan, 'Is everything going to plan?'

'Yes, Mrs Philips. Justin seems extra busy. Is everything okay elsewhere?'

Worried word of the poisoning had spread, I asked, 'Why do you ask? Have you heard something?'

I got an innocent expression back. 'No, Mrs Philips. It's just that we haven't seen you today. No one has. We were getting a little worried.'

Buster nudged my leg. *'I need to go outside.'*

I needed to go inside. I wanted to check on Justin and about a hundred other things, but it wouldn't do to have Buster lift his leg in the banquet hall. Not that I felt he ought to be in there anyway. I would have to deal with his needs and settle him in my room. These were all tasks I could do without but having sent Mindy away, I was going to have to attend to them myself.

With a glance inside the banquet hall to reassure myself everything was going smoothly, I caught sight of Justin. He didn't see me because his focus was on the guests. I could leave him to manage proceedings for a few minutes more.

'I mean it,' whined Buster. '*I gotta go!*'

Taking the hint, I got my feet moving. Buster never joked about his need to go outside and the little monster was only too happy to find a place to go inside if I ever failed to hurry myself at his first warning.

The instant I was moving, he was straining at the lead, all low-down muscle driving forward to pull me along whether I wanted to go or not.

Here's a thing about owning a bulldog: don't.

Or maybe just know what you are getting into first. They are headstrong, they are ridiculously heavy so that picking them up is like having a fight with a giant wilful bean bag, and they are filled with attitude.

Amber disliked him intensely and though I loved him to bits, I also understood her opinion.

Spotting a door that would lead outside, I made a beeline for it, yanking on Buster's lead in an effort to steer him.

'Go that way, Buster,' I begged.

'Why? Outside is this way. I can smell the garden.'

'What you can smell is probably an open window. I use my eyes and not my nose which is how I can see a door.'

'Oh, a door. You humans think you are so clever. How about if I just make my own door?'

'What?'

'Ha! I bet if I run fast enough, I can go straight through the wall.' Buster sounded worryingly excited at the prospect.

'Have you been watching cartoons again?' I enquired with a frown.

By sheer will of force I got to the door and shoved it open, cold air rushing in like an assault on my exposed skin. I was dressed to be inside.

Abandoning his quest to go through the wall, Buster trotted outside, sniffing the air with piggy snorts like only a bulldog can. Whether I could trust him off the lead was a big question. I was already cold, the late autumn air making a mockery of my elegant but thin jacket.

I wanted to throw caution to the wind, but experience dictated that letting Buster roam untethered was a recipe for an hour of yelling his name.

We were standing in a courtyard outside the building on stone tiles set out in an elegant mosaic. Buster wasn't going to do anything on these. Shivering, I crossed to where they met the grass that extended to the trees about two hundred yards distant.

'Go on,' I encouraged. 'Pick your outhouse.' Admittedly, this isn't the coolest part about keeping a pet, but generally speaking the trade-off is worthwhile.

However, despite his claims that it couldn't wait, he had a scent in his nostrils and his brain couldn't do two things at once.

'*There's something alive out there,*' he whispered like we were in a war movie or a horror film.

'It's probably just some rabbits,' I told him, wishing he would hurry up. I wanted to get back to the practice dinner banquet.

'It's not rabbits,' he assured me, sounding quite certain. 'It's too ... not rabbity.'

'Good description. It's probably a badger.'

He asked, 'What's a badger?' Inadvertently, I'd piqued his interest.

Thinking on my feet, I said, 'Big predatory mammal native to these parts. Very territorial and bad-tempered. You should hurry up so we can get inside before it picks up your scent.'

'I'm gonna kick its butt,' said Buster. 'I'm a bulldog. You know what the first part of my name is? Bull. As in, like a bull. Nobody messes with the bull, because when you do, you get the horns!' He was pawing the ground and giving the night his meanest stare.

It was tough talk for a creature that is basically a stuffed sock with a face.

'I think perhaps we should finish up out here and get back inside.' I was almost begging while simultaneously questioning if I could find some newspapers to cover the carpet in my room. If he didn't go soon, we were going inside anyway.

An owl hooted and Buster, tough dog that he is, bounced back two feet in fright.

'What was that?'

'An owl. You're about to ask what one of those is, aren't you?'

'No,' he replied a touch too quickly. 'Maybe we should think about getting back inside. It could be dangerous out here for you with all these badgers and owls around.'

If he wanted to pretend he was protecting me, I was fine with that. Just as long as we got to go back into the warm.

'Do you need to go or not?' I asked, giving him one last chance.

Two minutes later, I had a baggie held at arm's length and my eyes peeled for a bin of some form. We were not that far from the kitchens, there had to be a waste receptacle around here somewhere.

Starting to think I might just abandon it beside a plant and come back for it in the morning, a sight drew my feet to a stop.

## Worrying Clues

Ahead of me, at the leading edge of a row of parked cars, a Mini Cooper bore a number plate that read CHAB115. The figures were all pushed together the way people do to turn the government arrangement of letters and numbers into a tortured version of a word. In this case a name: Chablis.

Chablis left an hour ago. Or so I thought. She said she needed to get going or she would find herself in terrible traffic.

A twitch in my left eye as two neurons inside my brain connected told me something was amiss, and a memory surfaced as if summoned.

Chablis said she came to us from meeting a customer in Hastings, but to do that she would have needed to travel the same road the mushroom delivery driver got stuck on – the one out of Rye on the south coast. Also, she got to us fast. Too fast now that I was thinking about it. Even assuming she got through the location of the accident before it happened, there still hadn't been enough time to cover the distance. Not in the time between my first call to Barry and Chablis arriving.

Maybe she was already on the road I told myself.

As a tinge of doubt crept into my belly, I peered into the car. There were boxes of mushrooms stacked on the backseat. Chablis said she took the rejected ones away though, so that had to be what I was seeing.

It all made sense.

So why was her car still here?

'*Mine,*' said Buster.

I looked down to find him lifting a back leg to 'water' one of the wheels. In doing so he was claiming the car as his property. Quite why dogs wanted things once they urinated on them, I would never understand.

Ignoring him, I looked back toward the venue. The banquet hall was mood lit to create ambiance, but in the dark outside, I could see into it as clear as day. It was seventy yards away, a line of windows down one side showing me everything inside. The guests were moving to take their seats and as I watched, Justin came into view, effortlessly controlling the event as he always did.

My heart was beating faster than it ought to be. Why was Chablis still here? Come to think of it, how could Teagan have switched out the mushrooms? I'd jumped to a conclusion when I discovered she was only posing as a chef. There would be a devious reason why she'd done it, but could she have swapped the mushrooms?

Both the ones in the kitchen and the ones on the backseat were in the same boxes labelled with the same farm logo. It wasn't inconceivable for Teagan to know where they were coming from and to have intercepted them, but scrutinising the facts now, it just didn't add up.

My heart beat even faster.

I tried the door handle on the passenger's side of the car, and then the driver's too, though I thought it to be a pointless act even before I discovered it was just as locked. Moving around to the boot, my shoe mushed something, and I looked down to find a mushroom under it. There was another lying just an inch away that was intact.

Beginning to feel quite unnerved, I glanced at the banquet hall again. Everyone was sitting now. The servers would begin bringing the soup through in a few minutes.

Whipping my phone from my handbag with fingers that were starting to shake, I asked it to find me pictures of chanterelle mushrooms, then stopped. What was the other mushroom called? The one that looked almost the same but was poisonous? I couldn't remember.

Cursing myself, I dug around in my handbag for my reading glasses.

'There's something moving around in the bushes,' said Buster. 'I think it might be a bunny.'

With my attention focused on my phone, I couldn't spare the time to comment. I had bigger concerns than bunnies.

The picture on my phone looked just like the mushrooms I'd seen earlier. There was text beneath, my eyes whizzing left to right as I tried to speed read it.

*The Jack O Lantern mushroom is easily confused with the much-prized chanterelle, but one can easily be discerned from the other. The Jack O Lantern is more orange in colour, the chanterelle is the colour of straw. On the underside, the gills of the Jack O Lantern do not fork and present as a knife edge ...*

My breath came in gulps now as my heart started to bang in my chest. The description was the exact opposite of how Chablis described them earlier. I was holding a chanterelle in my hand. I couldn't get into the car, but I was willing to bet Chablis double switched the mushrooms earlier, taking the boxes of Jack O Lanterns away only to bring them back while hiding the replacement chanterelles in her car. She hadn't come from a meeting in Hastings at all, she'd been there for hours, making sure the mushrooms being delivered were deadly Jack O Lanterns!

She was the poisoner! Not Teagan.

I had to get to the banquet hall before anyone ate the soup!

Beginning to run, I screamed at the top of my lungs. 'Hey! Don't touch the soup!'

My screams could not be heard by the people inside the banquet hall. A string quartet accompanied by a harpist provided background noise, but the general hubbub of conversation plus thick double glazing made sure my voice couldn't penetrate.

The bunnies heard me though.

Just as I started to run - I could cover the distance to the banquet hall in a handful of seconds and hammer on the glass – several shadowy shapes darted in different directions across the tarmac.

Buster barked, '*Bunnies*,' and unable to resist, he shot off to follow them. That was bad enough, but the worst part was his trajectory. Going rearwards as I went forwards, both of us breaking into a flat-out sprint, his low centre of gravity took my left arm with it.

My upper body stopped for a split second then reversed direction but my legs kept going so that I sort of flipped in mid-air. Crashing painfully onto the ground, the lead came free and the last I saw of my dog was his fat, furry backside vanishing into the bushes.

'Buster!' I yelled like a madwoman. 'Buster, come back!'

There was no time. I would have to get him later. The wedding guests were all about to be poisoned.

Pushing myself off the ground, I screamed again, this time in pain because my left shoulder hurt like hell. Trying to get up despite the pain, I discovered my arm didn't want to work properly and a look made me believe my shoulder was dislocated. It was another thing that could wait. I would get to it later.

I broke into a run again, this one more of a shamble as I used my right arm to hold my left to my body. The servers were walking through the banquet hall now, each of them carrying two bowls of lethal soup.

I bellowed at them again with exactly the same effect as before. They couldn't hear me, but I would be there before anyone got to start eating. I could still save the day!

That was until Chablis stepped into my path.

## Reason to Kill

My feet screeched to a stop. I was forty yards from the banquet hall windows, but to get there I would have to go through a younger, taller, fitter woman who didn't have a dislocated shoulder. Any thoughts I had about trying it went south when the light from inside glinted off the edge of the kitchen knife she held by her side.

In the cold night air, I could see her breaths coming in rage-filled snorts like an excited racehorse on the starting line. Like me, she wasn't dressed to be outside, but unlike me she didn't seem to care.

'You're not stopping this,' she snarled at me. 'I won't let you.'

'But you're going to kill them all!'

'Good,' she snapped. 'It's overkill, but they all love her so I'm fine with some collateral damage.'

'Collateral ...?' I couldn't believe my ears. My eyes as wide as saucers, I watched the servers move in to place the bowls in front of the guests and I yelled another warning. 'Justin! It's poison!'

In response, Chablis swung the knife upward toward my face, narrowly missing me as I darted backward almost tripping over my own feet.

'You're not stopping this!' Chablis screamed. Now that I was a few feet farther away, the knife went back to her side. 'It will be too late soon.'

'Why?' I shrieked, horrified to have to watch. Buster was going to come back and save me, I just knew he would. That's what always happens on the television. So where was the stupid dog?

'She ruined my life!' Chablis raged, anger dripping from every letter.

'Who?' Honestly, I expected her to say Angelica Howard-Box. That someone might want to kill her almost seemed fair and just.

That wasn't the name Chablis had though. She said, 'Sasha. That's not even her real name, you know.' I didn't know but it came as no great surprise. Lots of public personalities have stage names just as authors have pen names. 'I came up with it. I called her Sasha Allstar. She is my invention. We were going to do it together. We made thirty shows as a couple and just when we were getting traction and our followers were growing, a big media firm stepped in and offered her a contract. Her, not me. AND SHE TOOK IT!'

'That's no reason to kill her,' I wailed, watching hopelessly as Justin led the guests in saying grace.

'It is every reason,' Chablis growled. 'Now if you don't mind, I think I would like to watch.'

I almost said, 'Go ahead,' but then I realised that what she meant was that it was time for me to die so she could watch in peace.

I shrieked and ran away. I couldn't get to the banquet hall, there was just no way, but I could get back inside the building. I ran to the nearest door.

Chablis swore at me, stringing profanities together as she gave chase.

'Buster!' I shouted for the dog again. 'Buster, Felicity needs you!'

My dog, stupid lump that he is, was off chasing rabbits and would probably be found later sitting by my body. He would be praised for his loyalty when want he needed to do was respond to my voice for once.

The door I came out through was ahead, but it opened outwards, and I knew from the sound of her heels on the stone flags of the courtyard that she was going to catch me when I got there.

I screamed in frightened relief when it opened outward just before I got to it.

The broad shoulders stepping out into the cold belonged to Vince Slater. An hour ago, I would have been happy to never see or hear of him again. Now I wanted to hug him.

However, my relief was short-lived. Vince got enough time to register what was going on, his eyes going wide as he threw himself outward from the building. Aiming for the woman chasing me, he simply didn't have enough time to do anything about the knife Chablis swung upward into his torso.

Bravely, or perhaps just because he didn't get a chance to think, Vince put his body between Chablis' and mine. As he folded around the blade, I screamed again, running for my life, and pumping my arms despite the searing pain in my left shoulder.

Chablis' torrent of profanity followed me, her heels clopping across the courtyard in my wake. The positions had reversed though, and she was behind me now as I ran toward the banquet room. All I had to do was get there!

If I could just stop them from eating, help would come. If Vince wasn't already dead, he would be using his radio to call for backup, I felt certain. I could see some of his men positioned strategically around the banquet hall.

Justin had finished saying grace and the bowls of soup were on the tables. Just behind my Master of Ceremonies, Mindy, my ninja niece, watched and learned. How I could use her skills right now.

Twenty yards to the windows and I swear I could feel Chablis' breath on my back. In the next second, I was going to feel the cold steel of the kitchen knife. Acknowledging it as fact before the event made my blood go cold and my legs shake.

A snarl came from right behind me and suddenly my head yanked back as Chablis grabbed my hair. I didn't know where the knife was, and there wasn't going to be a chance to ask, because as she pulled me off balance, she also shoved me to the ground.

I hit the ground completely out of control, my left shoulder leading the way. I swear I heard a pop as the socket went back together and I almost vomited when my head swirled from the pain it caused.

Chablis stood over me, breathing raggedly from the adrenalin and exertion. 'I lost the knife … I guess … I'll have to just … strangle you instead,' she announced between gasps of cold night air.

I wanted to scramble back to get away from her, but I had nothing left. I couldn't get to the banquet windows and they would be eating the soup in seconds.

Chablis took a step forward, looming over me.

Then suddenly she wasn't there. The space where she'd been, the space where my eyes were still looking, contained nothing but the inky black of a night sky.

'*Dun, dun, dah!*' yelled Buster. '*Superdog to the rescue!*'

I spun my head to find Buster skidding to a stop and trying to dig his claws in so he could come back for another pass. Between him and me, Chablis was tumbling to the Earth.

He'd used her legs like a cat flap, hitting them at his maximum velocity.

Chablis slammed into the stone tiles like a ragdoll, but she wasn't done. A cry of agony seemed to fuel her need to kill me. She was in pain, but she was getting up. With a growl of defiance, she got to her knees, her teeth gritted and murder in her eyes.

Vince punched her in the jaw and that was that.

A gasp of terrified relief escaped me, though my eyes refused to believe what I was seeing. Vince still had the knife sticking out through the front of his suit where it looked to be lodged in a spot at the bottom of his ribs. Buster had the left pant leg of Chablis' suit in his mouth and was ripping it to shreds. He might start on her leg itself if I didn't stop him.

Suddenly aware that I was gawping at the sight to my front when I had something far more pressing to do, I threw myself up and off the ground. On legs that argued against my demands to support my weight, I stumbled to the windows.

The servers were all beginning to move away, heading back to the kitchen, and I could see the bride and groom in the centre of the top table reaching for their spoons.

I hammered on the glass, both fists slamming into it as I screamed and hollered with everything I could muster.

Heads whipped around, finally hearing me.

## Enter the Real Sleuth

The paramedics gave me painkillers but said I didn't have to go to hospital if I didn't want to. I had already argued against it. I was bruised and battered. There was skin missing from both my knees. Chablis had pulled out a chunk of my hair and my left arm wasn't going to work right for a while. I also still had the carpet burn on my chin from falling over Buster earlier but how could I be mad with him now?

We were inside Loxton Hall where the police, led by Chief Inspector Quinn, were managing the situation.

Three of the chefs had tasted the soup before it was served – standard kitchen practice as they season and check their dishes. They were all on their way to hospital where I was assured they would make a full recovery, though it would take several days before they were completely out of danger.

It turns out that Jack O Lanterns are not lethal if treated quickly, even though they are poisonous. The effects are difficult to treat, one paramedic explained, telling me they would have intravenous drips and a cocktail of drugs combined with a strictly controlled diet to wash their systems through. Chef Olafson had died of a heart attack, his body giving out as a result off the mushroom poisoning, so it was still a murder charge Chablis faced.

Chablis, conscious again and also being treated because it turned out Buster broke both her ankles, cared not that she had killed a man. In fact, she seemed more put out to hear about the non-lethal nature of the mushrooms and that her attempt at mass murder might not have worked after all. I got to watch her be taken away in the ambulance with two police officers accompanying her plus two squad cars providing escort.

Vince came to find me, plonking himself down onto the chair next to mine where I sat idly scratching Buster's head with my right hand. My left arm was in a sling.

'How come you are not on your way to hospital?' I asked, surprised to see him.

He flexed a bicep. 'They make us Slater men tough, Felicity. A little stabbing isn't enough to keep me down.'

I eyed him sceptically. 'You were wearing a stab vest, weren't you?'

His cheeks reddened slightly as he murmured, 'Only a little one.' I laughed at him despite the horror of the last few hours. As if I had somehow encouraged him, he pulled open his jacket and lifted his shirt to show a wound dressing. 'It went right through the vest though.'

He got another doubtful look from me. 'Really?'

'Well, the tip did.' His cheeks coloured again. 'The fabric did its job and stopped the blade penetrating any farther.'

Anything else he planned to say was interrupted by Chief Inspector Quinn coming our way. He looked … I couldn't decide. It was somewhere between annoyed and relieved.

'You are both receiving the treatment you need?' he asked.

Vince showed the dressing over his wound again, and foolishly, I lifted my left arm in its sling to show that I had been patched up. A blast of pain from my shoulder, even through the dullness caused by the painkillers, convinced me to not do it again.

'Very good. Now,' he looked at me and then at Vince and then back at me, 'I seem to remember a conversation about amateurs not attempting to do police work. Do either of you remember that?'

A snort of sad laughter escaped me. 'I hardly think this was a deliberate choice on my part. I stumbled across the woman trying to poison everyone at the wedding by accident. And if Mr Slater hadn't shown up when he did, you would have my dead body, a hundred poisoned guests, and a killer yet to be identified. Ought you not to be thanking us?'

'Goodness, no,' replied the chief inspector. 'I shall thank you to report such suspicions in the future. Mrs Philips, in the statement you gave my detective sergeant earlier, you claim to have found evidence that led you to suspect Miss Chimera on the ground by her car. You then attempted to intervene in events in the banquet hall and participated in a fight with Miss Chimera. I put it to you that your first act should have been to call the police.'

'There wasn't time,' I protested.

'Your statement suggests otherwise,' he countered.

I could feel a head of steam building up. It had been a trying evening and the entire dinner, every single course, had been rejected by the wedding party on the premise that no one could guarantee another dish hadn't also been poisoned. As I understood it, the footballer friends of the groom and Sasha's bridal party had all called a local pizza place and were on their way to the indoor pool for a pool party.

Before I could blow my top, a familiar face, even if it had aged since the last time I saw it, appeared behind Chief Inspector Quinn. The familiar face was heading our way and already speaking.

'Chief Inspector Quinn, how lovely it is to see you again.'

Right in front of my face, the chief inspector closed his eyes and muttered something that probably couldn't be printed. When he opened them again, he had a smile on his face that didn't extend beyond his mouth.

Turning around to face the newcomer he said, 'Mrs Fisher, good evening.'

The End

## Author's notes

On the next page you will find the main story that you bought this book for. However, though the new characters: Felicity, Mindy, Vince, Buster, and more are not yet familiar to you, they are going to help me bring a new series to life.

Felicity Philips Investigates is a working title for the new series and about the sixth I have tried out so far. It probably won't stick, but I am scheduled to write their first full-length mystery next, so I had better come up with something.

Weddings struck me as a good backdrop for a series. There are a few definites in life, like dying at the end of it and cursing the taxman all the way through. Weddings, if not your own then someone else's, are another inescapable event. Felicity Philips and her team will uncover myriad mysteries as they arrange weddings for the rich and famous and possibly insanely murderous. Across my home county of Kent, where there are many castles and stately homes, they will move between venues and solve crimes as they go. Not because they want to, but because circumstance demands they must.

In this short story I use mushrooms as a murder weapon. Writing my fifth series and my fifty first novel, I feared I would begin to run out of ideas for methods of dispatch. How boring would it be if everyone got shot? Thankfully, I show no signs of repeating myself yet.

The chanterelle and Jack O Lantern are indeed close cousins in appearance, but as I describe in the story, the Jack O Lantern will make you quite ill rather than kill you.

No doubt you are itching to get on with the main story, so I will delay you no longer.

Have at it.

Steve Higgs

## My Curious Streak

Chief Inspector Quinn did not look pleased to see me. I knew our chosen professions put us a little at odds; we were coming at crimes from two different angles, but I was not aware that I had caused him any particular problems.

We knew each other because I own a private investigations business and had a habit of getting under his feet. Another way to look at that was to say I habitually solved crimes he was investigating and that irked him.

I neither liked nor disliked him. He is a lean, six-foot man with a strong sense of his own career path. He gives the impression anyone getting in his way on that path is likely to get trodden on.

My name is Patricia Fisher. I'm fifty-three-years-old, soon to be divorced, a few pounds heavier than I think I ought to be, and I learned this year that I can solve a mystery like no one else on the planet. Unfortunately, that goes hand in hand with attracting more trouble than I feel I deserve and the semi-regular appearance of freshly dead bodies.

Minutes after arriving at Loxton Hall, a plush stately home in the west of Kent where I was spending the weekend to attend the wedding of two good friends, I spotted an ambulance whizzing up the long driveway. Curious, I watched its path, leaning against the window as it neared the house and saw a dozen police officers rush out to meet it. Watching them was the unmistakable form of Chief Inspector Quinn.

I last saw him just before I fled the country more than a month ago and he was on my list of people I wanted to see now that I was back. Since he was here ... Well, I acknowledge that it might have been more pertinent to wait until whatever crisis he was dealing with was over, but I have a curious streak that demands to be satisfied.

The chief inspector stood up and turned around. In so doing revealed the people he'd been talking to.

I hadn't seen Felicity Philips in many, many years, but even though her face had inevitably aged, there was no mistaking who I could see.

'Felicity!' I cried excitedly, the words bursting from my lips as I closed the remaining distance to her. My feet stuttered when I saw her sling and the scuff on her chin. Next to her was a man with his shirt untucked and what looked like a wound dressing poking out from beneath it. Between her feet was a happy-looking bulldog, his tongue lolling out to one side. 'Goodness, what happened?' I asked.

Felicity snorted a tired laugh. 'There was an issue with the caterer.'

I suspected there would prove to be a lot more to the story, but I didn't press her now. Having brought a small entourage with me, introductions were necessary.

'Everyone this is Felicity Philips,' she's the one who pulled the strings to get us here this weekend.'

At my shoulder, my boyfriend, Captain Alistair Huntley of Purple Star Cruise Lines, said, 'We are very much in your debt, Felicity.'

On the other side of me, my good friend, Barbie, a stunning twenty-two-year-old blonde bombshell gym instructor from California said, 'This place is amazing. It's so beautiful here.' Then she gasped. 'Oh, my goodness, look at the bulldog! Isn't he the cutest?'

The bulldog tilted his head, looking displeased with the question.

Barbie had my butler, Jermaine, in her shadow yet he saw no need to add a comment of his own. He did strong and silent very well. It went well with his ninja skills. How I came to have a butler is a long story for another time, but I will tell you he is a six-foot four-inch Jamaican man who fakes his Downton Abbey English accent.

I quickly announced the members of my party – there were more in the building, but they were in their rooms still where they were … um, otherwise engaged – and I learned the name of the bulldog and the injured man sitting next to Felicity.

Chief Inspector Quinn had taken a pace to his right when I first squealed my surprise at seeing an old friend. Like Jermaine, he remained quiet, but when the first natural lull in conversation arose, he filled it with words.

'Mrs Fisher I must congratulate you on your recent exploits. To have successfully identified and then beaten what is being argued to be the world's largest criminal enterprise is no mean feat.'

He referred, of course, to my exploits with a woman called the Godmother and her desire to kill me and all my friends. I inadvertently triggered her wrath many months ago when I stopped several families of murderous gangsters in Miami. And again in Tokyo. And in London when I got back to England. They all worked for her and putting them out of business impacted her income. Sometimes, I really couldn't blame her for getting upset.

I nodded my head at the chief inspector's compliment. 'We were lucky,' I replied, being modest, but also telling the truth because I still marvelled at our survival.

Barbie leaned around me to fix the chief inspector with a frown. 'It didn't help that the special police officer you provided as a bodyguard turned out to be working for the Godmother all along,' she pointed out.

He had the decency to look embarrassed at least, but he said, 'Scotland Yard found no less than twelve percent of their staff were employed by the Godmother. Again, thanks to Mrs Fisher, they were all identified.'

I doubted the chief inspector enjoyed giving me the credit. I didn't know him well, and he was always respectful when we spoke, but I was quite certain he wanted me to take up knitting and leave the detective stuff to his team.

To change the subject, I said, 'Yes, well, we saw the strobe lights and thought we ought to investigate. Our friends are getting married here tomorrow so we are invested in the weekend going peacefully.'

Felicity made an oops face. 'You might not have picked the best venue for peaceful.'

Barbie asked, 'Is that because Sashatastic is here?'

CI Quinn nodded his head sadly, but said, 'I have fifty officers here to ensure the venue is not mobbed at any point. The well-wishers and fans camped outside will not be permitted entry, the staff here have all been vetted and checked, and the guests attending will have to pass through the entry process. There is no reason to believe anything untoward will happen.'

Barbie hitched an eyebrow. 'You know Patty is here, right?'

A scowl found its way to my face. 'Hey.'

Barbie giggled but defended her statement. 'We had been here less than twenty minutes when we saw flashing lights outside the window, Patty.'

'I didn't cause them.' My scowl stayed in place.

Chief Inspector Quinn chose that moment to cough politely. 'I must attend to matters here,' he told us while backing away a pace. 'There have been two arrests already today and one death that will most likely prove to be manslaughter. There is a heavy police presence at Loxton Hall. If anyone suspects a crime is taking place or may be about to take place, I insist that you alert my officers and make no attempt to deal with matters yourself.' He locked eyes with me for some reason.

'That seems perfectly clear,' I replied with a sugar-sweet smile.

Jermaine coughed loudly.

'Oh, yes,' I caught the chief inspector's attention just before he escaped. 'Given what you just said, you may wish to know about the two men we have tied up in our room.'

## Fair Warning

There followed a moment of stunned silence. Chief Inspector Quinn's face appeared to be deciding whether it wanted to laugh at my little joke or choke with outrage that I would do such a thing.

Before he could react, Alistair volunteered, 'They were following us and snooping around. We have learned to be cautious about such things.'

Sitting on the floor next to Felicity, Vincent groaned and closed his eyes. 'Are they both in suits with radio earpieces?' he wanted to know.

Alistair nodded. 'Yes. They claim to be part of a security team working here.'

I added, 'We were coming down to see what had happened to draw all the police officers and ambulances and figured we could see if there was any truth to their claim at the same time.'

'They're mine,' Vince admitted reluctantly.

'Was it your instruction to spy on us?' I wanted to know.

Vince levered himself back to his feet. 'It is my job to ensure there is no threat to the Howard-Box wedding. You are not on the guest list and I know for a fact that there are no other guests staying here this weekend because there are no other weddings.' He glanced down at Felicity where she remained sitting on a chair. A smirk flitted across his face. 'Of course, I am wrong about that. Aren't I, Felicity? You could have mentioned your hand in this earlier when I told you I was sending someone to watch them.'

Felicity said, 'I promised Patricia I would tell no one she was here.'

Chief Inspector Quinn interrupted our conversation. 'We appear to have strayed away from the part where you have kidnapped two people and are currently holding them captive,' he pointed out sternly. 'Since you are here, can I hope that they are still alive and not currently being tortured by whoever you left behind to guard them?'

He was being flippant, and quite unnecessarily so in my opinion.

'The bride and groom have them,' said Barbie with a grin.

'And the best man,' I added.

CI Quinn rubbed his temples. 'That failed to answer my question about their current condition.'

I started to back away, signalling for Vince to follow. 'Perhaps you would like to collect them? I'm sure that would set the chief inspector's mind at rest.'

'I rather think I shall come too,' Quinn insisted. 'There's a troubled voice in the back of my head that feels it might be prudent to assign a couple of officers to watch over the area where your rooms are located.'

I shrugged. 'If you wish, Chief Inspector.'

Seven of us with Buster the bulldog leading made our way back through the ground floor of Loxton Hall. It reminded me of my house in East Malling, the one the Maharaja of Zangrabar gave me. Loxton Hall was bigger by at least a hundred percent, and it was far older, but the interior finish and the sense of space the oversized rooms gave was much the same.

An ugly thought about my husband surfaced uninvited. On Monday, just three days from now, I was due to attend a meeting with him and his lawyers. I could opt to postpone the meeting or simply refuse to attend, but eventually I was going to have to deal with the issue of our divorce and ... well, I just wanted it done and behind me. If he wanted to split our assets in half, I was going to give it to him and watch as he choked on it.

'Everything okay, Patty?' asked Barbie.

I shot her a questioning look. 'Yes. Why do you ask?'

She curled a lip. 'You were muttering, and it looked as if you were plotting to kill someone.'

I chuckled. 'I was thinking about the divorce meeting,' I admitted. 'So ... I kind of was plotting murder.'

'Hmmm?' asked Chief Inspector Quinn. 'Did I hear you say murder?'

Barbie and I both shot him down with hard frowns. 'Listening to people's conversations is not polite,' stated Barbie flatly.

She got a derisory snort of laughter from him in return. 'It's my job, Miss Berkeley. Don't talk about murder and don't kidnap people and I might feel less inclined to listen.'

The conversation stopped because we had arrived, Jermaine knocking smartly on the door to the room containing the other four members of our party.

The door barked in response.

It wasn't the door, obviously, but my two miniature dachshunds doing what they always do. For some reason, and I'm sure it is not just my dogs, they view anyone knocking on the door as a foe to be thwarted until such time as the case can be proven otherwise.

Buster reacted to their barking, by doing the same in reply. Felicity needed a hand to haul her headstrong dog away from the door, Alistair –

ever the gentleman – moving to help only to get cut off by Vince who darted forward to get there first.

I could hear Lieutenant Schneider scooping my dogs on the other side of the door, easy since they weigh less than five pounds each, and the door opened to reveal the groom.

He was expecting us, not the three extra people we had collected.

'Everything, okay?' Lieutenant Martin Baker asked, keeping the door mostly closed so the police officer with us would not see the two men tied up and sitting on the carpet.

With a signal that he should back away and let us all in, I said, 'The chief inspector is curious to make sure we have not harmed our unexpected guests.'

When the door swung wide, it revealed two men in suits looking annoyed and embarrassed. That their boss was with us probably didn't help.

'They jumped us, Vince,' said the nearest.

Vince entered the room ahead of me. 'Then you should have done a better job of being invisible, shouldn't you.' He wasn't taking their side.

'You can untie them now,' said Alistair - the four lieutenants in the room all worked for him.

The dogs were all on the floor, Buster still being held in check by Vince, but his little stubby tail whizzed back and forth in excitement as he met my two dachshunds, Anna and Georgie.

Chief Inspector Quinn rubbed his temples again as if he were fighting a migraine. 'You ... you do know that you cannot just tie people up,' he mumbled.

'They were spying on us,' I pointed out.

Quinn looked around to find my face. 'That would give normal people cause to speak to the police, Mrs Fisher.'

I shrugged. 'This seemed more efficient.'

He closed his eyes while his eyebrows climbed to the top of his head.

The two men were freed of the plastic cable ties used to bind their ankles and wrists. Back on their feet, they looked like they wanted to start a fight but badly outnumbered and in the presence of a police officer, I doubted they would be so foolish.

'Come along, chaps,' said Vince, gesticulating for them to leave.

Chief Inspector Quinn raised a hand so everyone would stop what they were doing. 'I could arrest your men, Mr Slater.'

'For what,' Vince wanted to know.

Quinn snorted. 'Do you want a list? How about for carrying the weapons I can see that man,' he pointed at Lieutenant Anders Pippin, 'about to return to them?' Anders' cheeks coloured. In his hands were two batons, the telescoping sort that extend when the user flicks their arm.

Vince stopped arguing and Chief Inspector Quinn panned his gaze around the room.

'I could also arrest all of you.' He paused to see if any of us would be foolish enough to ask why. When no one did, he let a small laugh go. 'So you do understand that holding people against their will is illegal. Good.' He looked around again, making eye contact with everyone. Then he huffed out a sigh. 'There will be no more of this. You will act like normal people and give me and my officers no reason to pay you any attention whatsoever. I want no more acting like secret agents.' He narrowed his eyes at Vince and his two men. 'And I want no more trying to solve crimes by yourself.' He was looking firmly at me this time.

I smiled back at him. I had no intention of doing anything this weekend other than watching two friends get married and spending some quality time with Alistair. All too soon we would be back on the ship and altogether too busy. Here, at this wonderful stately home in the countryside, I was going to let myself unwind.

If only I had known then what the next twenty-four hours had in store for me, I might have packed my bags and left.

## Inadvertent Eavesdropping

Once the chief inspector had delivered his warning and departed, Vince ushered his men from the room too. They made a point of giving Baker and the other lieutenants a mean glare before they departed, a macho nonsense that required no words of translation: next time it will be different. Or something like that.

Deepa Bhukari, tomorrow's bride, clapped her hands together to make sure people were listening. 'Right, you men, get out. This is the bride's room and will only have ladies in it until someone convinces me to marry him tomorrow.'

Obviously expecting to get turfed out, Lieutenant Martin Baker made a big joke of how hurt he was to have to leave and dragged his feet.

'You too, Jermaine,' Deepa ordered. 'And you, sir,' she flared her eyes at her captain, Alistair.

Chuckling, he backed away to the door. 'Chaps, I dare say it is an appropriate time for us to frequent the bar.'

His suggestion was met with approval by all, including me. It had always been our intention to visit the bar before we retired for the evening. Now that we were here, the plan was to relax. The week had been filled with hasty arrangements such as a dress for Deepa because the one she had was on the ship still and thus somewhere in the Mediterranean. There were rings to be bought, vows to be written, food to organise.

It was to be a quiet ceremony, obviously since there were so few of us, but both had family arriving in the morning. Martin's were flying in from Northern Ireland, a short hop that would deliver them to Gatwick Airport at breakfast time. Deepa's family lived a couple of hours drive north of Loxton Hall and would also arrive around breakfast time.

Felicity had been instrumental in pulling everything together so quickly; her contacts made it all possible. I needed to thank her for that.

Turning to catch her before she too departed, I said, 'We're going to head for the bar. Will you join us? It would be nice to catch up and we really need to show our appreciation for all you have done.'

Felicity smiled in reply. 'You are welcome, of course. I would love to come for a drink, but I fear I have much to do yet this evening. Things have not gone to plan today. I must visit with my clients to discuss tomorrow and any changes they may wish to impose.'

Hovering in the doorway still, Vince said, 'Yes, dear, you and I have much to do yet this evening. No rest for the wicked, eh?'

Hearing his words and the way he said them prompted a fresh question. I hadn't seen Felicity in a long time, but she was married way back then. Now it sounded like she was in a relationship with Vince.

'Sorry,' I started. 'Are you two together?'

Felicity's mouth dropped open in abject horror. 'Goodness, no!' she cried indignantly as if I had suggested she were dating an entire rugby team.

Vince sniggered. 'I think she means to say not yet.'

Felicity rounded on the private investigator, striding the two paces she needed to get close to him where she promptly poked him in the chest.

'I mean no, Vince Slater. I don't know what daft idea you have got in your head, but you can jolly well get it out again. I am not looking for a man in my life and if I were, I should like to think I have better taste than to pick you.'

'Goodness,' Vince chuckled. 'I really get you all hot and bothered, don't I?'

Felicity made an angry noise of frustration. I had no idea what their relationship was, but Vince appeared to be right: he was getting under her skin. He was handsome and looked to take care of himself. Plus, he was about the right age. If she were no longer married, I wouldn't dare to ask what might have happened to Archie – her husband's name flashed into my head – then she could do worse than the man she was currently arguing with.

That said, she didn't need a man any more than any woman does.

With a final comment as she went out the door, Felicity said, 'I really must go. I'll see you at breakfast no doubt. Thanks for the offer of a drink. If I get the chance to swing by the bar, I'll do so.'

Then she was gone, Buster leading her away with Vince gamely following behind.

It left just the three ladies in the room. Five if I chose to include Anna and Georgie.

Deepa flopped onto the bed. 'I must say I did not expect to be using the plasticuffs this weekend. How do we always attract so much trouble?'

Barbie giggled. 'I like to call it the Patricia effect.'

I frowned at her. I wanted to argue that it wasn't my fault. In all honesty it wasn't, but I will admit that wherever I go something tends to happen.

Deepa stared up at the ceiling. 'Well, I hope that's the end of it. I want to see my parents and my sisters tomorrow. I want to finally meet Martin's family and I want to get married. Preferably without anything exploding or anyone getting murdered.'

Hastily changing the subject, I suggested, 'Gin, anyone?'

The bar was empty. I don't mean there were only a few people in it, I mean it was empty. The two young men working behind the bar were reading books, hunched over to lean on the counter.

Deepa, Barbie, and I looked around in confusion.

'Where is everyone?' asked Barbie. 'I thought Sashatastic and Bobbie H-B were here with hundreds of their friends.'

The question was aimed at the barmen who both looked up, eyes drawn to respond as customers arrived, but then those same eyes saw Barbie and Deepa – two unfairly attractive women – and everything about the two men changed. Gone were the bored expressions and vague disappointment at having their quiet reading time disturbed. In its place, keen enthusiasm to please arrived.

'Yes, they are having a pool party, I believe,' revealed the one on the right. His badge displayed the name Joe.

Not to be outdone in talking to the attractive ladies, his partner, Ken, spoke up. 'Something happened to their dinner.'

'I heard it was poisoned,' said Joe.

'I was just getting to that,' pointed out Ken with a frown. 'One of our colleagues, a girl called Teagan, was arrested for something.'

'We don't know what yet,' said Joe, earning himself another frown from Ken.

'She wasn't supposed to be working today but stole a chef's uniform and was working in the kitchen. Our guess is she was trying to poison everyone,' Ken told the girls as if it were a big secret.

'Can we get some drinks?' I asked.

The barmen weren't really listening though. Not to me anyway. They were entranced by Barbie and Deepa.

Behind me, Alistair came into the bar, Schneider, Pippin, Baker, and Jermaine on his heels. I got a broad grin from him.

'Hello, darling. Fancy running into you here.' He pulled me into a hug, looking over my head at the bar. 'Chaps, I believe some beverages are in order.' Somehow when he spoke, Ken and Joe saw fit to abruptly end their chatter and get on with the drink making.

A minute later, I had a Hendricks and tonic in a large balloon glass with ice and cucumber. It didn't last long.

I think we were all relatively tired, and all saw the sense in getting an early night. Tomorrow would be a big day for two of our party, and a joyous celebration for the rest of us. Nevertheless, we were all awake now and about as relaxed as we had been at any time since I first met the people around me. Sharing downtime with the lieutenants was a rare thing anyway – they were in uniform and working mostly, and when they were not, such as when Martin and Deepa came to Zangrabar with me, we were all too busy trying to not get killed to actually relax as we had hoped.

There was one topic I wanted to avoid, not least because we were attending a wedding and talk of divorce has no place there, but also because I didn't want my friends' scrutiny. Despite my best attempts to steer the conversation onto other subjects, Barbie got me in the end.

'When is the meeting?' asked Barbie. She referred to the imminent ambush my husband was planning with his team of divorce lawyers. My friends knew it was soon, but I had been deliberately tight-lipped about it for weeks.

I let my shoulders sag and decided to just tell the truth. 'Monday at ten o'clock.'

'Monday!' squeaked my blonde friend. 'Patty you don't even have a lawyer! What are you going to do?'

I huffed out a breath. 'I'm going to argue.'

Earlier this year I caught my husband in a compromising position in my best friend's bedroom. At the time I was shocked and horrified. I felt betrayed and filled with shame that it happened to me, but in retrospect, he did me a favour and my life was so much better now than it had been back then.

However, a number of things in my life changed after I walked out of our house and through accidentally solving a mystery that saw a priceless sapphire returned to the grateful Maharaja of Zangrabar, I came to live in a huge mansion and have access to a surprising amount of money.

Now that we were getting a divorce, my rat of a husband believed he had rightful claim to half of it. He hired a top law firm to ensure he got it, and I'd been too busy trying to stay alive to be able to think about finding a divorce lawyer of my own.

In truth, I'd been putting the task off when I knew I could resolve it with one phone call. Given the sums involved, I doubt anyone in the phonebook would have turned me down. Now, it was too late. I agreed to attend the meeting weeks ago and though I was sure I could find a legal reason why I should not attend, or simply duck the meeting, I wanted it done and put to bed.

However, I was determined that Charlie wouldn't get a penny, though I was yet to cement a method for achieving that. I had a wildcard that I might be able to play, I just didn't know if it was worth anything yet, not for certain, and we were getting close to the wire. If I didn't get an answer soon, there was a danger Charlie might win.

I was going to have to make another phone call.

My friends did not look happy about my stance on the divorce meeting but none of them were going to condemn me for the position I found myself in. Instead of finding myself a lawyer, which is probably what they thought I should have been doing this week, I had focused on getting Deepa and Martin ready for their wedding.

Alistair leaned over to take my hand. 'Nothing you lose will be of any concern, Patricia. We have all that we need and more.'

They were kind words and very true. I could let Charlie have everything and go happily about my life. I knew it would rankle me to see him win though. His smug face as he took from me all that he had done nothing to deserve would be enough to make me want to run him over and then probably reverse back and do it again. That image in my head was enough for me to squeeze my glass so hard I thought it might burst in my hand.

No. Letting Charlie have the Maharaja's house, cars, and everything else was not an option I could live with. It wasn't about what I needed. It was to do with the world being a fair and just place to live.

I was going to beat Charlie and his oh-so-clever team of lawyers. Or I was going to have Anna poop in his shoes.

Sensing that it was a delicate and unwelcome subject, Deepa swung the conversation around to the celebrities we were sharing Loxton Hall with this weekend. Had anyone seen a famous person yet? Who was it?

I forced the images of Charlie from my mind, putting my glass down so I could excuse myself to visit the restroom.

I left Anna and Georgie at the table; they were finding plenty of willing laps on which they could curl up for a sleep while idly getting a belly rub or an ear scratch. Outside the bar, I could hear female voices coming from my right. Thinking it was probably conversation drifting out from the ladies' restroom, I explored that way.

I didn't really need to visit the restroom; I was unsettled by the conversation and the uncertainty I felt over the likely outcome of the meeting on Monday. That was why I was going to make the phone call now even though it was late on a Friday evening.

Unsure whether he would even answer and feeling like I should lead with an apology for calling if he did, I let go a breath I hadn't realised I was holding when the call connected. 'Morris Worthington,' he announced. 'Is that you, Mrs Fisher.'

'Yes,' I sighed with relief. 'Yes, thank you so much for taking the call. I'm sorry it is so late.'

'That's perfectly all right, Mrs Fisher. I am still at the office.'

My eyes flaring, I choked out, 'At this time?' The voices I could hear coming from the restroom were getting louder. Two women were arguing about something.

I put my free hand over my right ear so I could better hear the phone pressed to my left. 'Many of our clients are not on Greenwich Meantime, Mrs Fisher. Case in point, I am waiting for a call from a partner in Zangrabar.'

His announcement made my heart pitter-patter, a nervous reaction to hear what he might say next. 'Is there any news?'

'Not yet, I'm afraid,' he replied, his voice solemn. 'I think though, that this is good news, Mrs Fisher.'

'Why is that?' I begged to know, holding my breath once more because I had so much riding on the outcome of his investigation. I had to turn away and back up a few paces, the argument in the ladies' restroom was getting to the point where I thought someone might throw a punch. I figured it was probably a couple of girls from the wedding party, a little tipsy and fighting over a boy or something.

At the other end of the phone, I heard Mr Worthington moving things about and the catches on a briefcase spring open – he was packing up to go home. 'Because if it were the case that you were, shall we say, out of luck, I believe the answer would have come back immediately. I am aware of the Monday deadline, Mrs Fisher. Fear not. I expect an answer before the weekend is out.'

All I could do was thank him for his diligence. I ended the call, tapping my phone against my lips in thought. I was either going to have an ace card to trump anything Charlie had, or I was going to have no cards to play at all. With two days to go, I had no idea which it might be and despite Mr Worthington's optimism, I refused to let my hopes swell.

A yell of anger came from the restroom. The two women were still arguing. I now needed to use the facilities, but did I go in and disturb them?

Pondering that very question, I heard fast heels coming toward the door. Whoever was coming out almost ripped the door from its hinges such was their mood. A cacophony of profanity lit the air as Sashatastic – I knew who she was only because Barbie showed me a photograph earlier – burst into the corridor.

She was the one doing the swearing and continued to fire insults over her shoulder as she stormed away. She came my way, passing me with the briefest of glances. The internet star was dressed for the pool in a bikini but sporting a long winter coat that fell to her knees and would have covered her near-nakedness completely had she buttoned it up. Her face, normally pretty I knew from her pictures, was a mask of rage that would scare a silverback into retreating.

Yet, somehow, I got the impression things had not gone her way in the restroom. My suspicions were confirmed when an older woman – roughly my age, I guess – stepped out from the restroom to shout a final warning down the corridor.

'Do as I say, Sasha, or there will be consequences.' The woman was smiling as if Sasha's display of emotion were amusing.

Sasha raised her hand as she walked away, a familiar hand gesture her parting response.

This time, the older woman sniggered, and catching sight of me standing uncertain in the corridor like an innocent bystander to a crime, she flipped her eyebrows and went back into the restroom.

I didn't know what I had just seen but it was not the happy night-before-the-wedding behaviour I expected. It was none of my business and I wasn't going to go looking for another restroom, so I got my feet moving.

Inside the ladies', the only occupant was washing her hands when I got there. Seeing me enter, she felt a need to explain what I had just seen.

'Sasha likes to think she got to where she is by herself.'

Not wishing to get involved but also not seeing a way to avoid speaking unless I chose to be very rude, I guessed, 'Are you her mother?' She was about the right age and though she was several inches taller, her hair and slender figure bore enough similarities for there to be a genetic connection.

My question got a laugh. 'Goodness, no. I'm Cara Fright, her manager. Sasha likes to live in the moment. Her internet blog, the concept of living her teen years on the air for everyone to see everything was inspired and it got her noticed. She wasn't the first, but she was the first to do it successfully. What she fails to realise is that others have come along, treading the path she created, and Sasha is no longer a teenager. She isn't even close.'

'And that means she is no longer relevant?' I joined the dots of what Cara appeared to be telling me.

Cara was watching me in the mirror. 'Not to the same audience. The fans she amassed ten years ago are mums now, or career women. Sasha needs a new angle, or she will be left behind and that's just not good enough. She has a team of people behind her, responsibilities, investors who expect to see a return for the faith they placed in her. Sashatastic was a highly commercial platform from which many successful products have been launched. But investors are turning away and now Sasha … well. You don't need to hear the whole story, I'm sure.'

I didn't think I needed to hear any of it, but I had. Cara dried her hands and turned to face me, her forehead wrinkling. 'Oh,' she made a startled face as she recognised me. 'I'm sorry. I didn't recognise you.' Her frown deepened. 'But you're not a guest at the wedding, are you? Are you here with Angelica?'

A laugh escaped me. 'No. I am not here with Angelica. There is another wedding here tomorrow. A small one. We will be on the other side of Loxton Hall and in a separate set of reception rooms.'

She nodded, bumping her hip away from the counter as she started to move toward the door. 'Well, it was nice to meet you.' She went around me to get to the door and finally I was alone. I would say alone with my thoughts, but while they ought to have been still focussed on Charlie and the imminent divorce, they were not.

I had an itch at the back of my skull, and I didn't like that I knew what it usually meant.

## Missing Persons

Coming back into the bar, I could see most of the glasses on our table were either empty or nearly empty. I could not ask for a clearer signal that people were ready for bed. It was a little early still, but while Schneider got up to go to the bar, determined to stay for another one before bed, everyone else looked to have been politely waiting for my return.

I knew for a fact that Alistair was tired, for he'd been out on an impromptu stag party the previous night. The chaps all behaved themselves, which is to say they all came home inebriated but not to the point that anyone was stupidly drunk. No one got arrested, no one got handcuffed naked to a streetlight, and I doubted very much that strippers had been involved in the event at any point. They just weren't those kind of men.

With my arm hooked into his elbow, Alistair guided me back to our room, where a four-poster bed waited our attention. I knew he was tired, like I said, but I wasn't going to let him get to sleep just yet.

Some time later, as I lay my head down to sleep, I believed I would enjoy many hours of uninterrupted slumber.

I got about three.

The soft but continuous knocking woke me, and blearily I levered myself onto my elbows. Blinking in the darkness, I could see shadows in the gap at the bottom of the door where a crack of light was trying to peek through.

Someone was outside. I blinked again and counted. It was more than one person, and they were talking. They were doing so quietly but not whispering and they knocked again, this time waking Alistair and the dogs.

Anna and Georgie habitually slept next to me in my bed on the Aurelia, or in their own bed next to mine if I was at my house in East Malling.

Tonight, they were under the bed and thus wrapped in blankets which was why they heard the door knock last and not first. Wired to repel whoever might be outside until such time as the intruders were proven to be someone they should welcome, they barked ferociously.

There were other guests to consider, not least the bride and groom who had to want a decent night of sleep in their separate rooms.

'Shhh, girls!' I insisted, rushing across the room to get them. Alistair was getting out of bed and looking for clothes to put on. I needed a robe which meant a trip to the bathroom as I hadn't brought one with me.

Anna and Georgie continued to bark and growl and wriggle to get back to the door so they could kill whoever was outside even as I carried them to the bathroom. I knew if I put them down they would both break into a sprint, so I juggled them until I had a hand free, grabbed a towel, threw it into the tub, and plonked both tiny dogs on top of it.

'Now be calm,' I chided them with a wagging finger. 'Or mummy will turn the taps on.'

The very fact that they were in the bath seem to be enough threat to quieten them. I snagged a robe and hurriedly pulled it on as fast as I could. Alistair was talking to someone.

Framed in the light shining in from the corridor outside, I could see Deepa. She had Barbie with her, both wearing the same Loxton Hall robes and slippers. They were supposed to be having a girly pamper night with facemasks and such, at least that had been their plan. Maybe they chose to empty the minibar in Deepa's room instead, but whatever the case they looked to have been asleep and were now awake. They had Vince Slater with them and two more of his security detail.

'What's going on?' I asked as I came up behind Alistair.

It was Deepa who answered, 'The two guards from earlier, Jones and Scarrat, have gone missing. They are not answering their radios.'

Barbie said, 'Mr Slater wondered if maybe we kidnapped them again.' She wore a tired and grumpy expression and made it clear by the tone of her words that she had not enjoyed being woken.

Vince tried to explain. 'It seemed plausible that they might have taken it upon themselves to do something silly.'

'Like get their own back for earlier,' Deepa filled in the words he didn't say.

Vince let a sigh go. 'Yes. Those two can be a little headstrong. I can see I guessed wrong, though I will say I am happy to be incorrect this time.'

I skewed my lips to one side in thought as the back of my skull itched again. 'You still don't know where they are though?'

Vince puffed out his lips. 'No. That remains a mystery.'

Barbie and Deepa were looking right at me, both of them wearing 'oh-no' expressions while simultaneously flaring their eyes.

'What?' I asked, my own eyes narrowed as I dared them to say what I knew they wanted to.

Barbie gave a half shrug of apology. 'Welllll.'

Alistair finished her sentence. 'You have a habit of poking your nose in whenever there is a mystery to solve.'

I narrowed my eyes further, boring my gaze into the back of his head. 'I do not,' I disagreed indignantly.

He choked on a splutter of laughter and turned around to see if I was being serious. 'My dear, Patricia, your ability … nay, your need to solve that which others find mystifying literally defines you.'

I folded my arms and scowled. 'Well, I am here for a wedding. The location of two security guards is no concern of mine. I expect they found somewhere warm to take a break and fell asleep.'

Alistair and the two girls looked at me as if waiting for me to deliver a punchline. Even Vince was watching me to see what I might say next.

'I mean it,' I insisted when everyone continued to stare.

Deepa couldn't hide her surprise. 'Okay.' She turned toward Vince. 'I think you should assume they are dead and speak to the police. You will want to have the building combed most likely.'

'Dead?' said one of the previously silent guards standing in Vince's shadow. 'Why would they be dead?'

Barbie could not stop her eyes from twitching around to see if I was looking at her. Catching her, her cheeks coloured, but she said it anyway. 'We um … we have found that one member of our party …' I was going to kick her in the knee. '… that is to say.'

'Oh, stop beating around the bush,' I snapped irritably. 'Barbie is trying to suggest that murderers gravitate toward me like I am some kind of mad killer magnet.'

Vince's eyebrows made a bid for the sky. 'So, based on past cases, you think my men are dead?'

I was getting quite grumpy. 'No,' I chose to repeat myself. 'I think they are holed up somewhere warm and asleep. My *friends*,' I made a show of the word, 'think they are dead.'

'It really is very possible,' said Deepa, backing up Barbie. I noted Alistair wasn't arguing against their opinion either.

Vince huffed out a breath. 'Righto. Well, they are not here so I think I ought to leave you all alone now. I am sure they will turn up. My apologies for waking you.'

We said goodnight to Barbie and Deepa once more and watched for a moment as they trudged back to their room on the other side of the corridor. Alistair worried an itch between his shoulder blades and closed the door with his free hand.

By the time I had the dachshunds out of the bath and back into the bedroom, Alistair was already asleep. His light snores were enough to keep me awake, but even without them I wasn't going back to sleep any time soon.

I tried, don't get me wrong, but whether Alistair's claim that I had a need to solve mysteries was on the money or not, I couldn't shift the feeling that there was something going on.

Felicity said they had an issue with the caterer, not that she expanded on her statement. It was clear, however, that someone had tried to do something to upset or ruin the Howard-Box wedding. A quick check of the clock confirmed it was now Saturday morning. Only just, but it was accurate to say the wedding was today.

The barmen, Joe and Ken, claimed another member of staff had maybe poisoned the food. I couldn't guess how accurate their statement might be. It sounded unworthy of consideration at the time, more like a wild speculation on their part.

Two guards were missing though, and my skull would not stop itching. I got up and walked to the window, both dogs bouncing out of their bed to follow me – you know, just in case I felt like feeding them something.

Silently, I drew the curtains apart enough to slip between them and stood on the other side looking outward. It was all quiet, as one might expect. Would the impromptu pool party have ended? I glanced at the clock again. The wedding guests, certainly the younger ones, were bound to still be going. Why book a private stately home if not to avoid licensing laws and such that would close the bar before midnight?

Young people would stay up until four, drink copious amounts of alcohol and then appear looking bright eyed and ready to go again a few hours later needing nothing but some greasy food and a Bloody Mary to revive them. I acknowledged that I was stereotyping and there were probably serious athletes in the building who went to bed early. Bobbie Howard-Box was a professional footballer so many of his friends would be too.

I found myself toying with the idea of taking the dogs for a late-night walk. We were all awake, after all.

Just as I was about to turn away from the window, the decision to go back to bed until sleep took me winning because I knew it was the sensible one, something moving caught my eye.

## After Midnight Excursion

Freezing in position, I watched a man in a black hoody slink along the base of the building beneath me. I had to put my forehead against the glass to be able to see him – it was clearly a man – but to my horror, I then saw two more men round the corner and give pursuit.

The two chasers looked like Vince's men. Not ones I had seen before but their generic haircut, suit, and curly wire over the ear gave them away.

The man in the black hoody didn't appear to have seen the men coming up behind him. They were thirty yards back but moving fast over the short grass of the lawn.

I raised my hand to bang on the glass but stopped myself before I made a sound. I didn't know what I was looking at. Was the man in the black hoody guilty of something? Was he being pursued for good reason? Vince's team were here as a private security operation to keep the celebrity wedding guests safe, or at least that was my belief.

In organising my thoughts, I identified how little I knew about who was doing what here and what dynamics might be in play. The hooded figure vanished into a shadow and was lost from sight, moments later the two security guards vanished into the same pool of inky black.

I watched for more than a minute, holding my breath though I did not intend to as I waited for a gunshot or a scream of pain or ... something.

Nothing came though and none of the three men reappeared.

It was enough for me. There was no chance I was getting back to sleep now. However, still wearing a negligee and nothing else, I faced a minor dilemma in my need to get dressed.

We were only staying two nights so as you might imagine, I hadn't packed a wealth of clothes. Sorry, I should say that Jermaine hadn't packed a wealth of clothes. My butler would get most disgruntled if I started doing things for myself.

Padding quietly across the room, I blindly snagged garments I couldn't see from my wardrobe, hooked a pair of shoes, and went into the bathroom. Only once I was in there with the door closed did I turn the light on. Ultimately, Alistair wouldn't try to stop me. At least, I didn't think he would, but he would frown on my after-midnight excursion.

The dogs buzzed around my feet, excited because something was happening even if they had no idea what it might be.

Thinking about Alistair brought up a line of doubts I had been trying hard to ignore. I couldn't deny that I loved him, which is slightly different from being in love, but ... well, I don't want to get into semantics. The point is, he is lovely, but do I really want to move in with him and live in his cabin on the ship a week or so after signing my divorce paperwork?

I'd just got used to being me as a singular entity. I wasn't about to break things off with him, not a chance, but I couldn't help wishing I'd crafted a more elegant solution than us living together in his cabin.

Doing so would take away a part of who I was. Worse yet, once I moved in, if I then found a better way for us to coexist, I would have to move out of his cabin and that would feel like a statement. Thinking about it made my head dizzy which was why I kept ignoring it.

The bottom line was that I couldn't afford to stay in the Windsor Suite on the Aurelia, and I didn't want to move into one of the below decks crew cabins if Purple Star offered me the job I'd asked for. There was no guarantee they would. I was attempting to create a whole new position – that of ship's detective, and it was all because I loved Alistair.

In a candid moment, I might reveal that I would rather he quit his job and move home to live with me. I couldn't tell him that though. One of us had to give, and I chose for it to be me. I compromised so that we could be together. I was happy that we would be, but my happiness had questions.

Because there was no job – not yet. Not until Purple Star agreed to it, my thoughts on the matter were moot.

The clothes I managed to snag were not the jeans and jacket I'd hoped for, but an alternative combination that would work just as well. Well, almost. I should have found an additional top – a blouse or something – but the jacket covered most of the negligee which mostly just looked like a plunge top with a frilly lace edge now it was tucked in.

Dressed, I picked the dogs up, balancing them both under one arm, and snuck out of the room.

Anna and Georgie were super excited to be out again, nipping at each other and colliding as they ran along the corridor. I hissed insistently for them to return, then gave up and went after them. Once they were finally on their leads, I made my way to the staircase.

Since the girls were up, I knew I would have to take them outside. It looked cold beyond the front door and I hadn't thought to get my outdoor coat. I was just going to have to brave the sub-zero temperatures. I wanted to get a look at the spot where the hooded man vanished anyway.

If the cold air bothered the dachshunds, they were putting a brave face on it and in no hurry to do their business as I walked them around to the side of Loxton Hall. Looking up, while hugging my jacket closed, I tried to work out which windows were the ones for my room.

The best I could do was narrow it down. I doubted it mattered though for the interesting bit was the path the men had taken. I tracked it along, finding the first tendrils of frost on the grass made it easy to see where the men had stepped. I followed their footsteps, walking on the balls of my feet so my heels wouldn't dig into the turf.

The building was lit all the way around, except for the part I was heading toward. Whether through poor maintenance, or deliberate sabotage, the floodlight mounted high on the eaves to illuminate this section of the building was out. No light came from it and thus the inky blackness that swallowed all three men was able to exist.

However, down at ground level, the dark was not so all encompassing, and I could see where they had gone. They had walked into a shrub.

I stopped and stared. The trail of footprints was really easy to see, even in the dark, but when I got near to where it ended, all I found was a big bushy thing. On her extendable lead, Anna sniffed her way to it and then vanished.

Barely able to believe my eyes, I followed her and found, much to my surprise, that the bushy thing was in fact an overgrown trellis. It jutted out perpendicular to the wall where it cast a shadow that hid a door.

Casting the beam of light from the torch on my phone downward, I could see the footsteps leading all the way up to it. Though it was freezing out - I was beginning to shiver uncontrollably – the mud in which the footprints were preserved was not yet frozen and I had to position my feet carefully so as not to disturb it.

The door was mounted flush to the wall, and it bore the look of a maintenance entrance. I tried it, finding it locked as I imagined I would.

With the light of my phone, I examined the footprints – they all went in the same direction: in. None of them faced the other way so all three men went inside, and none came out again.

Was I paranoid? Did this mean anything at all? The man in the hooded top might have been the maintenance guy on his way to fix the broken light creating the shadow in which I stood. The security guys might have been jogging to catch up, there to make sure he got the job done.

I had no way of knowing, but I felt certain seeking out Chief Inspector Quinn to report my concerns would result in yet another tired and boring lecture.

The cold was biting into my skin, so when a breeze blew along to accentuate how cold it was outside, I decided the girls' opportunity to do what they might need to was at an end. I hurried back to the doors.

Of course, they were locked.

## M.I.L.F.

I looked around to see if there was anyone around. There wasn't. Both Anna and Georgie had decided they wanted to get out of the cold too and were nudging at the door with their little noses as if reminding me that I was supposed to open it now.

I couldn't even see in because the doors were solid oak. Did I knock? That seemed like a fruitless gesture that would sting my knuckles and be heard by no one. Standing at the front of the stately home and shivering before the giant double wide, double height entrance, I couldn't even find a doorbell.

I kicked the door a few times, and yelled, 'Little pig, little pig, let me in!'

No one came. I won't claim that I was dangerously cold, but the dachshunds were visibly shivering, and they are so small I have often worried about how long it might take for the cold to really penetrate their bodies. Neither has a lot of fat to insulate them.

With no alternative I could see, I went looking for a different way in. The side of Loxton Hall my room was on had no entrance that I had seen save for the one which I knew to be locked. There had to be other ways in though. Around the back, I would find kitchens and such; offloading areas for supplies to be delivered.

I didn't get that far though. Halfway along the other side of Loxton Hall a large addition or extension jutted out. I could see even as I approached that it contained a sports complex. Behind windows illuminated by the moon sat a dormant row of cardio machines: treadmills, rowers, elliptical bikes.

If the pool party were still going, I would find people there. I guessed it was on the far side of the extension and was proven right when I rounded the corner. Light spilled out through windows and I found myself mercifully in the lee of the building where the breeze couldn't get me.

I hurried on, drawing level with the windows to find several young people still fooling around inside. They were mostly young men, but two women were with them. I counted eight in all: six men and two women. No one had any clothes on.

There were several empty champagne bottles upended in ice buckets and though no one was staggering drunk, I suspected they were all really rather well oiled. Preparing to hammer on the glass, I told myself to feel lucky the naked party hadn't yet moved on to other activities.

Rapping smartly on the glass as I continued to make my way along the building toward an alcove I prayed would hold a door, I got their attention.

Their heads shot around, some a tad slower than others as the effects of alcohol numbed their senses and coordination, but they saw me and were clearly discussing the woman outside as I motored along the side of the building.

Finding a door in the alcove, I gave myself a mental fist pump, but it too was locked. Mercifully, the people inside understood my plight and were already coming to my aid.

Except they weren't.

'Can I help you?' asked a cocky young white man on the other side of the glass door.

'Let me in, please?' I begged.

'Sorry, love. Private party,' he replied with a grin to a chorus of giggles and guffaws from the other idiots around and behind him.

'I'm going to freeze,' I growled, having already suffered enough of their nonsense. 'Please open the door.'

Neither the cocky white man nor any of his friends moved to help me. He reached up to rub his chin. 'I dunno. What do you think, guys?' he asked his idiot drunken colleagues.

'Make her pay a toll,' suggested one with a cheer.

It got the popular vote. 'Yes! A toll!' echoed one of the girls, bouncing on the spot with glee to make her boobs jiggle.

Idiot white male rubbed his chin again. 'Hmm,' he nodded, liking the idea. 'I supposed she is kind of a Milf.'

'Yeah,' echoed a young black man as he came to stand beside his friend. 'She's even wearing something saucy under that jacket. I can see the lace and silk, man.'

White idiot cast his eyes down, making me feel uncomfortable.

Frowning, and doubting I would like the answer, I asked, 'I'm a what?'

He explained what the abbreviation meant.

I slammed my fist into the glass. 'Let me in, you horrible little pervert!'

Far from having the desired result, I made them all laugh, and I was beginning to think I was going to have to look for another way in. It would not go well for them if I did because I would then find the kitchen and come at their tiny todgers with a meat tenderiser.

Just when I was about to grab the dogs and move on, the white idiot came forward to get the door.

I almost thanked him, but he paused with his hand on the handle and didn't open it.

'About that toll,' he started. 'It hardly seems fair that we are all naked and you want to join us but have all your clothes on.' In my head I mentally crushed one of his testicles. 'How about you open that jacket and give us all a look at the goods?'

'Yeah!' cheered the girl with the jiggly boobs. 'Show us the goods! Show us the goods!'

An angry snort of air left my nose. Had it not been for Anna and Georgie I might have turned tail and looked for the next door. Instead, I unfolded my arms, grabbed the edges of my jacket, and pulled them apart. My negligee covered me, but in that alluring way that silk does, clinging to every part of my skin. In the cold night air, my nipples were so hard I could have used them to chip ice.

I got wolf whistles and nods of appreciation from the idiot cohort inside. Wondering if he was going to now demand something more, young white idiot decided he'd had enough fun at my expense and unlocked the door. He was opening his mouth to say something. Maybe he was about to apologise. I was far too angry to wait to find out.

With a grin, I let go the two dog leads and shouted, 'Girls! Get them!'

The big smiles and laughter evaporated instantly. They hadn't seen the two dog leads I held or the dogs themselves because the lower three feet of the door was opaque. Now the drunken idiots were all trying to back up, turn around, and run away but the ones at the back didn't react at the same speed.

The inevitable pile up shot one girl out of the side. Anna chased her, the little dog's teeth gnashing and growling. It was sufficient to convince the girl to jump into the pool.

Georgie bit someone, I heard the squeal of pain that came from one of the men though I couldn't see which one.

Coming inside, I slammed the door behind me, relishing the warmth. I wanted to get back to my room and get some sleep, so I wasn't going to dally. However, I could spare enough time to teach a few manners.

Young white idiot was sprawled on the floor. Having bounced off the man behind him, he'd twisted his legs around one another, got them confused and landed on his butt. Now he was trying to escape backward over the bodies behind him and wasn't getting very far.

I stalked forward.

Anna and Georgie were snapping at the seven naked humans, darting in to try to bite and zipping back again as a limb came to swat them away. All in all, they were doing a great job of corralling the idiots. Had they been sober, I doubt the dogs could have achieved such an effect, but in their inebriated state, the humans just couldn't move swiftly enough to defend themselves.

I called the girls back to me and secured them once more. However, I kept them facing the horde of drunken fools as I started my lecture.

'You were not very polite,' I pointed out. 'That made up word you used to describe me is nothing short of disgusting.'

'Don't you know who we are?' asked young white idiot as if it should matter.

'Yeah,' echoed the girl in the pool, holding on to the edge but not brave enough to get out. 'Don't you know who he is?'

'He is a rude little boy,' I snapped. 'Beyond that, I have not the slightest care who he might think he is. It is of no importance. A more pertinent question might be to ask if you know who I am?'

Young white idiot was getting to his feet. He'd recovered from the initial shock of the sausage dog assault and his confidence was returning.

He was five or six inches taller than me so when he lifted his right arm to jab a finger at me, he probably felt quite superior. 'Listen, old lady. I did you a favour calling you a Milf.'

I'm not sure if it was his repeated use of the word, or the fact that I could see something jiggling in free air just below my field of vision as I looked up at his face, but something snapped, and I did something I couldn't remember doing in a very long time.

I kicked him.

Right where it hurts, you might say.

There was a gasp from his friends and a horrified profanity from the girl in the pool who had the best angle to see my strike find its target. Maybe I learned a few things watching Jermaine hand out a beating or two when criminals were in need of one, or perhaps I was changing again. Whichever it was, I felt nothing but triumph as young white idiot sunk to his knees cupping his wotsits and groaning like a hippo pooping a pineapple.

'Learn some manners,' I suggested, as I tugged the dog leads and led my dachshunds from the pool.

Striding around the collection of shocked faces, my head high and my jacket firmly held in place once more, I couldn't help the corners of my mouth curling upward in a devilish grin.

I left my room to investigate what I saw outside, but heading back to my room, sleep deprived and failing in my determined attempt to have a relaxing weekend, I had to acknowledge that I would have been better off staying in bed.

What had I seen? Three men vanished but what did that mean? I wasn't going to speak with Chief Inspector Quinn because he would get excited about me poking my nose in, and the only place I knew I could find Vince Slater - if I wanted to ask him about his men - was via Angelica Howard-Box's room. I'll admit I quite liked the idea of knocking on her door just to see if she would answer it and have a heart attack on the spot from seeing me here.

I dismissed the notion. Though I loathed the woman, this was a special weekend for her, and I had no good reason to wish to spoil it. I also dismissed the idea of going to the Hall's reception area to find out what room I could find Felicity or Vince Slater in. I doubted either one would wish to be disturbed.

At breakfast I would find out how wrong my assumption turned out to be.

## The Cake

The morning of a wedding, when things are still quiet and people are excited but not yet nervous, has always been a wonderful time in my mind. I have attended the nuptials of a number of friends and relatives over the years. On many occasions that required travel and thus I would find myself somewhere new on the morning of the big day. With no active part to play, I could enjoy the surroundings I found myself in.

Today was exactly that and I woke up next to a man I love. How's that for a good start?

We had tea in bed and read the papers we found tucked into a slot outside our door as requested upon arrival. Though it was cold outside, the sun shone through the windows to show a clear blue sky as the last of the night fled for the horizon.

It looked like one of those glorious autumn days that people call crisp. The air has an almost magical quality to it, and trips outside to walk the dogs were filled with the promise of a warm indoors to which a person could return.

We dressed for the day, not in the outfits we would wear for the wedding – I insisted Alistair have Purple Star send him a captain's uniform since his was on the ship – we would change into those after lunch. Our loose plan for the morning was to take the dogs for a nice countryside stroll through the stately home's grounds and then, once the dogs were worn out and wanted a sleep, we hoped to visit the on-site leisure centre.

I omitted to mention my earlier visit; Alistair didn't need to know. I believed he'd slept the entire time I was out of the room. If he had, in fact, woken and noticed my absence he was choosing to not mention it, so I did the same.

Taking my shoes from the wardrobe, where I carefully placed them in the early hours of the morning, I noticed a layer of thick red mud around the base of each. Screwing up my face in disgust, and glad I'd had the sense to take them off before coming into the room, I used a makeup wipe to tidy them up.

'Ready to go, dear?' asked Alistair, looping an arm around my waist so he could nuzzle my neck playfully.

His stomach gave an audible rumble, making me chuckle. 'I still need to walk the dogs,' I laughed. 'I'll make it a quick one if they are willing to cooperate.' I almost pointed out that they'd had plenty of exercise in the night and only just managed to stop myself.

'We'll walk the dogs,' he replied, taking my hand, and tugging me along after him. 'Let's hurry up though, eh? I'm really rather peckish.'

Intuitively aware that it was time for walkies, both dogs were at the door, nipping at each other and dancing about with excitement.

Twenty-five minutes later, Alistair and I took our seats for breakfast. We were early but we were not alone in the restaurant. As I understood it from talking with Felicity, Loxton Hall had several kitchens to accommodate the many weddings held there. Each wedding had a separate set of rooms assigned to it and the guests were, in general, kept in separate wings depending on the size of the party.

Breakfast, however, was served from a single kitchen run and managed by the on-site chefs.

Perusing the elegant, embossed breakfast menu and letting my waistline argue with my tastebuds, I felt certain I was going to order the light but nevertheless tasty smoked salmon and scrambled egg when *it* happened.

If you are wondering what *it* is, then I shall tell you that *it* is the thing that happens all too often around me.

Me and everyone else in earshot heard a blood-curdling scream of utter horror. It was the kind of scream that one does not associate with pain, so it wasn't someone being murdered, rather it was the scream of someone who had just found the freshly murdered body.

Alistair was already up and on his feet; years of being ready to deal with situations as they presented themselves made his reactions instinctive. In contrast, I closed my eyes for a two-count and huffed a breath of annoyed disappointment.

Around the room, guests and the staff serving them were frozen in place, questioning eyes searching for answers in those nearby.

When the scream was followed by an angry shout of rage, which was not the sound I expected to follow the first utterance, I opened my eyes and started moving. Someone was having a bad day but my initial assumption that there was a dead someone to be found was now shifting. More so as the person who started out screaming was now swearing loudly in fluent French.

Alistair and I were not the only ones rushing toward the voice. It was coming from behind a door marked 'Staff only' - advice we duly ignored, pushing through it and into the kitchens beyond. Inside we found a gaggle of chefs, but they were not crowded around a murder victim, or anything else, we discovered. They were peering through a hatch into the room on the other side.

These were the chefs working on breakfast for the guests drifting into the restaurant and they were just as curious about the screaming and swearing as we were.

I spotted a door that appeared to lead into the next room, but as I went for it, one of the chefs called out.

'I wouldn't go in there if I were you.'

It gave me pause. 'Why not?'

The chef, a big man in his forties with a big belly, sucked in a breath of warning. 'Chef Dominic has an explosive temper, and he is looking for someone to kill.'

I almost got to reply to the effect that such situations are my specialty when another door clattered open and Felicity appeared. At her shoulder was a younger woman, a teenager perhaps. Their features were similar though the girl – if I dare call her that – was attired more like a ninja whereas Felicity was dressed for a wedding in a dark floral print dress, stockings, heels, and a designer jacket. There would be a matching hat somewhere I had no doubt.

Catching my eye, Felicity made a grumpy face. 'I can only guess that this is the cake.'

I had no idea what she meant but following her through to the next room, I soon found out.

Entering just ahead of me, the young woman with Felicity said something rather colourful in response to the sight my eyes could not avoid.

In the centre of the room stood a seven-tier wedding cake. Iced in the purest white and decorated with intricate swirls to look like it was covered in lace, the central focus was a cascade of bright blooms sweeping from the very top to the very bottom. Each had been crafted from icing and must have taken many, many hours of painstaking work to create.

Someone had taken an axe to it.

Standing just a few feet away and visibly quivering with rage, a pencil-thin, five-foot-tall man in chef's whites with a big floppy hat and a waxed moustache swung his head in our direction.

'What ees this!' he demanded to know in his thick French accent. 'Madame Philips, tell me oo would do such a thing to such a masterpiece?' He jerked his head back to the cake and resorted to more swearing in French.

I turned to look at Felicity, wanting to know if she had any idea what was going on, and that was when I saw *it*. Yes, I know, it's another *it*.

Spray painted onto the wall behind us in bright red letters was a clue to the why at least.

*You will not*

*marry him!*

The letters were mashed together but we could all read what it said. Felicity saw me gawping and turned her head to see what might have caught my eye. What startled me most was the lack of surprise on the wedding planner's face.

Felicity closed her eyes as if saying a silent prayer. Or perhaps she was cursing instead, but when she flicked them open again, she was looking at me.

'Patricia, I may need your help,' she said. It wasn't begging, and it wasn't a plea. It came out like a statement of fact.

I found myself replying instantly. 'Of course, Felicity. Whatever you need.' Looking at the diminutive wedding planner, my brain finally caught up with itself to tell me why I thought there was something incongruous about her. 'What happened to the sling?' I asked. She'd had one supporting her left arm last night.

Felicity grimaced. 'It was too impractical to keep on. I've taken some hardcore painkillers and I'm trying to not use my arm.' She wriggled the fingers of her left arm. 'I'll put the sling back on once the wedding is done.'

Any further discussion of the subject was interrupted when Chef Dominic kicked the stand on which the cake stood. Once, twice, and with savage intensity. The leg he struck withstood the first blow but shifted with the second. The third saw the leg fold in under the stand and the whole cake fell to the floor like a white icing avalanche.

I doubted it could be saved before, but there was no question now.

The angry man stormed from the room before Felicity could stop him, her hand to get his attention flailing briefly in the air as she considered calling for him to wait and decided it might be best to let him cool off.

'Poor Chef,' Felicity commented. 'This was one of his biggest. He doesn't get many requests for seven tiers.'

'You don't look surprised,' I observed, an eyebrow raised in question.

Felicity held up a finger to beg a moment's grace and turned her head to speak with what I guessed was her assistant.

'Mindy, could you be a dear and fetch Justin. He'll have had a late night and is probably still in bed. We have much to do and very little time to do it.'

As the young woman rushed away, her fast and effortless movements reminding me of Barbie, Felicity faced me once more.

'Justin is my master of ceremonies. He's the public face that interacts with the wedding party. I move in the background seeing to their needs. Normally, he would get the morning off after the big rehearsal dinner the night before but there's no hope of that today.'

'What's going on?' I desperately wanted to know. Was there an issue here that might affect Martin and Deepa's wedding later?

Felicity sucked in a deep breath, held it for a beat and let it go again, her body deflating like a balloon with a leak. 'Someone,' she began explaining, 'broke into the bride's room last night and took a knife to her wedding dress.'

I heard myself gasp.

'Someone also broke into the best man's room and stole the wedding rings. And someone put the best man in hospital last night,' Felicity added. Pointing to the message on the wall, she added, 'The same message is in the bride's room. Whoever is behind this got happy with a spray can of red paint and really wants to stop Sasha marrying Bobbie.'

I looked again at the message. It was crudely done, the paint running down the walls where the artist applied too much of it. Was the colour choice deliberate? If I didn't know better, I might think it was blood.

My heart went out to the bride and groom. The bride especially. I could not imagine a worse thing to happen.

Felicity said, 'It gets worse.' Seeing our expressions, she explained. 'Six of Vince's security guards went missing in the night. Two of them were guarding Sasha's room which is how the vandal managed to get inside.'

Six of them were missing, not just the two I knew about. My memory flashed to the two I'd seen following the man in the hood. There was no doubt about it, I was going to have to reveal my midnight excursion now.

Felicity gave a shudder. 'Sorry, I keep imagining Sasha asleep in her bed while a crazy person is in her adjoining dressing room carving up her dress with a knife. It would have been so easy for them to attack her instead.'

'What is Mr Slater saying?' asked Alistair.

Felicity made a grim face. 'He's mostly dumbfounded. He was on his way to speak to the police again when I last saw him. That was about twenty minutes ago. He came here with a dozen men, now he has six and they are being spread thin and managing without sleep. Vince is doing the best he can but he's catching a lot of heat from the client. Mrs Howard-Box,' she clarified. 'She thinks everything is his fault, but I don't think she has been honest about why she hired him.'

Nothing about Angelica causing additional drama surprised me but Felicity's statement required further inspection.

'What makes you say that?' I wanted to know.

Felicity tried to lay out her thoughts. 'This is just a celebrity wedding. I've managed hundreds of them, and none have ever required this level of additional security. There are dozens of police officers on site to manage the influx of guests and the crowds of well-wishers outside. Mrs Howard-Box said Vince's team were just precautionary, but I think it was in response to a direct threat she won't admit to.'

Alistair picked up on what she was saying. 'You suspect there to be a credible and known threat and that the client, Angelica, is sitting on information that might be of use?'

Felicity said, 'Exactly that. I wouldn't be shocked to discover she knows who the vandal is. What if the missing guards are all dead? She's so desperate for a perfect wedding where she gets to pose as the mother of the groom that I think she would kill people herself if they got in her way.'

'And probably feel justified to do so,' I agreed. I knew Angelica well. She did everything in the steadfast belief that it was for the good of everyone around her. That her actions were often cruel and would adversely affect other people had no bearing on her decisions.

'What do you want me to do?' I asked the direct question.

Felicity looked right into my eyes. 'Help me find out who is behind this before they manage to do something I cannot undo.'

## Back on Track

Incredibly, Felicity believed she could undo all the damage wrought thus far. She couldn't bring back the missing guards – I think we all knew there was going to be a pile of bodies at the end of that search, but through a large pool of talented contacts she was going to fix everything else.

Just before we left the room with the destroyed cake, her master of ceremonies arrived.

'Justin Cutler,' he introduced himself, shaking first my hand then Alistair's. Handsome with a strong jaw, a good head of hair and deeply blue eyes, Justin was very nearly six feet tall, clean-shaven, and both confident of himself and instantly easy to like.

He was dressed for the day in a turquoise tweed three-piece suit. Complemented by a silver pocket watch, an orange tie that matched some of the fine thread running through his tweed and a pair of snazzy white spats, he was certainly going to stand out from the crowd.

Any crowd.

He was going to collect the virtual baton Felicity already had in motion. His task was to run it around the next leg while she came with me to speak to Chief Inspector Quinn and Vince. The bride was to move rooms, a team were dealing with that now. The advantage of having a place designed to cater multiple weddings was that it had more than one honeymoon suite.

The dress was to be remade, something Felicity assured me could be achieved in just a couple of hours. The gown shops she most regularly used would move Heaven and Earth to meet her needs, but it was still a good thing the bride had chosen a simple design and not one that looked like a giant meringue.

The rings had been specially made but placeholders were on their way to the venue, being rushed by a gold dealer Felicity knew well. The woman had all the contacts, that was for sure. I thought the cake to be the stumbling block, yet I was proven wrong once again. Felicity took a minor detour on our way to visit Chief Inspector Quinn.

Pushing through a set of double doors to come into yet another kitchen area – this one not currently in use – we found Chef Dominic muttering to himself as he inspected another giant cake.

As Alistair and I paused just inside the doorway, Felicity continued onwards, crossing the room. 'Chef, I knew I would find you here.' She wrapped her arms around him as he turned her way and held him in a hug.

'I cannot let a vandal beat me,' he huffed, waving an arm flamboyantly. 'It is my name on the cakes.'

'Chef Dominic makes almost all my cakes,' Felicity revealed as she let him go again. 'We have been working together for years and understand each other. Isn't that right, Chef?'

The short, thin man shrugged despondently as he inspected the cake. 'I suppose.' With a tut, he said, 'I still 'ave to bake the seventh tier for this one and I will need a whole team to complete the icing and decoration.' He said it as a lament, but it was clear he planned to get the job done and was just having a whinge.

Only now that he mentioned it did I notice there were only six tiers.

Felicity grabbed his head with both hands, kissing his cheek, then pausing to rub off the smidgeon of lipstick left behind. 'I knew you would rally to the challenge,' she said. With a pat of his arm, she spun on her heels and started back toward the doors.

'All good?' I asked.

I got a nod of approval. 'We are back on track, but whoever is behind the vandalism is still at large. I hate to even consider what they might do when they realise the wedding is still on. 'Let's go see the cops, shall we?'

My feet twitched, but I make it a rule to always know more than the other person and Chief Inspector Quinn could be a tricky monkey when he wanted to be. I wanted to quiz him, and I needed to let him know what I saw last night, but I was going to confront Angelica first.

## Collision Course

At my request, we made a short detour to check out Sasha's original room. I felt a need to see the dress. According to Felicity, they had moved the bride to a new honeymoon suite, but the dress obviously stayed where it was – Sasha would not want to be reminded by the sight of it.

Seeing the wreckage of the dress, the rage that had been visited upon it, I found myself questioning how it was that Sasha had survived unscathed. Someone had come into her room while she was sleeping and trashed her dress with feverish hate. The same message I saw by the cake covered the wall in high letters.

It was the same message and yet somehow it also wasn't. The way it was sprayed was completely different. Where the one downstairs was crude and almost every letter had paint running downward from it, this one was stylised and elegant. Artistic even.

There was something undeniably wrong about it. About the fact that the two messages didn't match even though they contained the same words.

I poked around the room but there was nothing else to see. Feeling time was not my friend and knowing Felicity had many other tasks to which she needed to attend, we pushed on to find Angelica.

The issue between Angelica and me went back more than four decades and was entirely her fault. At least, it was her fault that the rift still existed. At school together, we fell out over a boy when our ages could still be measured in single digits. That she continued to hold a grudge was just ridiculous, but as we continued through school, she became the bratty little princess with the money and a club of followers while I played football and often had dirt on my clothes.

My world and her world continued to clash but after school, I rarely saw her. When I married a few years later and failed to have children, she smugly popped out three. She left me alone though, as if I were beneath her. To be honest, in many ways, I was. Not because of position or money, but because I had allowed my self-esteem to drop to a point where most people were above me.

When that changed earlier this year, and my adventures brought fame (of a sort), she started a hate campaign against me. She was the well-to-do woman in East Malling and there was no room for another in her opinion. Most especially since I appeared to have more of everything than her now. She was divorced, one of the few things we had in common, and though she insisted she kicked him out, I personally doubted that was the truth.

I came to Loxton Hall this weekend knowing she was here but with the solemn intention of doing nothing to interrupt her special event. Now I felt I had no choice, but I also knew how she would receive my appearance.

Her foul attitude placed the two of us on a collision course long ago. I wondered if today would end in wreckage for both parties. Because I knew he would stop me from doing anything silly, like slapping her face, I collected Jermaine on my way to her suite.

Felicity knocked on the door. There was a guard outside; one of Vince's men. He glanced at Alistair and me, giving us a quick check, but seeing nothing that set off any alarm bells, he lifted his right hand and spoke into his cuff.

The door opened, another guard inside the room responding to the all-clear from the one outside.

Felicity let herself in, turning left in the entrance lobby part of the suite and through another door, this one open, to reach the central area of Angelica's room.

I followed close behind, Alistair right on my shoulder and I admit a flutter rose in my core because I knew a fight was about to ensue.

The room had a dozen people in it. I recognised Bobbie Howard-Box from seeing him around the village as a boy. He was a man now and had a light stubble that was carefully maintained at a precise length. His facial features were unchanged though. His older sisters were also both in the room, lined up facing inward on chairs while hairdressers did fancy and complicated things with their hair.

Bobbie spotted me and frowned slightly; an expression I took to mean he recognised my face but couldn't work out why. His bride-to-be, Sasha, AKA Sashatastic, was curled into one corner of a couch, her feet tucked up under her derriere. Her face was devoid of makeup and she wore a grey flannel warm-up suit. It was a mile from the glamorous image she portrayed publicly, but she was also in tears, a small pile of damp tissues mounded on the floor by her feet.

Standing beside her was a man wearing an abundance of makeup and a garish outfit that screamed gay BFF. Next to him was a plus-size woman in her mid-twenties, and by Sasha's feet, another woman roughly her age. The woman held Sasha's free hand, the one that wasn't currently wiping her eyes.

'What if someone gets hurt?' Sasha asked.

Our arrival occurred partway through a conversation.

'No one has been hurt yet,' said the woman on the floor in a soothing tone.

'But they were in my room with a knife, Gloria,' snivelled Sasha. 'My dress was sliced into ribbons.'

'But they are making you an exact copy,' replied the woman on the floor.

Bobbie put his hand on Sasha's shoulder. 'I hate seeing you upset like this, babe.'

Sasha sniffed and wiped her eyes. 'It's bad luck for you to see me before the ceremony,' she burst into a fresh bout of snivels.

Striding into the room through a door to the left, her hair in curlers and a bathrobe wrapped around her, came Angelica Howard-Box. She had a fascinator in each hand, holding them up to the light in the window as she tried to decide which she favoured. The bride was in tears, the groom looked miserable, but Angelica acted as if nothing were happening.

'That's just a lot of superstitious nonsense,' she snapped, not bothering to look at the people whose feelings she didn't care about.

'We can postpone,' growled Sasha, instantly angry at her almost mother-in-law.

Angelica sounded amused when she replied with, 'Poppycock!'

Bobbie stood up straight to address his mother. 'What if there is a maniac loose in here, mum? What if their next step is to hurt someone? What if they come for Sasha next? She seems to be the target here.'

Sasha sobbed again.

'What if you tell us the truth about why you hired the security firm?' I asked, my voice loud enough to ensure no one could miss it.

At the window, still facing outward and scrutinising her headwear options, Angelica froze.

An inappropriate smile played across my face.

'No,' gasped Angelica, refusing to turn around because that might make it true. 'No. You can't be here. It's not possible.'

'What's going on?' asked the tearful internet superstar bride-to-be, looking around the room in confusion.

Angelica turned around, hate filling her eyes as she spotted me.

I gave her a pinky wave.

'Get out!' she screamed with enough volume to make the room vibrate.

I didn't move.

'Get out!' she repeated this time going red in the face. 'Security! Security! Get this woman out of here! Right this minute! I want her gone!'

The man manning the inside of the door dashed around the corner, his extendable baton drawn as he looked about to identify the source of threat.

Jermaine whipped out an arm, removing the baton and giving it a deft flick so it telescoped back into itself.

'Probably best if you put that away, sir,' Jermaine advised.

The security guard looked like he wanted to get in my butler's face, but another impatient scream from Angelica refocused his gaze.

'Get her out of my room!' she screamed.

Alistair and Jermaine fixed the guard with easily interpreted looks and now stuck for a course of action that wouldn't result in a fight, he dithered.

'Angelica,' I started.

'Don't you talk to me!' she yelled.

I carried on as if she hadn't spoken. 'Angelica what is the real reason you have a security team here?'

Bobbie, Sasha, and most everyone else were looking my way.

Bobbie asked, 'Mum, what is she talking about?'

Angelica growled. 'Just ignore her. She is a troublemaking, fame-hungry conspiracy theorist. This is Patricia Fisher, the woman from the village I told you about.'

Bobbie blushed. 'You mean the one you ran that awful poster campaign against?'

'I was doing a public service!' Angelica snapped. Far from calming down, she seemed to be getting angrier. 'She does nothing but cause trouble.' Then she gasped as a fresh idea hit her. 'This was you, wasn't it! You broke into Sasha's room and carved up her dress. You stole the wedding rings. What will you do next?'

'The cake has been destroyed,' supplied Felicity. The shock of her statement shut Angelica up for a moment if nothing else.

'My cake!' wailed Sasha, a fresh supply of tears leaking down her cheeks.

Bobbie got onto his knees to hug his fiancée.

Angelica turned her hate-filled eyes on the poor security guard again. 'Get her out of my room or I'll fire the whole lot of you!'

The man, caught in an impossible situation, reached out to grab my arm. He did so without any commitment behind the move, but Jermaine slapped it away nevertheless. As my boyfriend and my butler moved to form a physical barrier that would prevent any further foolhardy attempts to remove me, I strode forward.

Now in the centre of the room, I stopped and looked about.

Felicity joined me. The two of us standing side by side to face Angelica down. I was going to try to reason with her for the sake of the couple planning to marry in a few hours, but Angelica got a question in first.

It was aimed at Felicity. 'Mrs Philips, perhaps you would care to explain how it is that Mrs Fisher is even here this weekend. I block booked the entire venue, did I not? It occurs to me that there should be no reason for her to even be able to access Loxton Hall since the police are only allowing those on the guest list to enter.'

A tinge of pink warmed Felicity's cheeks for a moment though she quickly regained control and forced it away.

'There is another wedding here this weekend,' the wedding planner revealed.

Angelica looked like she had been slapped. 'I booked the entire venue,' she repeated.

Felicity nodded. 'And you gave me carte blanche to employ the rooms as I saw fit. There was no stipulation that no other event could take place. In fact,' Felicity added quickly as Angelica opened her mouth to begin arguing. 'When I asked you about the empty rooms, your advice was to do with them as I pleased. I have that in writing.'

Angelica shut her mouth again, but she was seething. 'You are fired,' she growled from between gritted teeth.

'Fired?' Felicity hitched an eyebrow. 'I thought you wanted me to rescue the wedding now that you have a deranged stalker on the premises trying to ruin it.'

Sasha wailed again but we left her to it.

Angelica's lips twitched. She wanted to rage and throw things, but she was stuck too.

'I have a dressmaker feverishly sewing as we speak. Shall I tell her to stop?' Felicity asked, knowing the answer full well. 'I have a goldsmith on his way here now with two replacement rings. Do I turn him around? Oh, and if I am fired, you might like to consider that you paid me in full up front for a five percent discount.'

'I will ruin you!' Angelica snarled.

Bobbie kissed Sasha's cheek and stood up again. 'Mother don't be so dramatic. With all the guests arriving today, we still only half fill the place. There is more than enough room for Mrs Fisher to be here. Did I hear you say there is another wedding?' he addressed me.

'That's right,' I nodded.

'It is yours?' he asked, looking between Alistair and me and sounding genuinely interested.

I was about to shake my head when Alistair said, 'Not yet.' A flutter zipped from my stomach to my head, making me feel faint. 'It is for two friends of ours,' he added. 'Just a small family thing with a few friends. About thirty of us all in. I doubt you will even know we are here.'

Bobbie waved the suggestion away. 'There is more than enough room for all of us. I hope your event goes better than ours.' Turning his head back to meet his mother's eyes, he said, 'Seriously though, mum. Is there a reason why you brought in the additional security? What are you not telling us?'

'Nothing, dear,' she lied.

I don't think a single person in the room believed her and I was in the habit of assuming anything she said was a lie.

'Mother,' warned Bobbie.

'There is nothing to tell,' Angelica snapped at him. 'I thought additional security would be prudent. You are both so famous,' she tried to sell the lie.

I'd had enough. 'Angelica I am going to leave shortly, and I am going to do as I have been asked and try to figure out who is behind what is going on here.'

She was horrified by the idea. 'You'll do nothing of the sort! You'll go away and stay away. I don't want you poking your nose in where it isn't wanted, even though that is your speciality.'

Fixing her with a hard stare, I said, 'I think you mean you don't want me finding out what you are up to.' I knew she would scream something at me, but I was no longer listening. Just as I turned away, ready to escape the awful woman's presence, I spotted the unhappy couple.

They both looked a little lost, a little miserable, and very much bewildered. Catching their eyes, I did my best to impart some confidence in their day. 'I will do my very best to catch whoever left the messages and damaged the cake and dress. I know I don't have much time, but I am going to speak with Chief Inspector Quinn next. He is the officer in charge today and a close, personal friend of mine.' Okay so I was stretching things a lot with that statement, but he's been in my house and that means we were friends, right?

'I don't want you anywhere near us,' snarled Angelica, voicing her opinion yet again.

I didn't bother to show I had heard her speak. Instead, I was watching the bride and groom and wondering why my skull was itching again.

A nod toward Jermaine got him to move to one side which created a path around the guard. I checked to see if Felicity was following me and led the way to the door, the four of us exhaling gratefully once we were back outside.

Alistair caught my hand, making me look back to see what he wanted.

'Patricia, dear,' he started, 'how do you manage to find such loathsome characters?'

I laughed. I couldn't help myself, and it proved infectious because a second later all four of us were laughing. Even the guard positioned outside the door started to chuckle, probably guessing who we were talking about.

'Come on,' I encouraged, pulling on Alistair's arm. 'It's time we had a chat with a chief inspector.

## First Body of the Weekend

On the way to the stairs Felicity got a call on her phone; her master of ceremonies needed her.

'Go,' I reassured her. 'We've got this. I'll find you later. Go fix this wedding.' She gratefully hurried away in a different direction, but as she left us, I changed my mind about where we should go next.

'Shall we check on the others?' I asked.

'You mean our bride and groom?' clarified Alistair.

Not breaking my stride, I said, 'And the best man and page boy too.'

Lieutenant Pippin wasn't the page boy at all, of course. He's a grown man, not someone's child even though he does look barely old enough to shave. The page boy thing was a joke the other lieutenants were playing on him. Of the four, we had bride, groom, and best man. Pippin made the mistake of asking what his role might be.

I knocked first on the room for the big Austrian, Lieutenant Schneider. We heard a rumble from within, followed a few seconds later by the door opening.

'Hey, everyone,' he beamed out at us, throwing the door wide in a welcoming gesture. 'Are you heading down to breakfast?'

His question served as a stark reminder that Alistair and I never got ours. I jinked my wrist to check my watch. It was twenty-five past nine. They stopped serving breakfast at ten so we either hurried up and got there or we got nothing until some point this afternoon.

My stomach rumbled its emptiness. Shooting a glance at Alistair, I said, 'I suppose we ought to give it another go.'

'I could use a cup of coffee if nothing else,' he agreed.

Schneider hooked his keys from the edge of the desk in his room and shut the door behind him. A few doors along, another door opened, Deepa poking her head out.

'I thought I heard you,' she left the room, Barbie exiting behind her.

Waving, my blonde friend said, 'Hey, Patty. Hey, guys. Did everyone get a good sleep?'

Her question prompted an explanation of the early morning events the late risers were not privy to. Since we were gathered in the corridor, Schneider did his best man duty and knocked on the groom's door.

Pippin poked his head out of his room one door along, but there was no answer from Baker. A sliver of worry chilled my blood.

Deepa poked my arm. Getting my attention, she said, 'You were telling us something about the other wedding. I take it something happened in the night. Did someone get mercilessly drunk and end up in hospital? Barbie and I snuck down to spy on the people in the pool and they were all hammered. We just went for a little celebrity spotting. All the big names had gone by then though.'

'Except that soccer player you like,' Barbie reminded her.

Deepa rolled her eyes. 'It's called football here, but yes, okay, Lennie Larsson was there and so were a few of his fellow England players.'

I heard everything they said, but my eyes never left Baker's door. I needed it to open and for the groom to appear. I didn't care if he was hungover, or still drunk, or looked like death warmed up. I needed him to be okay.

He didn't come to the door though, and Schneider was looking at it now as if wondering how to open it to check on his friend.

The sliver of worry was becoming a spear of ice. Martin Baker was a lot like me in many ways, he had a habit of snooping when he wanted to get an answer to a question. Had he gone out last night too? There were missing guards from Vincent's team and someone looney enough to steal rings, smash a cake, carve up a dress and scrawl messages on walls. That whoever it was wanted to convince Sasha from tying the knot with Bobbie was clear. What length they might go to was not and though I had nothing to suggest the missing guards and the other events were linked, I believed they were.

If the groom chose to roam Loxton Hall last night, did he meet the vandal?

Noticing my expression, Deepa asked, 'What is it, Patricia?'

I swallowed. It felt like I had a bowling ball stuck in my throat and my vision was starting to prickle as an inability to get a breath in properly threatened to make me faint.

I took a stumbling step toward the groom's door, Lieutenant Schneider giving me a curious look as he gave up and stepped away.

Before I could take another step, Alistair and Jermaine came to grab my arms. They could see me wobbling. A sense of dread was taking over my whole body and it was when I let the men take my weight that a police officer came into view.

The solemn look on his face was too much and I don't remember what happened next.

## Not as Dead as I Thought

What happened next was my brain failed to get enough oxygen and I passed out. I came to a few seconds later being carried to my room by Alistair. In his arms I felt secure and reassured, but that was only until I remembered why I fainted.

'Martin!' I cried.

'Hello?' he replied as if surprised to hear me calling his name.

Alistair was still carrying me but as I struggled to sit up and look around, he shifted my weight to plop me, as daintily as he could, back onto my feet.

Lieutenant Baker was right there. Utterly unharmed, dressed in casual clothes and looking at me with mildly amused concern.

'Everything all right, Mrs Fisher?' he asked.

Unable to order my thoughts now that he was here and clearly not lying murdered somewhere, I darted my eyes around until I spotted the police officer.

Seeing me lock eyes on him, Alistair said, 'Ah, yes. The chief inspector has requested your presence. There's, um ... there's a body.'

I sighed and sagged against the wall. 'Of course there is.'

As a group we traipsed after the young officer, a man called PC Llewelyn. He'd been sent by Chief Inspector Quinn to locate me, though I was yet to find out why my presence was needed. Martin Baker had risen early and gone to meet the family and friends he had flying in. He had the Range Rover from my collection back at the house in East Malling, not that he could get everyone in it, but drove the few miles to the airport so he could be there to greet them and make sure everyone found the venue without trouble.

Coming back into Loxton Hall with his family in tow, he stumbled across the police who had just recently stumbled across a body.

'Who is it?' I had to ask.

Martin didn't know and PC Llewelyn said, 'I think it would be best if I let the chief inspector fill you in on the details.'

It meant I had to wait until he led us to the site of the body which thankfully was inside the building and not outside in the cold.

Deepa got a call on her phone, squealing with excitement despite the recent grave news of a murder because her own family were just pulling up outside.

'You should go,' I insisted. 'You should all go. Especially you,' I pointed at the groom who seemed to think he was duty bound to accompany me since he'd brought us the news. 'And you,' I patted Alistair on the arm.'

'My place is with you,' he argued.

'Jermaine will remain at my side. Won't you, Jermaine?'

'As you wish, madam.'

Alistair looked less than convinced, but as the rest started to move away, I lowered my voice to say, 'Darling, they get married in a few hours. They shouldn't have to find themselves involved in a murder investigation.' I called it that because I was sure PC Llewelyn wasn't taking me to see someone who had a terrible accident. 'Be with your crew members as only you know how. I know you have a secret you've been keeping from Baker. You should think about telling him soon.'

I got a surprised expression. 'How on Earth do you know about that?' Alistair wanted to know.

I gripped his chin and pulled it down so I could kiss his lips. 'You talk in your sleep, sweetie.'

He snorted, laughing at himself, but said, 'Don't worry. I have a plan for Lieutenant Baker.'

I certainly hoped he did. He kissed me again before he went, then made fast steps to catch the others as they rounded a corner. I was left with Jermaine. It felt like old times in many ways. However, the addition of an impatient-looking young copper prevented me from taking a moment to enjoy reminiscing.

I gave the dogs a pat and shooed them into their bed. They would need more exercise this morning, but a murder scene was not the place to take them.

Forging ahead, and leaving the PC behind, I called over my shoulder, 'Come along, Constable Llewelyn, let's find out what Chief Inspector Quinn wants, shall we?'

## The Body in the Bog

It turned out that yes there was a body, but Chief Inspector Quinn wanted to see me for something entirely different.

I got as far as the crime scene cordon set up in the corridor before I was stopped by PC Llewelyn.

'Please wait here,' he instructed politely.

We were back near the bar, in the same corridor where I saw Sasha for the first time last night when she stormed out of the ladies' toilet. Looking over the heads of officers filling the corridor, I could see the ladies sign jutting out from the wall.

PC Llewelyn returned less than a minute later. 'You can follow me, Mrs Fisher. Please do not touch anything and no photographs. Please leave your phone in your bag at all times. That goes for you too, sir,' he made sure Jermaine understood the rules applied to both of us.

He led us through the press of officers, half a dozen of them filling the space in the corridor, and into the ladies' restroom where I spotted the chief inspector talking to two sergeants.

PC Llewelyn approached his boss and then waited patiently for the top man to finish his conversation and turn his attention our way.

Chief Inspector Quinn actually looked pleased to see me. 'Ah, Mrs Fisher. Thank you for coming to me. It saved me a trip and I am awfully busy.'

'You want to ask me about whoever you have found in here?' I questioned, truly curious as to why he might have summoned me given his lecture about leaving it all to the police yesterday.

There were crime scene officers on the floor, half in and half out of one of the stalls. Peering between their shoulders, I could see the victim's feet and ankles. Lying flat on the floor, her head had to be next to the toilet itself. Beyond the stalls, a handbag – the victim's I guessed – had been upended. Lipstick, tissues, a phone, keys, and more were strewn across the floor. Was it a robbery? How had she died? Questions were queuing in my head and I missed what the chief inspector asked me.

'I'm sorry, can you say that again?' I requested.

He gave me a broad smile. 'Of course, Mrs Fisher. I said that England striker and best man for the Howard-Box wedding, Lennie Larsson, was taken to hospital in the night having suffered terrible bruising to his ... um, nether region.' I felt my cheeks begin to burn. 'I believe they said he'd suffered a dislocated scrotum. You wouldn't happen to know anything about that, would you, Mrs Fisher?'

I took a moment to run through my response options. Felicity told me the best man had been taken to hospital. I hadn't realised it was me that put him there.

The chief inspector continued talking. 'I ask because one of the rather inebriated witnesses provided a description for his assailant and it matched you rather well.' He was toying with me, clearly already certain I was to blame and waiting for me to confess.

So I did. 'He was rude, and he came at me while drunk and naked. I took the action I thought appropriate.' The heat left my face, the embarrassment fading as righteous indignation replaced it.

Chief Inspector Quinn pursed his lips and nodded. 'I suspected as much. You'll be pleased to know he had no desire to press charges. Shall I consider the matter closed or do you wish to file a charge of your own?'

My previous statement made it sound like I might have been defending myself from a sexual assault. In a way, I was, but I wasn't going to make a headline out of it.

I shook my head.

'Then I think that will be all so far as Lennie Larsson goes.' The chief inspector's attention was back on the crime scene guys kneeling over the body.

I heard the subtext in his words. 'You have something else you wish to discuss with me?'

He pursed his lips again. 'We have established that you were out of bed last night, Mrs Fisher. Can you tell me what time that was, please?'

I felt my eyes narrowing but answered his question as accurately as I could. 'I left my room around twelve thirty this morning and returned a little after one.'

Beside me I felt Jermaine's body tense up. He was waiting for the chief inspector to accuse me of something and he didn't like it.

CI Quinn said, 'I see.' He wasn't watching me, as I would be him if I thought he'd been up to something suspicious. For me body language is one of the biggest tells for when a person was hiding something or just plain lying. So he either did things differently or he just didn't suspect me. 'What was the nature of your excursion, Mrs Fisher? I assume you didn't leave your room just to cause injury to Mr Larsson.'

'My dogs needed to go outside,' I bent the truth. 'The front door closed behind me and I had to find another way back in. That was via the pool where I met Mr Larsson and his friends.'

CI Quinn nodded his head yet again. A repetitive movement each time I answered a question. 'I see.'

Certain he was about to ask me another question, I got in first. 'Whose body is that?'

Finally, he turned his head in my direction, fixing me with an unreadable expression. 'I was rather hoping you might already know, Mrs Fisher.' He was daring me to give him an answer.

'All I can see are some feet,' I pointed out.

Inviting me to take a closer look, he stepped to one side with a sweep of his arm – go see for yourself.

I wrinkled my nose. I wasn't a fan of dead bodies. Who is? 'Is she icky?' I asked.

The chief inspector raised an eyebrow, somehow surprised by my reluctance to see the victim. 'She was strangled from behind. It suggests a male attacker, but a female killer cannot be ruled out.'

One of the crime scene guys sat back on his heels and turned around to face me. He had one of those face shield things on to help stop him contaminating the scene.

I recognised the face. 'Hi, Simon,' I chucked him a wave which he returned.

His partner, Steven, looked up, confirming the other crime scene guy was the one I always saw Simon with. He got a wave too.

'The attacker had small hands,' Simon shifted position, giving me an almost complete view of the body. 'Almost certainly a woman. From the angle of the post-mortem bruising, I would say the killer was roughly five feet and five inches tall. It looks like she was grabbed coming out of the stall. There are marks on the floor where the victim's shoes fought for purchase and marks on the door and frame where she grabbed it in trying to fight her attacker off.'

I stared down at the victim, wishing I didn't recognise her. 'That's Cara Fright,' I murmured more to myself than to answer the chief inspector's question.

Predictably, CI Quinn nodded. 'Quite so. You knew her?' he asked.

Answering his latest question, my mind filled with the image of her argument with Sasha the previous evening. 'I met her last night. We exchanged words. Nothing more.'

Simon and Steven exchanged a glance before Simon continued to explain his findings. 'There is a contusion on the rear of her skull, just above her neck. It's likely the attacker intended to knock her out first. We will need more time to determine the nature of the weapon, but a small bat or something similar is likely. Once subdued, she was strangled.'

Facing me, Chief Inspector Quinn wore a serious expression. 'During your nighttime excursion, Mrs Fisher, did you by chance happen to spot Miss Sasha Allstar out of her bed?'

I shook my head, an automatic reaction and an honest one. 'No.'

I got yet another nod.

'Where is she?' came a cry of despair from outside. 'Is she in there? I want to see her!'

The shouting came from a man, a mature man if my ears could be trusted. He sounded Canadian and he was causing some bother for the officers outside. They were refusing him entry and doing their best to keep him calm. I had no idea who he was, but I could guess: Cara Fright's husband/boyfriend.

His anguished cries echoed against the walls of the ladies' restroom.

Looking over my head to the door, Chief Inspector Quinn said, 'I must break the news of Miss Fright's death, though I fear it may have already leaked. Please do not leave Loxton Hall, Mrs Fisher. I have further questions for you.' He walked by me, heading for the door which left me with Jermaine at my side like a big comfortable blanket of reassurance, and the two crime scene guys at my feet either side of Cara.

Checking to make sure the chief inspector was out of earshot, I hissed, 'Guys, why did he ask me about Sasha being out of bed?'

Simon and Steven exchanged a glance, and then both stared at the door to make sure their boss was no longer in the room. I knew they had no love for Chief Inspector Quinn, I believed few did even if he was a man who got results, so I expected them to give me the inside tip and I was right.

Stealing another glance to make sure no one could hear, Simon licked his lips nervously and told me, 'There was a note stuffed into Cara Fright's back pocket.' Steven reached across to retrieve a clear plastic evidence bag from a box. In it a single piece of yellow paper with a big pink heart embossed on it – Sashatastic's emblem. 'It asks to meet here at one o'clock.'

I read the handwritten note.

*'I'll do it. But I want half the photos first. Meet me at the restroom outside the bar at one.'*

On the face of it, this one piece of evidence pointed directly to Sasha Allstar. Chief Inspector Quinn might not jump to a conclusion, but he would be heading up to interview her soon. If she didn't have an alibi, she would be getting arrested. It was the morning of her wedding, on top of the disaster the day was already turning out to be, her manager had been murdered and she was going to get arrested for it.

Was she guilty?

I had no way of knowing, but Felicity asked me to work out what was going on and this definitely fell into the same task. Using my phone, I took a picture of the note and thanked the two forensic scientists.

Now I needed to be somewhere else. Chief Inspector Quinn's request was to stay in the building which I had every intention of doing anyway. I had no intention of remaining in the ladies' restroom with the cadaver though. With a nudge, I got Jermaine moving.

'Come along, Jermaine. We have much to do.'

'Yes, madam.'

I waved goodbye to Simon and Steven and beat a hasty retreat. Outside the restroom, we slipped around the back of Chief Inspector Quinn and went the other way. Silently escaping, I risked a glance at the man whose voice we heard.

He looked distraught for sure, but I couldn't help noticing that he was far shorter than Cara. In fact, I'd put his height at about five feet five inches – small for a man. Not only that, but I also saw his hands and they were delicate little things.

## Charlie

Breakfast still hadn't happened, and I didn't feel that I had time for it now. Jermaine insisted I eat something though, steering me toward the restaurant where he popped inside to scare up bacon sandwiches. I would have gone with him, but just as we arrived, my phone started ringing.

I expected to find Alistair's name displayed on the screen, or Barbie perhaps. Alas, I was disappointed because it was neither. Nor was it anyone I wanted to speak to even though it was a name I knew well and had used often.

Clenching my teeth, I thumbed the green button and put the phone to my ear. When it connected, I said, 'Charlie.'

'Where are you?' he demanded to know, skipping over the parts where he ought to apologise for calling me, apologise for trying to screw me out of everything I own, and probably apologise for even existing.

Thinking my glare might form two laser beams like Superman if I gave it any more juice, I asked, 'What business is that of yours?'

My question tripped him up because he had no way to reply unless he was going to admit it was none of his business. Instead of doing that, he tried a different approach. 'I am at your house, Patricia. I want to talk to you.'

'We are talking,' I replied coolly. I could hear the ice in my words so no doubt he could too. 'Are you calling to tell me you have come to your senses and want to drop this ridiculous quest to split everything down the middle.'

'We agreed to an even split, Patricia,' he spat. 'Why are you being so unreasonable?'

I choked in response to his insane question. 'Unreasonable. We agreed to split our joint assets evenly. When we made that agreement, I didn't even have a place to live. I was staying in a bed and breakfast, or rather I was supposed to be, but had moved back in with you because I didn't think I was safe there. The point, Charlie, is that we made an agreement before the Maharaja's generosity came into the picture. You have no right to claim anything beyond that which we accrued together in our marriage.'

'Together?' he laughed at me. 'What did you ever contribute? I made all the money. What I have in my bank account, the house, everything up to and including the money you stole to take that cruise around the world came courtesy of me. You are the one who has no right to claim what you have.'

I bit my tongue, fearful for what might come out of my mouth if I spoke another word. He took my silence as a prompt to tell me why he wanted to speak to me in the first place.

'Look, Patricia,' he softened his tone so he sounded friendly at least. 'The meeting on Monday probably won't be nice for either of us. My lawyers assure me that you still haven't employed legal representation of your own and they are a pack of sharks. I don't want to come out of this as enemies.'

I choked again. 'And you think this is the way to go about it, do you?'

Reacting to my comment he dropped the friendly tone. 'I came here to get you to sign the paperwork in advance of the meeting. I was trying to save you the pain of attending a meeting where my lawyers might tear you to shreds. I was thinking of you.'

My jaw began to ache from clenching my teeth together. 'What utter nonsense!' I raged at him. 'You were thinking about what you can get for yourself, you greedy little pig. Are you looking up at my house now and thinking about how you might redecorate? Do you think you will be able to force me out because I cannot possibly afford to pay you the half of its value your lawyers will demand?'

'Well, can you pay me?' he asked, his question deadly serious.

A smile curled the edges of my mouth. Charlie couldn't see it, but he would hear it when I said, 'You should listen to the last piece of good advice I ever plan to give you, Charlie Fisher. Walk away with what you have. Keep our house. Keep what is in the bank and keep everything in the house. I want none of it. All our belongings are tainted by the memory of you. You can have it all. But if you come after what is mine. If your lawyers try to get the Maharaja's house and all that came with it, then so help me, Charlie Fisher, I will destroy you.'

I heard him draw a deep breath, a sigh of his frustration. 'I thought I would be able to make you see sense,' he whined.

'I'll see you on Monday at ten.' With my final words spoken, I punched the red button to end the call and dropped the phone back into my bag.

Jermaine was standing a few feet away, politely not listening to my call. He could not help but have heard it though. In his hands, he held two plates, both stacked with slices of toast between which juicy, thick slices of bacon were poking.

'Ketchup?' I enquired.

'Already applied, madam.' He was ever such a good friend.

Hitching my bag into the crook of my left elbow, I gratefully accepted a plate and took a bite, toast crumbs dropping from my lips to the floor like fairy dust.

Though he was too polite to ask, I knew he had to want to know. 'You are wondering if I have a plan to deliver on my boast to destroy my husband, aren't you?'

'I heard nothing, madam.'

I squinted at him playfully. 'Jermaine you are such a terrible liar. I do have a plan. It's just not one hundred percent there yet,' I admitted. It was nearing lunch on Saturday which gave me less than forty-eight hours in which I needed Mr Worthington to confirm or deny a singular piece of information.

I thought about it all the way back to my room, by which time I had devoured my bacon sandwiches, and a good thing too because there were two dachshunds on the other side of the door, and they could smell bacon across a county line.

As I dug around in my bag for a tissue – I wanted to get the grease from my fingers before I touched anything else – I heard Felicity call my name.

## The Ex-Girlfriend

'Patricia! Patricia, I've just seen someone!' she gasped, a little out of breath. She was running along the corridor, which is to say she was trying to slow down while her dog, Buster, attempted to make her go faster.

Buster's tongue lolled from the left side of his mouth, the squat, muscular dog panting from the exertion though he looked happy.

I wiped my hands and opened my door so the girls inside could rush out. The three dogs sniffed and circled and sniffed again while I waited for Felicity to get her breath back.

'Teagan,' she managed between gasps. 'I saw Teagan.'

Had I heard that name already? I couldn't be sure, but I wasn't able to say who Teagan was. 'Should I know what that means?' I asked.

Getting another lungful of air, Felicity supplied an answer. 'Teagan is Bobbie Howard-Box's ex-girlfriend. She took a job here working in the bar just to get close to him, then because she wasn't on shift last night, she stole a chef's uniform and claimed the agency sent her to help out with my kitchen staff. We thought she was the one who tried to poison the wedding party. We know it wasn't her now, but they arrested her and took her away at the time. I didn't think she would dare to show her face again – I assumed Loxton Hall would fire her, but I swear I just saw her.'

I joined the dots. 'She could be the one who hacked up the dress, smashed the cake, stole the rings and left the messages.'

Felicity put an arm against the wall to support herself and gasped in another breath. 'I need to do some fitness training,' she wheezed.

I snorted a small laugh. 'Don't let my friend Barbie hear you say that.' Remembering that Felicity had most likely missed the latest piece of news as she tried to fix the earlier problems, I said, 'Are you aware there was a murder?'

Her eyes popped out on stalks. 'No! Here?'

'Sasha's manager, Cara Fright,' I supplied. 'Did you meet her?'

Felicity shook her head. 'What on Earth is going on here? I've never had a wedding like this. I mean, I've had one where the groom dropped dead on the morning of the wedding. He was eighty-seven though and his bride, the little gold-digger, was twenty-two. The family were over the moon because she was about to get everything, and the police got called in to investigate but it turned out he just had a heart attack.'

Refocusing her on the point she raised, I asked, 'Where did you see Teagan? Where was she going?'

I got an oops face back at me. 'She was outside. I was in my room trying to gather my wits; I needed a minute to myself with all that's going on. I spotted her crossing the grass toward the building. She could be anywhere now. I need to tell the police, don't I?'

'I think so,' I agreed. 'We need to tell them, and we need to speak with Sasha because Chief Inspector Quinn will be on his way to her soon and I want to get there first.'

Jermaine had the dogs on their leads, and we were ready to move on again. Felicity was coming too, but asked, 'Why will the chief inspector need to talk to the bride?'

I puffed out my lips and wriggled them about as I thought about what to say. In the end I went with, 'Because she might have murdered her manager.'

As you might expect, my statement shocked the wedding planner walking next to me. 'Why?' she begged. 'Why would she do that?'

I didn't know the answer, but I did say, 'I heard them arguing last night. It was quite loud and rather unpleasant. I'm not sure what it was about but Sasha's manager levelled an ultimatum at the bride. "Do as I say or there will be consequences."' I quoted her words verbatim. 'Sasha did not act as if she intended to comply.'

'That doesn't make her a killer,' Felicity challenged.

I agreed. 'It does not. That's why I want to talk to her before the police do. If I don't get in first, she might be arrested before I get a chance to hear her side of things.'

Felicity shook her head in horror. 'That's all this day needs: the bride being led away in cuffs.'

I had nothing to say on the matter. Felicity was absolutely right, assuming that is, that the bride hadn't killed her manager to avoid doing whatever it was Cara Fright was trying to force her to do.

My day was getting away from me. Deepa and Martin were due to wed at three this afternoon and it was gone ten thirty now. I had four hours to get out from under this so I could stand next to Alistair in the lovely dress I'd had made for the occasion. It accented the stark white and the gold brocade of his uniform and we would be a handsome couple. I did not want to stand next to him with my feet twitching because I felt I needed to be elsewhere trying to stop a killer.

I was already missing out on the fun my friends were having so I could help Felicity, and I wasn't going to let myself complain about it. Focusing on the problem in hand, I asked, 'What time is their ceremony?'

'Three o'clock,' came her prompt reply. 'I could have done with it being a little later. The rings will get here soon, and I'm confident the dress will be done in time. The cake isn't needed until the reception this evening, so that isn't a problem either – probably,' she added with her fingers crossed. 'It's what else our wedding vandal might do yet that worries me. If the same person who trashed the dress and the cake also killed Cara Fright, do you think they will kill again?'

That was a question I could answer. 'In my experience, the first murder is the hard one. After that, it seems to matter less.' I got a strange look from Felicity. 'What I mean is, after the first murder, the killer knows they are stuffed if they get caught. Going to jail for one murder or two or three doesn't make much difference. Often the second murder is an attempt to stop people finding out they were responsible for the first.'

I thought about the likelihood that the vandal and the killer were the same person. I could make it fit, but it didn't feel right. 'In this case,' I continued, 'The vandal seems to want to stop the wedding. Killing Cara Fright probably won't do that, so if it's the same person, killing Cara wasn't a premeditated act.'

'You think it might have been ...' Felicity stuttered, trying to join the same dots I was. 'It might have been that Cara knew something and it got her killed?'

I shrugged. 'I don't know enough about anything yet. I'll make wild guesses later.'

We were at Angelica's door again. Would they all still be inside, or would they have dispersed? I let Felicity talk to the guard still stationed outside. It was the one who'd been inside last time, the two had swapped positions I discovered when the door swung open.

Jermaine got a sideways look from the guard outside; still sore about Jermaine disarming him earlier no doubt. The dogs led the way inside, but we found the room to be mostly empty.

Mostly.

Angelica heard the dogs panting, or possibly she can sense my evil presence. Whichever it is, as we came into her suite's main living area, she stormed out of her bedroom.

'What are you doing back here?' she screeched.

'Investigating whatever it is you are hiding,' I replied with a smile.

'I brought her with me,' said Felicity.

Angelica didn't like that answer either. She still had on the robe over her underwear, but her face and hair were complete. She looked good, truth be told. Felicity's makeup girls had taken ten years off her.

Before she could get up a head of steam, I said, 'There's been a murder.'

Whatever she was about to say died on her lips as stark horror gripped her. 'Bobbie!' she squealed, jumping to a conclusion that made me want an explanation. I wasn't going to get it though. The shock of my statement slammed into her, her eyes rolled upward, and she fainted.

Honestly, I could have caught her. I wasn't that far away, but weighing up my options, I decided to watch instead. Guiltily hoping she might bounce her head on something as she fell, I was silently disappointed when she just folded into herself. Her knees went first, and she just sort of flopped into a heap where she'd been standing.

Felicity made a startled sound and started to dart forward. I grabbed her arm, holding her back just long enough to be able to get my phone out. You might think bad of me, but Angelica has been the bane of my life for many years. In recent months it has gotten even worse and seeing that she was breathing and not injured I took a second to savour the moment.

'Should I carry Mrs Howard-Box to her bed, madam?' asked Jermaine.

I considered his offer, but said, 'Nah, stuff her.'

Still holding Felicity back, I took Buster's lead from her hand and shooed him over to investigate.

Felicity cackled, her hand over her mouth to stifle the sound. 'Patricia, you are awful!' she squealed as Buster licked Angelica's face. I took a few last pics and popped my phone away, kneeling to help Angelica up when she let out a groan.

As her eyes fluttered open, and Buster was innocently watching her from across the room again, she asked, 'Oooh, what happened?'

'You fainted,' I told her flatly.

She started to lever herself up from the carpet. Felicity had the girls' leads too so I offered my worst enemy a hand to get back to her feet.

Angelica slapped it away in disgust. Then she remembered why she fainted, and the blood ran from her face again. Starting to hyperventilate, she stared up into my eyes. 'Who was murdered?' she begged to know, her voice fearful.

'Sasha's manager.' I gave her the honest answer straight away because I am not cruel enough to lie about such a thing, even to someone like Angelica.

Angelica breathed a huge sigh of relief. 'Oh, thank goodness.'

I didn't think that was an appropriate phrase to employ but I let it go. 'Why did you think it might be Bobbie?' I asked it as a question, but it came out like an accusation. 'What are you hiding, Angelica? Is there a threat against your son?' She said nothing, waving her arms to make me step back before getting shakily to her feet. 'Why won't you tell us so we can help?' I pleaded with her, desperate for knowledge that might help me make sense of things.

'I don't want your help!' she spat. 'I have my own private investigator and he will get to the bottom of the vandalism and theft we have suffered, not you. His men and the police will catch whoever is behind the crimes. Just you stay out of it, Patricia Fisher!'

I laughed at her. I didn't know what else to do. 'Even when your son is in danger; I'm guessing that is the true reason behind your private security, you still won't accept my help. If the killer strikes and neither Vince nor the police were able to prevent it, will you blame me still?'

She thrust an arm at the door, her index finger pointing. 'Get out!'

I nodded at her, accepting that there was nothing I could do to help a person who didn't wish to be helped. I would find Sasha and Bobbie and I would help anyway. I was doing it for them, and because Felicity asked me to, and because it was the right thing to do.

Turning away from the ridiculous woman I motioned to Felicity that I was leaving. She paused, eyes wide, and when I got close to her, she whispered, 'Do you think we should tell her?'

I shook my head. Not a chance.

I guess Felicity felt it was her duty as the wedding planner or that she had a responsibility to her client, but Angelica's awful attitude overruled both those things. Following me to the door, Felicity chose to keep quiet too.

Neither of us were going to tell Angelica that Buster had licked off all the makeup from one side of her face.

## Sasha's Lies

Felicity already knew which room Sasha had been moved to because she arranged it with the venue management. Another of Vince's guards was positioned outside the door.

'Is the bride inside?' Felicity asked as we approached the door.

She got, 'Yes, Mrs Philips,' in reply, plus, 'Mr Slater is in there too along with several police officers.'

I groaned inwardly, cursing myself for wasting time on Angelica. The door opened from the inside, and permitted to enter, we went in search of the bride.

I could hear Chief Inspector Quinn's dulcet tones before I saw him. The honeymoon suite was a touch larger than Angelica's suite as you might imagine and commanded a corner of the stately home with windows on two sides. I observed its dimensions as I came through the door from the entrance lobby and into the main living area. The bedroom would be off to the left, I guessed, and the bathroom through the closed door to the right.

I stayed quiet, slipping just around the doorframe and into the room where my eyes were instantly confused. Ahead of me, with his back facing my way was Chief Inspector Quinn. His lean runner's frame was easy to pick out, and besides, he was the one doing the talking. Flanking him, were two sergeants. I'd seen them both last night and a niggling voice at the back of my head argued that I almost always saw him with male officers.

Was there a sexist streak running through the chief inspector? It was a question for another time.

Across the room I saw Vince. He looked to be fighting the fatigue he was probably feeling, I knew he carried an injury; I saw the dressing on his abdomen last night. All four men were looking inward to the persons sitting on two couches where they faced outward and thus could see me.

It was the two seated figures that were confusing my brain because they were both Sasha.

Because their eyes were pointed in my direction, they both saw me come into the room, and the shift in their focus was noticed by the men looking at them. All four men tracked the eyes of both Sashas to see Felicity and me now gawping at them from across the room.

Chief Inspector Quinn grimaced. 'Yes. It occurs to me now that I should have assigned a constable to the door to prevent access.'

'Hello again, Chief Inspector,' I replied even though he hadn't actually addressed me. 'I hoped I might get here ahead of you. Are you accusing Sasha Allstar yet, or have you not got that far?'

The senior police officer gave me a deeply worried frown. 'Will I have to have you removed, Mrs Fisher?' he asked.

I couldn't stop the smile that reached my face. 'That will depend upon your agenda, Chief Inspector.' Before he could react, I raised my hands in supplication. 'I came only to observe, if you will permit me. My good friend,' I indicated Felicity standing to my right, 'is performing miracles to keep this wedding on track. If you are going to derail it for good, I think it only fair she be informed so she may react accordingly.'

He narrowed his eyes as he considered my words. 'If you wish to observe you may do so,' he agreed. No sooner had he made the comment than he turned around to address the Sashas once more.

'Sorry,' I interrupted. When heads turned my way again, I jinked a finger at the two Sasha's. 'I didn't realise you had a twin.'

Both Sashas looked inward at each other and burst out laughing. It went on for several seconds, their joke shared between no one but themselves. When her giggling subsided, the one on the right said, 'I'll take that as a compliment.'

The other said, 'You should, Gloria. You really should, but I've been telling you for years that people think you are me for a reason.'

I was confused, because I wasn't in on the joke, but their language made it clear my assumption had been false - they were not twins at all. Gloria was one of the women in her entourage; I'd seen her in Angelica's room the first time I went in there.

'Gloria is my double,' Sasha explained still giggling at my foolish mistake. 'She does public appearances for me when I cannot be two places at once.'

They were dressed identically in what I had come to recognise as Sashatastic's signature look. It started with a pink wig though I believed Sasha's was her real hair. The hair was braided to fall in a single tail between her shoulder blades. The dress was a pink creation that was both futuristic and impractical. Sleeveless, it stopped four inches above the knee and bore a see-through plastic panel a foot wide around the midriff. Anyone wearing it needed to commit to performing a lot of sit ups. The legs were bare, and on her feet were a pair of black army boots that looked utterly incongruous to the outfit.

Chief Inspector Quinn cleared his throat, the sound very much intended to cause everyone else to fall silent.

Squinting at the Sasha I could now identify as the real Sasha, he said, 'You were seen out of your bed last night at a time that places you as a suspect in the murder of your manager. I have three witnesses that will testify to seeing you, not only out of your bed but on the ground floor, far away from your room and in the vicinity of the crime scene.' He paused to let his statement sink in. 'I will shortly start interviewing the people connected with the victim and those closest to you, Miss Allstar. When I do that, will I find that you had motive to wish Miss Fright's permanent silence?'

He was asking the question because he already knew the answer. It was a trap he wanted the internet superstar to walk into. I already knew there was something untoward about her relationship with her manager, but I couldn't tell if she would see it as motive for murder. I wanted to find out for myself. To do that, I needed to head off her answer.

I jumped in quickly. 'Chief Inspector, are you sure it was Miss Allstar who was seen last night?' I let my question hang for a few seconds because I knew he wouldn't be able to come up with an immediate answer. In front of him were two women with the same hair and the same clothes. With the same makeup applied, they were impossible to tell apart. 'Was she reported to be wearing the outfit we currently see her in?'

I got no answer but saw it when the chief inspector's face twitched in annoyance.

I pressed on. 'Given her unique hairstyle and look, any woman of roughly the same dimensions might be mistaken for Miss Allstar.'

Chief Inspector Quinn swivelled on his heels to glare in my direction.

I carried on as if nothing had happened. 'How reliable are your witnesses?' I asked him, feigning innocence in my face now that he was looking at me. 'As you know, I was up and about at the same time. Everyone I saw was distinctly inebriated.'

I stopped talking. My point had been made. He might have witnesses, and they might have accurately identified the true Sashatastic. He couldn't be sure of it though and that was going to buy me some time to figure out a few things. Things that would be far harder with Miss Allstar on her way to a cell at Maidstone police station. I needed to quiz her. And Bobbie too and maybe several other people for that matter.

Quinn's lip quivered in annoyance.

Pressing on, I said, 'I only point this out because her lawyers will do exactly the same. It does none of us any good to arrest her if she is innocent. Given her popularity and the way the press chase her, the public outcry could be most damaging to reputations. I would not want to be the one to falsely accuse her.'

The look in his eyes let me know I had won. Not that it was a contest. The point is I was right, and it would be easy to argue the Sasha the witnesses saw at night from a distance while under the influence of alcohol could have been anyone wearing one of her wigs with the Sashatastic dress and boots. If she did murder her manager, the chief inspector was going to have to gather proper evidence before he made a move.

Quinn lifted his head and eyes, looking skyward for a moment and drawing in a deep breath through his nose as he considered his next move.

'Very well,' he brought his gaze back to Sasha. 'Do you deny that you were out of your bed last night between the hours of midnight and two, Miss Allstar?'

Sasha leaned down to collect a handbag from the carpet. It was one of those oversized ones with a designer label and probably cost more than most people made in a month. She shoved her hand in, digging around as she said, 'I think I should call my lawyer before I answer any questions, Mr Policeman.' It was a derogatory response though I knew Quinn was too calm and in control to react to it. Failing to find what she was looking for she upended the bag in frustration. The contents tumbled out.

Chief Inspector Quinn reacted at exactly the same moment as me – when a little notepad with a stylised pink heart motif fell free.

'Take that, Sergeant Travis,' he ordered, pointing to the notepad.

Sasha frowned as the man darted forward to retrieve the object. 'You want my notepad? I have a bunch of them around here someplace. Take some.'

'This matches a note found in Cara Fright's back pocket,' said the chief inspector.

Sergeant Travis donned a pair of blue latex gloves to carefully pick up the notepad. I knew why the chief inspector wanted it. If there was an imprint on the top sheet that matched the words found on Cara's body, he would have evidence and reason to arrest. It was clear from the sergeant's face that no such imprint was visible.

'I'm calling my lawyer,' Sasha announced to the room.

Eyeing her suspiciously, Chief Inspector Quinn said, 'Yes, Miss Allstar. I believe you should do that. My investigation will continue.'

'Are you going to stop the wedding?' Felicity wanted to know. I could see how much anxiety the doubt was causing by the way she gripped Buster's lead so tightly.

The chief inspector looked heavenward again, sniffing in his next breath slowly before answering. When he lowered his eyes again a few seconds later, he was still looking at Sasha. 'Not at this time,' he replied.

Sasha ought to have gasped a sigh of relief at the news. Felicity did, but from the troubled, sorrowful look on her face, the bride had too many other problems on her mind already.

With a nod to his sergeants, Chief Inspector Quinn made his way around Felicity and me to get to the door. On his way, he called over his shoulder. 'I should ask your lawyer to hurry if I were you, Miss Allstar. You may need legal representation sooner than you think.'

It was a threat as much as it was a warning. He wanted to make sure she felt ill at ease and would probably have someone watching her like a hawk now to see what she did.

I stayed silent and continued to watch Sasha myself. Like the chief inspector, I had to consider her a viable, possibly even likely suspect. Once we heard the door close, I looked around the room. Vince was still here, and I was beginning to wonder what role he might play in the shenanigans we were witness to.

'I thought you were supposed to be investigating. I didn't hear you ask any questions,' I accused him.

I got a smile in response. 'If I dedicate time to investigating, I will not be protecting. Both things are not possible simultaneously. I can look into what happened here later. I still have missing men; the police have not been able to locate them, and replacements are coming who will need to be briefed upon arrival. There is already much to do without wasting effort and energy trying to work out what happened to a cake.' He switched his gaze to the wedding planner by my side. 'Besides, the lovely Felicity appears to have cakes and dresses and things in hand.'

Felicity wrinkled her nose and groaned at his flirting.

'So you are just going to focus on keeping Sasha and Bobbie safe?' I asked.

He dipped his head. 'That is what is important.'

'What do you think happened to your men?' I asked him.

He didn't like the question and made a show of looking away from me. 'The police are yet to find them,' he said, which wasn't really an answer, I noted.

Switching my attention back to Sasha, who didn't seem inclined to call her lawyer, I asked, 'What was the fight about last night?'

Sasha hiked an eyebrow. 'Who are you? I get that my imminent mother-in-law doesn't like you … that's probably a reason to trust you, actually,' she commented to herself. 'But I don't know you from Adam. Why are you asking me questions?'

I crossed to a spare armchair and sat, picking up my dogs so I could scratch their ears while I observed the internet superstar. 'I'm Patricia Fisher,' I gave her my name but didn't expand. 'Someone is trying to mess with your wedding, and I have been asked to work out who that is so they can be stopped. Your manager was murdered a few hours ago. If you don't mind me saying so, you don't look particularly upset.'

'Cara was a disgusting leech,' spat Gloria, answering for Sasha. 'She would work Sasha to death if she thought it would turn a profit.'

I looked for confirmation from Sasha. She looked at the carpet as a tear rolled down her cheek. 'She used to be nice. I think she was being squeezed by the parent company who own my name and the right to use it.' I frowned my lack of understanding. Seeing it, she explained. 'I rebelled against my parents and signed a contract the second I turned eighteen. It made me a lot of money very fast but took away all my freedom. I was ... still am owned wholly by a Japanese media corporation. Everyone thinks I live this amazing life, but it isn't my own.' She grabbed at her dress. 'This ... this stupid thing. Have you any idea how many of these I have? How many times I have worn it? How much I hate the sight of myself in it?'

Gloria chipped in, 'They tell her what to do and when to do it. They control every part of her life. Just look at today.' I hitched an eyebrow, wondering what she was referring to.

'What about today?' asked Felicity, equally curious.

Sasha wafted a hand at her outfit. 'I'm getting married in a few hours but first there is an event for my fans. Cara organised it. It's being live streamed to televisions around the world. They are changing up my brand and have a whole new host of shows planned. This one is all about my BFFs. People get to dress up in this ridiculous outfit,' she wafted a hand at her dress, 'and meet me. We chat and play silly games. I hate it.'

'In half an hour,' Gloria checked her watch. 'We have to meet two hundred Sasha wannabes downstairs in the ballroom.'

'I have to meet them,' Sasha corrected her friend.

Gloria gave Sasha a sad look. 'I'm not letting you do it alone. Not today. You should just let me go in your place.'

'These are diehard fans,' sniffed Sasha, dabbing her eyes with a tissue. 'They would spot the difference and cry fake.'

I felt sorry for the bride; she appeared truly miserable on what ought to be a very happy day. I was going to make things worse because it was time to hit her with a question that would blindside her. 'What pictures has Cara got?'

Both Sasha and Gloria reacted as if I had slapped their faces.

'It was on that note found in Cara's pocket. The note said, "I'll do it. But I want half the photos first. Meet me at the restroom outside the bar at one."'

'You think I wrote it?' growled Sasha, angry now. 'You think I killed Cara? I might have disliked her. Hated her even at times, but I'm not a crazy person. I don't go around killing people because I don't like them. I think you should leave.'

'Yeah,' echoed Gloria. 'You need to leave now.'

Sasha stuffed her things back into her handbag so no one could see them, snatched it into the air and got to her feet.

'I have to get married shortly. Is it too much to ask that everyone leave me alone?' The question came over her shoulder as she stormed from the living space and into her bedroom.

Gloria glared at me, getting to her feet so she could look more imposing. It didn't really work because, like Sasha, she is only five feet and about five inches tall.

I had overstayed my welcome, that was for sure, but I had learned something useful. As I moved to the door, Felicity, having a terrible time as the wedding planner, felt a need to say something.

'The dress will be here by noon,' she called out. 'I'll come up with the dressmaker to make sure it fits.' No answer came back from the bedroom. 'Okay?' she asked, hopeful of an answer or even an acknowledgement.

None came.

Waiting for her by the door, I looked down, and it was then that I spotted a patch of dried red mud. It was the same stuff I had to wipe from my shoes. The same red mud I stepped in last night outside the door the hooded man led the guards to. I needed to find out where that went, and I berated myself for not yet telling Chief Inspector Quinn about it.

I would attend to that shortly, but why was the mud in Sasha's room? I remembered the hooded figure – I'd been convinced it was a man, but I believed Sasha really was out of bed last night. That didn't mean no one else was …

I went back through to the living space only to bump into Felicity as she tried to catch up to me. The dog leads tangled but Jermaine shot out a steadying hand to catch me and for once I didn't end up on my bottom.

Calling out, I asked, 'Sasha where did this red mud come from?'

I heard footsteps stomping across her bedroom. Gloria wasn't in the living room so one of the two was coming to answer me.

That proved to be an incorrect guess though. Sasha stormed back out in the suite's main space where, once clear of the door, she threw a lamp at me.

I squealed in fright, jumping back into the entrance lobby a half second before it sailed through the space my head occupied a moment before. It struck the wall, exploding into pieces of pottery and glass as the light bulb went too. Only the shade mounted on top remained intact, but I was through the door and outside before it hit the carpet.

Our ears still ringing, Felicity and I hurried away. I wasn't going to label Sasha as Bridezilla – she'd had a tough and trying day and it wasn't yet noon. However, I also wasn't going to take my eye off her. That Angelica was lying to me was commonplace and normal. The bride was lying too and with all that had happened since I arrived yesterday, it made me deeply suspicious.

'What was that about the red mud?' Felicity asked.

Her phone rang before I could answer, and I waited while she looked to see who the caller might be.

'I have to take this,' she said, turning to walk away a pace.

It was her dressmaker, that was instantly clear, and they were stuck outside Loxton Hall because a procession of Sasha wannabes, all dressed up to look like the superstar were now entering the grounds. The police were checking them all, the murder no doubt making them extra diligent.

Ending her call with a tut and a sigh, Felicity said, 'I'll have to go down there and collect her on foot. She can abandon her car at the side of the driveway. She won't be here long.' Like so many other people at Loxton Hall, Felicity had a lot on her mind, and it showed in her face.

I placed a hand on her shoulder as a show of support. 'A few more hours and it will be behind you.'

'Until the next one,' she joked. 'Honestly, I don't know why I do it to myself.'

'They're not all like this though, are they?' I hedged.

The question made her chuckle. 'If any of them had ever been like this one, I would have quit years ago.' She tugged at Buster's lead. 'I really must go. I'll catch up with you later.' Her feet stalled. 'What are you going to do next?'

## Footprints in the Mud

It was a great question. It was not, however, one for which I had an immediate answer. When I shrugged and made a face, Felicity hurried on her way, the ever-exuberant Buster powering along the corridor with his owner demanding he slow down.

I needed to find Vince. I needed to tell Chief Inspector Quinn about the door on the side of Loxton Hall where I saw the guards vanish last night, and I needed to watch Sasha. I probably also needed to see what Bobbie knew and maybe talk to everyone in the wedding party.

There wasn't time for the last one and I could only do one thing at a time.

'How do you feel about splitting up?' I asked Jermaine.

I got a doubtful frown in return. 'I rather think I should remain at your side, madam.'

It was as I expected. 'Then we need to recruit some help,' I replied as I started walking.

The corridor took us to one of the main staircases, a huge, wide, and overly ornate structure that looked to have been erected when the house was originally built. I could admire the wood panelling and the workmanship that went into the elegant scrolling of the banister, but my eyes were drawn through the windows to a bus now depositing people outside the front entrance.

These were the Sasha BFFs here for the television show. It was easy to tell because they all had the same ridiculous pink dress held in one hand. Some were already wearing their pink wigs, and while many had their dress on a hanger and inside a cellophane wrap to keep the dirt off, others were less particular and had it draped over an arm.

The Sashatastic BFFs were all shapes and sizes and ages. But what startled me most was that a good portion of them were men. It had to be over twenty percent, and some had beards! They would look great in the dress and wig.

Mind boggling, I hurried down the stairs. Which thing should I do first? Do I find Quinn first or is the door on the side of the building a red herring?

I needed to check it out again in the daylight. Hurrying on, Anna and Georgie under my arms because they don't go down stairs very well if at all, I asked Jermaine, 'Can you call Barbie, sweetie? I think I might need a small amount of help, but I don't want to involve too many people. Not now that Deepa and Martin have their families here.'

'Very good, madam.'

I heard him speaking to our blonde friend as I got to the bottom of the stairs and could put the dogs down again. They shook their coats out and looked up to see where we were going next. They were having a fine old day – going here and there instead of sleeping the whole time.

It occurred to me that they hadn't been outside for a while and that tipped my decision. I wanted to speak with the chief inspector again. No, I'll correct that statement. I felt I had a duty to inform the chief inspector about the door. I knew I ought to tell him about the argument I overheard between Sasha and Cara too, but if I did that, he would take it as further evidence and probably arrest her. If she weren't guilty, I would never forgive myself for ruining her wedding.

My skull itched again the moment I thought about her wedding being ruined. Why was that? Heading for the door, I searched my thoughts.

Paying too little attention to the world around me, I was almost trampled when the Sashatastic BFFs surged through the front doors of Loxton Hall like a tidal wave. Had Jermaine not gently steered me to the side as they barrelled in, I might have been swept up and along like so much flotsam.

'Where's the buffet?' asked a man. He was in his forties and jumping up to get a better look over the heads of the people in front.

'Yeah, I'm starving,' moaned another. 'You'd think the TV people would have fed us breakfast.'

A harried looking young woman with a tablet and a headset shoved her way through the crowd while shouting for everyone to keep going. There was a cloakroom for them to put their outfits in and a room set up with a buffet. They already had assigned group numbers. Group A would be first and should proceed directly to the changing rooms in the leisure centre.

The harried looking woman was joined by others, all discernible by their headsets and tablets as they appeared ahead of the BFFs to guide them where they needed to go.

I watched for a second, unable to tear my eyes away from the incredible sight. The cloakroom was just off to the left, the ballroom where they would film was on the opposite side of the main hall we were in, and the leisure centre with its changing rooms could be accessed through a door at the back. The restaurant where I almost got breakfast had been repurposed to house the BFFs for their buffet.

The hungry man in his forties was first to get there, throwing his dress, wig, and boots at the cloakroom ladies before running to get to the food.

Whipping them into a frenzy was not necessary, but one of the TV people did it anyway. He looked to be the man in charge, standing back and giving orders to the other TV people.

'Keep moving, everyone,' he shouted to be heard. 'Sashatastic is super excited to meet you all, let's not create any hold ups. Remember we are live streaming today's show!'

The mere mention of the star's name produced a deafening cacophony of cheers, whistles, and shouts of joy.

Loxton Hall staff appeared, ready to assist the hundred or more potential BFFs to get to the right place. As the sea of people coming through the front doors started to dwindle, Jermaine and I slipped out.

Anna and Georgie merrily snuffled along, their noses to the ground as we left the path and stepped onto the grass. My heels dug in instantly. Despite all my complaints about how cold it was last night, it hadn't reached freezing and the ground was squishy and soft from recent rainfall. Walking on the balls of my feet, and using Jermaine's arm for support, I tottered around to the side of the building, following the path I took only a few hours ago. It had been dark then, and the door invisible until I was almost upon it.

In the daylight, I could see the trellis that hid it the moment I turned the corner. A flat steel door with no ornamentation looked out of place against the backdrop of the beautiful building, but painted letters at head height claimed it to be 'Pump Room'. That it led to a maintenance area no guests would ever see explained why the door was left plain, and also why it was locked.

It didn't tell me why footsteps went into it and not back out again. Although, now I looked more carefully, I could see one set of footprints going the other way. I asked Jermaine's opinion.

He examined the marks carefully before speaking. 'Madam most of the prints are made by an Oxford style man's loafer. I cannot find a set that appear to exit the building; they all go in but do not come out. I can detect several different sizes of shoe which would indicate at least three or more people - probably men given the shoe size,' he hovered his own giant foot above one print to demonstrate, 'went into the building. The one set of prints that do not match are from a running shoe and they do come back out again.'

I followed his hand as he tracked the footsteps in and then out again. 'More than once,' I pointed out. There were two left footprints side by side, squelched into the thick red mud which preserved them.

'Incidentally, madam,' Jermaine continued, 'The red in the soil is due to these plants.' He tugged at the frond of a broad-leafed fern-looking thing. 'Asponicus Decimosia,' he even knew its name! 'grows in Mediterranean countries, most notably Greece and into Turkey where it has adapted to survive in the nutrient deficient loam on mountain sides. If they planted the shrubs in any other soil, they would have swiftly perished.'

It was amazing what my butler could find inside his head.

'This means Miss Allstar was here last night then,' he concluded.

I pursed my lips. It was the wrong assumption. 'What we can believe is that someone who got mud on their shoes last night was in her room earlier today.'

'She only just moved rooms, madam,' Jermaine reminded me.

He was right. Her original room had a spray-painted message on the wall. It meant the shoes that left the mud had been worn by someone last night and again today and they were in Sasha's room earlier.

'What size would you say that shoe is?' I asked, drawing Jermaine's eye back to the imprint of the running shoe.

Again, he used his foot as a guide. 'I am a fifteen,' he revealed, which explained why his shoes looked like canoes to me. He looked across at my feet, which prompted me to do as he was and hold my foot next to the print.

I didn't need to tell him I wore a size five, he knew everything about me.

'I would guess this is a size ten, madam.'

I had to concur. 'That makes it more likely the print is from a man. It's wide too, I pointed out. Sasha is too petite by far so the only way she made those prints is if she wore someone else's shoes.'

I didn't say it, but I thought that was most unlikely.

'Hey, guys!' The excited cheer made us look up and caused the dogs to spin around. We all knew the voice belonged to Barbie, but I was surprised to see Deepa, the bride to be, jogging along next to her.

Barbie grinned as she approached, pausing to pat the dogs as they bounded out to intercept her.

'What'cha doin'?' she asked, one eyebrow lifted in question.

Jermaine and I both had a foot off the ground still. We lowered them and I took a moment to explain what I saw in the night and what my friends had missed so far this morning.

'So that's what the police were all doing inside,' said Deepa. 'That's terrible; a murder at your wedding. What's the likelihood Sasha did it?' she asked.

I shrugged. 'That I cannot yet answer. It's possible, for sure.'

Barbie asked, 'Do you think all the missing guards are dead too?'

It was another question I had no good answer to. It made me feel like I was failing. 'There's no sign of foul play. No blood, no sign of a struggle that I am aware of. Vince didn't ...' I squinted as something occurred to me.

'Vince what?' prompted Barbie. 'Come on, Patty. You're doing that secretive thing again. Did you just work it all out?'

I got the skull itch again when I thought about Vince and the way he acted earlier. His guards were going missing. Half of his force, in fact. Their numbers had been replaced with more he was able to call in at short notice, but ...

'I need to speak to Vince,' I announced, setting off back across the grass.

'Oooooh, Patty!' Barbie stamped her feet. 'You are so annoying. What did you just work out?'

I was going to answer her, I swear I was, but the sound of someone furiously banging on a window got everyone's attention. It was Felicity. She was inside Loxton Hall and her face betrayed utter panic.

We couldn't hear her, the glazing was too good for her voice to reach our ears, but the message was clear nevertheless: get here now!

We ran.

## BFF Barnstormer

I am by far the slowest in our group. I am also the oldest unless you count the whole group and then Alistair has me by more than a year. Being fair to myself, there are professional athletes Barbie would leave in her wake, and neither Deepa nor Jermaine are slouches.

I got to watch the three of them rocket across the grass as they ran back for the front doors. Felicity saw us coming and vanished from the window. I guessed she was on her way to meet us inside.

Anna and Georgie were held in check as they attempted to sprint after my friends - even a sausage can run faster than me, and I was in heels, let's not forget. At the door, I found Jermaine holding it open, dutiful as ever, and Felicity running toward us from the other direction.

'I saw Teagan!' she blurted. 'I swear it was her.'

'Where?' I needed to know.

There was very little colour in Felicity's face, the panic gripping her had stolen it away. 'What if I was right all along and she was here to ruin the wedding?' she wailed. 'She said she was in love with Bobbie!'

'Who is Teagan?' asked Barbie, gripped by the urgency we all felt but having no idea what significance the name held.

'A former girlfriend,' I said quickly. 'Felicity, where did you see her?'

'Heading for that thing with Sasha!' Felicity yelled as she started running back through Loxton Hall. 'The daft BFF thing. She was dressed the same as everyone else!'

We were all hard on her heels, my mind spinning. Where the heck were the police when we needed them? Spotting one of Vince's guards, I yelled for his attention.

'Hey …' What should I address him as? *Guard* just sounded dumb, but he hadn't even looked up to see who was shouting.

At my shoulder, Barbie saw me trying to get the man's attention and called out to him, 'Hey, gorgeous.'

Yeah. Obviously, that worked. He didn't hear me at all, but the voice oozing sex appeal attached to a chest that defied gravity somehow broke through his deafness and I got to watch his eyes light up with hope.

Stopping right in front of him, I puffed breathlessly, 'Do you know who Teagan Clancy is?' Then, when he didn't even look down to see who had spoken because he was too busy smiling at Barbie, I sucker punched him in the gut. It didn't hurt him, but it was enough to break his concentration. 'Teagan Clancy?' I demanded.

'What? No,' he replied, annoyed that I was getting in his way when there was a goddess he needed to talk to.

Felicity, Deepa, and Jermaine hadn't stopped and were now trying to get into the ballroom.

'Teagan Clancy was arrested yesterday for stalking Bobbie Howard-Box. She's an ex-girlfriend apparently.' I was getting a confused look from him. 'Look,' I snapped, 'I know there is a threat against the wedding or against the bride or the groom. The exact detail doesn't matter, but that is why Mrs Howard-Box hired in extra security. I am telling you there is a person here dressed as Sasha Allstar and it may very well be her intention to harm the bride. Get on the radio and get your colleagues here.'

When a half second passed and he hadn't moved, Barbie yelled. 'Now! Idiot.'

Her angry face was enough to jolt him into action. That would get the cavalry moving, but as I started running again, I yelled, 'Get the police too. She might be armed!'

I ran next to Barbie, my dachshunds tearing along excitedly ahead of us at the limit of their leads. Ahead of us we could see Deepa, Felicity, and Jermaine arguing with the TV people. They had their own security, and they were not going to let us in because they were filming and live streaming the event inside the room.

Deepa was in the face of a man who was giving her an amused, disbelieving look. It was the one from earlier who I thought was in charge.

'That is a very interesting story, but you are not getting in. I'm sure you are a big fan of Sashatastic, and she is very grateful for your enthusiasm. However, we have all the contestants we need.'

Deepa growled, 'I'm not here to take part, you moron. I've just told you Sasha might be in danger. We have to get in there right now!'

He didn't like the name calling and was giving her angry eyes now. 'And I told you there is no threat to Sashatastic. We have our own security guards in there with her and all the BFF entrants are thoroughly vetted. Please go now before I am forced to call the police,' he threatened her smugly.

Deepa's lips pulled back away from her teeth as she prepared to rip the man a new one.

Barbie grabbed her arm. It was enough to stay whatever comment Deepa had queued, but she didn't step away, merely turned her head so she could mouth, 'What?' in silent miscomprehension. She was about to hand someone their butt and Barbie was interrupting.

'There's a better way,' Barbie said, signalling with her eyes that she couldn't say anything else without giving whatever it was she might have planned away.

As Barbie backed away, she took Deepa's arm, pulling her away from the TV executive. He just smiled and shook his head as if he met crazy people everyday and this was just one more example of how the chance for some fame made some of them go nuts.

Forming a huddle on the other side of the great hall we found ourselves in, Barbie started to explain. 'The BFFs are going through in blocks. That's the first load in there now, the rest of them are in the restaurant,' she nodded her head toward the frosted doors that led to the buffet. From behind them a continuous hum of conversation echoed out. 'The only way we are getting to Sasha is if we dress like her BFFs and pretend to be the next cohort.'

It was as simple as it was ingenious, and the costumes were there for the taking. Well, not quite for the taking, there were a pair of venue staff managing a cloakroom with a barcode system. I guess it was so the BFFs didn't have to keep hold of their dresses, wigs, shoes, and accessories.

As you might imagine, distracting the venue staff would normally fall to Barbie, with Deepa thrown in for good measure. However, the targets were both women and that created a fresh challenge.

'Maybe they like girls,' said Barbie hopefully though she didn't sound convinced.

'I could try,' Jermaine volunteered, sounding equally unconvinced that he might succeed. I doubted he had much experience chatting up women.

We had no time to lose, and no plan for how we could achieve the simple task of swiping a few costumes. I turned to ask Felicity if she had any idea, but she was kneeling next to Buster, saying something to him. I wondered if maybe there was a back way into the changing area.

Felicity came back to her feet, leaning in so she could whisper. 'Get ready. Buster is about to create a distraction.'

Unsure what she meant, I peered around Barbie just in time to see Buster picking up speed. The white and tan bulldog was hurtling toward the front of the cloakroom where the two girls were chatting. They didn't see him coming which made his efforts all the more effective.

Barbie, Deepa, and Jermaine all tracked my eyes and therefore all watched in mute fascination as Buster went through the table they were using like it was some kind of obstacle course. It was a fold out table, erected so they could better manage the BFF's belongings, and sheathed in a velvet cloth bearing Loxton Hall's Coat of Arms.

Or rather, it had been sheathed in a velvet cloth. Buster snagged it as he ran beneath the table from one end to the other. Everything on the table, which included a vase of flowers, two cups of coffee, and a laptop, went skyward and he shot out the other end trailing the tablecloth like a cape while he barked raucously. The two young women yelled surprised curses as they gave pursuit.

'No, Buster! Bad dog!' called Felicity just about loud enough for people around us to hear but not so loud that the dog might turn around. She was trying very hard not to laugh.

'How did you get him to do that?' I wanted to know.

She didn't answer, her cheeks flushing red as she pointed to the disarray and the now unguarded cloakroom.

'Quick,' hissed Barbie and all five of us plus two dachshunds rushed for the door.

'What about Buster?' I whispered as we dashed into the cloakroom.

From the side of her mouth Felicity hissed back, 'He'll take care of himself.'

Just as I got to the cloakroom, the frosted glass doors opened outward – the next tranche of BFFs were leaving the waiting room and on their way to get their outfits. I ducked inside the cloakroom before anyone saw me, the last of my group as the others were already inside trying to find something that might fit. As I cast my eyes frantically around, and the dachshunds danced with excitement, I could hear the confusion outside.

Where were the cloakroom girls? How would they find their things now?

I moved a little further inside, broaching an aisle where I found a mostly naked Jermaine shimmying into a dress that was too big for him.

'Can you zip me up, please, madam?' He asked, spinning to present his back. 'It's hardly flattering but everything else here might be too small.'

Whichever of the BFFs owned it, they were big because it floated on Jermaine. Barbie and Deepa bounced into sight at the end of the aisle, both dressed the same and wearing Sashatastic's trademark pink wig. It looked better on Deepa, suiting her darker skin tone.

Behind me, the BFFs were coming in. So too the cloakroom staff. It sounded like Buster gave them the slip. Or they heard the BFFs coming and returned to do what they could with the wreckage of what had once been organised on their table.

Our eyes flared and we each found a spot in which to hide as the room began to flood with the mixed bag of humanity all wanting their fifteen minutes of fame.

The cloakroom ladies were trying to control the chaos while at the same time the TV executives could be heard calling instructions from outside because they needed everyone to get moving.

The BFFs, encouraged by the demands of the people running the show, were filling the cloakroom, all trying to work out which might be theirs. Buster had scrambled the ticketing system which was all managed on the laptop. I could only guess whether that still worked after its trip through the air.

The confusion provided us with the opportunity we needed though. I grabbed the first costume to hand, bundling it and heading for the door. Barbie, Deepa, and Jermaine were with me but already in their costumes. Like me, Felicity was going to have to hope what she grabbed would fit.

Across from us, the first tranche of BFFs looked to be finishing up whatever daft task they'd been expected to perform. They would be out soon, and the next lot would go in, us along with them.

In the hurried confusion – I guess live-streaming creates a degree of stress, everyone was moving faster than they wanted to be and the TV people were perpetually in motion as they tried to restore order from the chaos.

Funnelled into a changing room, I hurriedly tore my clothes off. I still had the dachshunds with me, both dogs eyeing me with some confusion. 'Girls, mummy needs to leave you here for a few minutes, okay?' I got two tilted heads, Anna and Georgie attempting to make sense of my jabbered words, but they didn't argue and that was good enough for me.

The dress was way too big, the shoulders so wide that the outfit I grabbed had to belong to one of the many men vying to be at Sashatastic's side. The shoes were a size twelve and like walking in snorkelling flippers. Even the wig was too big, smothering my head like a hood, but it was going to have to do.

'Quickly, Patty,' urged Barbie, helping me into my outfit. 'Wow! That is a little roomy on you,' she observed of my dress.

I lifted a foot and my boot just dropped right off it.

Outside, we could hear the TV people calling for the BFFs to line up and there was music playing.

Felicity's dress and wig fit like they were made for her, until she turned around that is, and I spotted how far up her boobs had been shoved.

Seeing my eyes flare, she looked down at the flesh trying to escape toward her chin and shrugged. 'I guess the owner has a flatter chest than me.'

To say the least, I thought, but we had to get moving, there was no time for talk.

The TV people were hurrying everyone along again. I heard someone shout. 'Leave phones behind! Anyone caught taking a phone inside will be removed and banned from future performances. Please hurry now, you are about to go in.'

Clumping out the door in my clodhopping boots, I had to hold my stupidly big dress onto my body with my right hand. There were BFFs still over at the cloakroom complaining they could not find their dresses. Thankfully, they were blaming the poor ladies managing the cloakroom and not looking for a thief yet.

Ahead of us, the ballroom doors opened, and the Sasha BFF wannabes began to file out.

One of the TV people with a headset and a tablet in hand called, 'Two minutes to reset. Can we get Miss Allstar some water, please?' A junior member of the team jogged away to find refreshments.

Nothing had happened to Sasha so far, which had to mean Teagan hadn't been in the first group. Nudging Felicity with my arm, I whispered, 'Do you see Teagan anywhere?' We had to get to Sasha so we could warn her but spotting Teagan and isolating her would be even more effective.

Frustrated, Felicity, whispered back. 'Everyone looks the same! Apart from the men, of course.'

Deepa, Barbie, and Jermaine were just ahead of us, but they didn't know what Teagan looked like any more than I did.

'Everyone places!' called the man with the tablet and the headset. Still looking smug and in control, we had to hope he didn't recognise any of us as we passed him. The doors were opening, the BFFs, us included, lined up and ready to sweep in. There were fifty of us, and the level of excitement around me was palpable. Like everyone else, I have seen celebrity frenzy on the television; scenes of Beatlemania replayed across the decades as each new pop group or film star to catch the global eye would swoon the crowds. This was little different.

'Annnnnd go!' shouted the smug TV man, sending the front of the column into the room with a sweep of his arm.

Hissing to Felicity, I begged, 'Anything?'

She was standing on her tiptoes to see over the top of everyone else and failing miserably. From behind, we could see shape only. Everyone had the same hair and dress. 'I thought I did a moment ago,' Felicity hissed back, 'but it wasn't her.'

'Eyes peeled everyone,' I begged of our group. We had to rely on Felicity to find our target, the rest of us were going to watch for danger and try to get to Sasha. The line of BFFs surged forward, Felicity and I going with them though my dress threatened to fall off my shoulder constantly.

Jermaine and Deepa, our two butt-kickers, if such a thing were to be needed, were making a beeline for the star already.

Unfortunately, so was everyone else.

'Hi, everyone!' yelled Sashatastic. Dressed just the same as everyone in the room, she would be easy to lose if I didn't keep my eyes on her face. No sooner did I think that, than a six-foot man walked in front of me. I darted around him, but she was gone from sight. 'Thank you so much for coming. I'm sooooo looking forward to getting to know you all!'

I didn't know much about the young woman, but the version I could hear now was nothing like the one I met earlier. Everything was super exciting like she'd drunk a case of energy drinks and might have sparkles coming from her nose if she became any more animated.

The BFFs weren't able to get within touching distance; the TV security people flanked her, but the BFFs could get really close. How difficult would it be to get a weapon in here?

The crowd kept moving.

'I want to introduce you all to my good friend, Gloria!' shouted Sasha in her crazy-excited way.

Gloria bounded out from the wings.

'Hi, everyone!' she waved enthusiastically. I saw a few people do a double take.

Near the front, Deepa and Jermaine were trying to get beyond the security line and to get Sasha's attention. They were competing with the noise of the crowd and losing.

'Ha!' laughed Sasha. 'Gloria is my official double. You may have heard rumours that I don't do all my personal appearances myself.' A mumble of agreement went through the BFFS. 'Well, it's true, but I hope you can believe that this is the real me, because the only slightly less real me is here as well.'

It was a confusing statement, but the BFFs were whipped into such a frenzy they cheered anyway.

Where the heck was the backup I asked for? Had the security guard outside failed to call the police? Where were Vince's men? They ought to be storming this place right now.

Felicity grabbed my forearm, her grip like a steel vice. 'I saw her!' she gasped.

'Where?'

Felicity tried to point, but the constantly heaving mass of people in a small space combined with everyone looking the same from the back made finding her target again impossible.

She swore, and still holding my hand, tried to weave through the people ahead of us.

'We need to be where Sasha is!' she yelled. 'Looking back at their faces. That way we might stand a chance.'

I had to agree, but how would we achieve that?

Just as our efforts saw us swallowed between a press of sweaty, over-excited bodies, I heard shouting coming from the entrance door. I turned my head, weaving around to see if it was Chief Inspector Quinn arriving, but my view was obscured.

It sounded like a fight breaking out. Felicity was pulling me forward still even as I tried to look back. The man's voice favoured the use of profanities, a torrent of them rising above the noise of the BFFs.

It probably wasn't the chief inspector, I decided. As heads began to turn to see what was causing the noise, and TV people rushed to intercept, Jermaine and Deepa saw their chance and ran forward to get to Sasha.

The TV security, a pair of men in suits positioned either side of Sashatastic moved swiftly to intercept my friends and the chaos that had been at least partially organised, now fell into utter disarray.

The shouting behind us increased in volume; I heard something about a dress being stolen followed by another tirade of expletives. More people were turning to see what was happening there, but as they did that, and security moved to intercept Jermaine and Deepa, the front row of BFFs saw a clear path to get to their idol.

And they went for it.

'There!' yelled Felicity. 'That's Teagan!'

This time I could see who she was pointing to - an attractive woman with doe eyes and a killer figure. It was only a glimpse, neither Felicity nor I getting a prolonged look but she was in that front line of BFFs surging toward Sasha.

The two guards realised their mistake and ran back to protect their principal; a glance showed both men yanking Sasha by her arms, but they were running out of places to go to escape the onrushing and overexcited horde. A glance to the left showed Deepa and Jermaine hadn't been able to get around the front row of BFFS who now cut off their path to Sasha.

Then I spotted Teagan again.

Bobbie's ex-girlfriend had something in her right hand. I saw the glint as the light caught on it and my heart did a double beat – she had a knife!

I screamed the words, but no one heard me; there was too much noise. At three different points of the room, commands were being shouted and counterarguments roared back. It was bedlam, but we had to get to Teagan.

Sasha's escape route was blocked off by more BFFs. They'd gone around the BFFs at the front coming at Sasha from the sides and the back to cut off the internet star as she fled. Gloria was next to her, both girls getting manhandled by the guards.

'Patty!'

The yell caught my attention.

Barbie was to my right, in the clear, and where Felicity and I had no hope of stopping Teagan's charge, I knew she could.

I jabbed an arm, pointing out her target as best I could. What was I to yell though? How could I possibly hope to describe Teagan when everyone looked the same?

There must have been something about the way Teagan was moving, or maybe Barbie saw the knife in her hand because I saw Barbie's expression freeze. The next second, she exploded into motion. There were a dozen BFFs ahead of her, but as I watched, Barbie put her shoulder down and went through them like a professional rugby player using humans as skittles.

Cries of surprise and pain echoed out, but like mowing a lawn, Barbie cut a path to Teagan.

Sasha, Gloria and the two guards were backpeddling. There was nowhere for them to go now. Pressed from all sides, the over-excited BFFs probably just wanted to touch the superstar, but she could get trampled in their rush, crushed, quite literally, by their adoration. Would Teagan be able to get to her still? Was she crazy enough to just start hacking at the BFFs that blocked her route to Sasha?

We didn't have to find out because Barbie, nimble little minx that she is, leapt into the air. I don't know who it was, but someone got used as a springboard as she jumped onto them and launched herself high over the crowd.

Teagan and Barbie were coming from right to left as Felicity and I watched. With open mouths, we got to see the whole thing.

Just as Teagan got within a few feet of Sasha Allstar, she raised her knife, the thin blade of shiny steel catching the light again. Then Barbie hit her from behind. Now, I don't know what Barbie weighs. There's no body fat on her, but she is lean and sinuous like a track star and she is tall. Like a missile coming down at an angle, she hit Teagan at the top of her shoulders and took her to the floor like a piledriver.

With the exception of the man swearing his head off by the doors, everyone else fell silent.

'She's got a knife!' I yelled. 'Everyone get back!'

To my surprise, they obeyed, the BFFs stepping away from the two women on the carpet as if there were a toxic spill leaking outward.

There were cries of anguish and fear, and shouted commands from the two men still fighting to get Sasha to safety.

'Clear the route!' demanded one of the men.

Behind me, the door clattered open, and this time it was Chief Inspector Quinn. Police surged into the room, the smug TV executive still doing his best to argue they were not allowed inside.

'Everyone, stop moving,' commanded CI Quinn.

No one paid him the slightest attention.

I was pushing forward, dragging Felicity with me now instead of the other way around. Barbie was grappling with Teagan, which came as a surprise because I thought she would be too strong for almost any woman.

I heard Barbie cry out in horror. 'Oh, no!'

Bursting through the leading edge of the BFFs as they continued to back away, I was sick with terror for what I might find. No matter what nightmare I could have imagined, what I saw was somehow worse.

It wasn't a knife.

And it wasn't Teagan.

You might be about to remind me that I don't know what Teagan looks like, and you would be correct. However, the person pinned face down between Barbie's muscular thighs was transgender. She was pretty, but also clearly possessing a set of male chromosomes. The silver thing I assumed to be a knife was an elegant pen.

The BFF we confused for Teagan had been trying to get an autograph.

'Clear back!' shouted Chief Inspector Quinn, his officers forcing a route through the crowd. Just as he arrived, bent on taking over, Sasha squealed in fright.

Her high-pitched scream reverberated around the room, pulling every eye her way. We all saw the blood smear down her face and across her shoulder, but as Gloria pitched forward, a knife handle sticking out from her back, Sasha wasn't the only one screaming.

Directly behind her and the two guards, a Sasha BFF was running away. Easy to spot because this BFF was the only one not facing the real Sasha, the stunned guards took a second to react and when they did it was to crowd their principal, not give chase – they were guards not law enforcement officers, and they were guarding.

I wasn't the only one who saw the BFF trying to escape, Barbie, Jermaine, and Deepa did too because like me they were all looking for a killer.

With shouts, they all gave chase. I started running too.

Then my oversized boots reminded me I could only just about manage to walk in them, and I fell flat on my face, almost losing the stupid dress in the process.

## Dire Panic

If there had been worry about being trampled earlier, it quadrupled now. My friends' attempt to give chase went south fast and the killer BFF vanished among the herd of lookalike Sashas. The police might have given chase too, but just arriving, they were too far away to have any hope.

Panicking, the BFFs ran for cover and they went in every direction. Most went for the main entrance, but some ran for the back of the ballroom where the Sashatastic BFF backdrop led to the star's private changing area. It's where her security had tried to escort the star but right now the safest thing the guards could do was stand still.

Besides, Sasha wasn't going anywhere unless they dragged her. She was going nuts over Gloria.

In contrast to almost everyone in the room, I was heading toward the victim and not away from her. I wanted to see whatever there was to see. I scanned around for the killer, but who was I kidding? It could be almost any one of the Sasha lookalikes in the room.

Quinn's officers were swift to react, closing the main doors again to seal everyone inside, but they would have to chase down those who escaped behind the backdrop.

Seeing the stab victim himself, Chief Inspector Quinn directed officers to her aid and was on the radio to bring paramedics and first aid gear the next second. I had to get out of the way as officers rushed to Gloria. She was alive, or so they said, but the knife handle was in her back between her shoulder blades – the wound was life-threatening.

It was also delivered by someone left-handed. I mimicked the angle of thrust required and couldn't make it work with my right hand. It was a small clue, but more than nothing.

There was so much going on all at the same time it was enough to make my head spin. My stupid Sashatastic dress was still threatening to fall off, I'd abandoned the dachshunds in the changing room, and the sweary man who started the disturbance that led to the killer stabbing Gloria was now storming across the room in my direction.

Now I realised why. It was his dress I had on. The man looked like a rugby second row.

He saw me clock him and grinned with evil intent.

'That's my dress!' he shouted. 'And those are my boots!'

If I didn't have enough drama to deal with already, I was about to get attacked by a human/bear hybrid. Then he ripped his top off, presumably because he planned to put the dress on, and he was as hairy as a … as a … I was struggling for a simile but all I could come up with was a man covered in glue and rolled on a barber's floor. Let's just leave it with he was hairy, and it tiered from his head into a beard and down his neck to vanish like a rug under a door when it met his trousers.

I backpeddled a step, bumping into Felicity. 'Jermaine!' I yelled, panic staring to rise.

My butler was already crossing the room, but Chief Inspector Quinn got to me first. Stepping between me and the sasquatch. His uniform and glare gave the beast cause to at least slow his pace.

'I want my dress back,' the man/bear snapped.

Chief Inspector Quinn hitched an eyebrow, looking the man up and down. 'I dare say you do, sir.' It was a good, old-fashioned police officer response.

'We need to find Teagan Clancy,' I said out loud, believing Chief Inspector Quinn would know why. 'She was in here.'

'I want my dress,' insisted Jabba the Hairball.

Quinn held up an index finger, demanding patience. 'You are sure of this?' he asked me.

Felicity said. 'I saw her in the hall outside,' she chewed her lip for a second. 'I would have sworn she came in here, but ... well, the person I thought was her turned out to be a man, but when I saw her outside, she almost walked right by me. I'm certain it was her. She was dressed ... well, like the rest of us.' I could see and hear how disappointed Felicity was that she might have got it wrong and led us in here by mistake. It wasn't a bad call though. I probably would have made the same one.

'What about my dress?' asked the wax shop's worst nightmare. He was getting surlier by the minute and becoming a distraction. There were more important things to focus our attention on and quite frankly I was bored holding my dress up.

I threw the wig at him. 'Thank you for the loan. Sorry I didn't get the chance to ask first.' I apologised and I meant it. Whatever I might feel about his hairy naked body, I wronged him, not the other way around. To get the boots off, all I had to do was angle my ankles and pull my legs up. Thankful I had a petticoat and slip beneath the dress in deference to the cool temperatures, I let the daft pink Sashatastic outfit go and watched it fall to the floor.

I was covered, though technically I was also now in my underwear in public. Chief Inspector Quinn turned away, one of the few men who did, and Jermaine arrived, screeching to a halt at which point he began dutifully taking off his dress so I could have it.

Seeing what my butler was trying to do, the chief inspector threw his hands in the air. 'Dear Lord, what did I do to deserve such a plague of amateur sleuths?' Quick as a flash, he unbuttoned his own tunic, passing it to me so I was at least better covered. It came below my bottom, mercifully. Eyeing me and Jermaine and Felicity, he asked, 'Now, can I ask that no one else attempt to get naked for a few minutes?'

The BFFs had been calmed, the stampede to leave no longer threatening to trample anyone and peace was being restored. Those who had fled around the backdrop were now returning, the police officers having caught them, or perhaps coordinated a response that would head them off from the other direction.

Or so I thought. I was close enough to the chief inspector to hear when an officer reported at least one or more got away. They didn't have enough bodies to cover every avenue of escape.

That wasn't the interesting thing I heard though. They'd spotted a blood trail. It wasn't a dangerous amount of blood like one might get from an arterial wound, but it wasn't nothing either. Had Gloria's attacker cut themself?

Chief Inspector Quinn asked where it went only to be told that it stopped in one of the corridors. The killer had most likely found something to stem the bleeding and the trail ended. It was disappointing but that the killer might be wounded was a helpful thing to know.

Paramedics burst through the doors. I didn't realise they had some on site, but the question was whether they could save Gloria. The live-streaming event was a washout, but only because Chief Inspector Quinn made them shut off the cameras. The smug TV exec argued until he was blue in the face. It was already their greatest viewing rate and still climbing. I could believe it. How often do people get stabbed on TV?

Quinn stared at the man until he backed down, the senior police officer barely needing to say a word.

Knowing I had a duty to tell him about the door and the footprints, and that to leave it any longer when I probably should have told him about it hours ago would be even worse, I took a deep breath and stepped into his field of vision.

## The Door to Nowhere

A look flashed across the chief inspector's eyes that made me worry he might be about to throttle me. His hands remained by his sides though I did see them clench and unclench a few times.

With a twitch of his head, he locked eyes with one of his sergeants and another twitch brought the man across the room at a jog.

'Get two constables, Sergeant Travis. We need to investigate a possible location for the missing private security members.' There was some dread in the way he said it, my brain conjuring visions of multiple bodies stacked on the other side of the pump room door. 'Mrs Fisher will show us where to look.'

When I requested politely to fetch my clothes and dogs, the chief inspector provided an escort. They helped me carry clothes for Barbie, Deepa, Jermaine, and Felicity and we took it in turns to go behind the backdrop to change.

Anna and Georgie were none the worse for being abandoned in the changing room and I found Buster sitting obediently with them. He trotted along after me to find his owner when I called his name.

'He's ever so obedient,' I observed.

Felicity raised one eyebrow. 'Is he now?' she asked, looking down at her dog.

Chief Inspector Quinn cleared his throat, impatiently demanding I get a move on, adding, 'If you please, Mrs Fisher.'

I mugged an oops face at Barbie and Jermaine, made sure my hastily donned clothes were straight, and gave the dogs a whistle to get them moving.

'This way, Chief Inspector,' I called over my shoulder as if I were waiting for him, not the other way around.

Sergeant Travis had the two constables ready at the door to the ballroom, poised and waiting for me to be ready. I led them all back to Loxton Hall's main door and around to the left, retracing steps I'd taken twice already.

Here and there, indentations in the grass showed where people had gone before. Some of the footprints had to be mine. Just as before, upon approach the door was impossible to see, shrouded cleverly in climbing plants over a trellis as it was. I could see the cops exchanging glances as they wondered where the crazy woman with the sausage dogs wanted to take them.

'Are you sure this is where you saw the missing private security go, Mrs Fisher?' Chief Inspector Quinn wanted to know.

I had to answer him carefully. 'I cannot say that it was the missing security guards I saw, only that I saw two of them heading this way as they followed what I believed to be a man in a dark hooded top. When I checked, I found their footprints went up to the door but did not come back out.' Everything I said was one hundred percent accurate.

Getting nearer, the indentations in the grass became more obvious and I could see the door. The police officers could too, and they were making comments about how this could have been overlooked in their search earlier.

Chief Inspector Quinn said nothing, reserving judgement until we got to the door.

'It's locked,' I advised just as we got to it. 'You'll need someone from the Hall's maintenance team to get into it, I guess.'

Obscuring my view of the door as they funnelled into the shadow cast by the trellis, the constables got there first.

'The footprints go both ways,' one said. 'Did I misunderstand something?'

I looked down, my eyes widening as I saw the truth of it. Where before, the mens' Oxford shoeprints had all pointed one way, now the individual prints were almost indiscernible from being walked over yet again in the opposite direction.

'The door is open too,' said the other constable, swinging it wide to prove his claim.

Feeling guilty, I shot my eyes up to see what expression the chief inspector might be wearing. His face was unreadable.

He said, 'Very well. Proceed with caution. Mrs Fisher, you may wish to wait here.'

I almost said, 'You can get stuffed,' but managed to reel myself in at the last moment. I needed to see what there was to see. If it was a pile of dead men I would run away again quickly, but I had a feeling we would find something else inside.

The officer at the front flicked a light switch just inside the door. Nothing happened. Five yards in, the dark swallowed the narrow concrete corridor completely. We saw why when the officer took a torch from a pocket – there were stairs leading down.

I picked up my dogs, doing my best to angle their muddy paws away from my clothes, and followed Chief Inspector Quinn as he followed his officers.

More torches created plenty of light to see by, not that it did much to scare away my growing anxiety. Reaching the bottom of the stairs, the lead constable called out for anyone inside to identify themselves.

No answer drifted back out of the dark.

Was that good or bad?

We were beneath Loxton Hall now, in part of its cellar. Built many centuries ago, I felt certain the cellar would have been divided to create this pump room in the twentieth century. The gurgle and churn of water moving through pipes, and the faint humming of electrical motors played backdrop to our footsteps on the damp concrete floor. The cellar possessed the same damp stone scent I associated with such spaces. It wasn't cold though.

The stairs brought us down into a corridor with bare brick either side. In the torch light, I could see the floor, but no footprints were visible save for those the officers' boots were leaving as they spread out. They moved away from the stairs in multiple directions to explore the entire space.

The chief inspector paused. 'Wait here, please, Mrs Fisher,' he requested in a tone that expected compliance.

My natural inclination to argue fought against an equal desire to not be in the dark dingy place. I said, 'Very well, Chief Inspector,' and took my phone out to enable the torch on it.

No sooner had I done so than the lights came on.

'I found a switch that works, sir,' said Sergeant Travis somewhat redundantly since we were already bathed in light.

Extinguishing the light on my phone, I decided the chief inspector's request to stay put no longer applied and put the dogs down since they were getting heavy in my arms. They snuffled in the dust, snorting along as they followed their noses.

'Sir,' called one of the constables, sticking his head back out from a doorway. I call it a doorway, but there were no doors, just gaps in the brickwork where a door could go if such a thing were necessary.

No one else had found anything of interest, his fellow officers converging on the young constable as he led them to his discovery. I went in behind Chief Inspector Quinn wondering what I might find, but my rising trepidation was to be disappointed.

It was an empty room. Or rather it was a room with a small table and several old sofas dotted about. My immediate assumption was that the groundsmen or gardeners used it to hide from the rain or cold weather when they needed to.

Chief Inspector Quinn jinked an eyebrow at his subordinate. 'Am I missing something, Constable Stanley?' he asked.

The constable sniffed. 'It smells like beer, sir.'

I sniffed the air, as did everyone else. He was right, there was a scent of beer on the air. A sort of stale, old smell that might not have been beer at all. Fermenting yeast when a person bakes bread produces a similar smell. Not that I thought anyone had secretly been down here baking bread.

When the chief inspector said nothing but held his gaze on Constable Stanley, the younger man felt a need to expand his explanation for alerting his colleagues. 'There are fresh marks in the dust, sir.' He pointed to scratches on the floor. 'It looks like something was scraped across here and here,' he shifted position to show another mark, 'and that must have happened recently, sir.'

Quinn crouched to get a better look, taking interest in what his constable had found. I heard him draw in a deep breath through his nose, contemplating the evidence, but when he stood up again, he said, 'There is nothing here. I expect this is nothing more than a hidey hole the gardeners or the maintenance chaps use to get out of the cold or rain sometimes.' His response brought a wry smile to my face. 'Someone spilt some beer at some point and the marks on the floor could be where a machine once stood or where the same gardeners or maintenance chaps placed some tools.'

His assessment made perfect sense.

Where were Vince's missing security guards then? I backed out of the room we were in, quickly moving to the next room and the next to explore the space we were in. There was a toilet, which surprised me. I almost didn't go in but seeing the layer of dust on almost every surface, I couldn't help but spot there was none around the sink and the toilet had clearly been used recently; the dust on the floor around it had been disturbed.

'Mrs Fisher?' the chief inspector's voice echoed into the room. I opened my mouth to answer but the thoughts swirling in my head demanded my focus.

I could not dismiss the notion that the beer smell and the recently used toilet were nothing more than visits by the ground staff as the chief inspector suggested, but I also didn't believe it. I saw two men come in here. Or, more accurately, I saw them follow a man in a hood in this direction and when I checked I saw shoeprints going in but not coming out.

Had I drawn a false conclusion?

I didn't think so. They were in here. Maybe all six of the missing guards were in here. However, if they had been in here, they had moved on, and it happened in the last thirty minutes between visiting with Jermaine, and then coming back with the chief inspector.

'Mrs Fisher.' The chief inspector's voice, loud as he came level with the door into the toilet, broke my concentration. I got a raised eyebrow as he looked around the dirty old restroom. 'Perhaps you would like to wait until we get back inside Loxton Hall proper,' he suggested. Oh, lord, he thought I was going to use the facilities! It was grim in here. Perfect for groundsmen and maintenance guys who probably thought farting was a sport. I should be surprised there were no posters of topless girls on the walls.

Wordlessly, I went around the chief inspector and back to the stairs. Anna and Georgie bounded up them and back into the ground level corridor at the top. The light there was still off but one of the constables was holding the door open to let in light.

I nodded my thanks as I passed him, my head back to thinking about Vince's missing guards. Another question surfaced: Why wasn't Vince more worried?' Six of his men had vanished.

The guards had been in the pump room, I felt certain of it. Whoever was messing with the celebrity wedding had lured them in there, but they were not then murdered. There was no sign of their bodies and I knew the police had scoured the building and its grounds already.

I found my face starting to ache as I squinted into the distance, my eyes on nothing but the inside of my head. I was missing something vital and it was all to do with the reason the guards were here in the first place, or why someone was messing with the wedding. Cara's murder was throwing me, but was it connected? Was it part of the same thing? Or entirely separate?

By the time we returned to the ballroom, the police officers there had identified everyone in the room and could confirm Teagan Clancy was not among them. They could also confirm no one had a fresh wound so whoever cut themselves did escape.

We had rushed into the room with good intentions, but ultimately helped no one. Maybe I could argue that the disruption we started resulted in the killer missing their target because the wrong person got stabbed. That was small comfort though.

Everyone had seen everything yet at the same time no one had seen anything of use. No one could identify the attacker. I wanted to label that individual as Gloria's attacker, but no one thought Sasha's double was the intended victim, not even Sasha. Gloria had been too close and looked too similar to the internet star. Would it cost her life?

Suddenly noticing that someone was missing, I spun around on the spot to ask, 'Where is Felicity?'

'She was permitted to leave, madam,' said Jermaine. 'Mrs Howard-Box came to the door complaining bitterly that her wedding planner was being detained when the ceremony is due to start in less than three hours.'

'What?' I gasped. 'Surely even that mad cow can see the wedding is off now.'

Barbie shrugged at me. 'It didn't seem that way. Sasha cried and said she couldn't do it, but Angelica just made soothing noises and told her to put a brave face on it.'

'A brave face?' I could not believe my ears.

Barbie was frowning deeply. 'It was like ...' she tried to find the words. 'It was like she got to make the calls and was daring Sasha to argue. Either way, Felicity left to find her master of ceremonies and her assistant. She said there was a lot to do still.'

The wedding was still on. At least Angelica was acting as if it was. I couldn't be sure - I didn't know how far Chief Inspector Quinn's powers might extend, but I doubted he would be happy to see the ceremony continue. Or would he? Was his best chance to catch the killer to keep everyone here?

The more I spiralled around the issue, the more upset with myself I became. Not for the first time in my recent life I was chasing my tail instead of the killer. On top of that, I still couldn't shift the worry that all the wedding vandalism was something unconnected to Cara's death and now Gloria's attack.

My friends had already given their statements to the police, and now that Chief Inspector Quinn was back to take charge, the BFFs, the TV people, and my group were all allowed to go.

Chief Inspector Quinn wasted no further time with the witnesses. They were proving wholly unreliable and even though he wasn't showing it, he had to be feeling the pressure. A murder and an attempted murder in the space of a few hours, both committed right under his nose with a force of police officers on site. He needed to solve this, and that was when I realised he'd duped me.

A smile tugged my mouth. In the cellar he'd acted as if there was nothing suspicious about the beer smell, but he made those comments for my benefit. I nodded my head, certain it was true. He wanted to solve this. Or, more to the point, he didn't want me to solve it first.

My friends and I were heading for the door, free to go now, but I paused to look back at where Gloria had fallen. Was it the same killer for both crimes? Gloria had been rushed from the building and might already be on her way to surgery but calling it one murder and one attempted murder just seemed pedantic – the intent to kill was there.

Conscious that Deepa's wedding was only just more than two hours away, I tore myself away from the crime scene, catching up with my friends outside. I could see on their faces, the elation and excitement we all ought to feel just wasn't there. We ought to be upstairs sipping champagne and getting into our finest clothes. Instead, we all felt deflated. Me most of all.

Waiting for us outside, I saw Alistair beside Deepa's groom, Lieutenant Martin Baker. They were at the head of a larger group consisting of both the bride and groom's families. Pippin and Schneider were among them too.

Spotting us, they came as a single body, crossing the space outside to meet us.

Alistair pulled me into a hug. 'Patricia are you all right?' he asked, his voice a soft rumble as I lay my head against his chest.

I sighed, allowing myself just a short moment to wallow. 'Yes. I am,' I admitted. 'Of course I am. Nothing bad happened to me or to my friends. I just wish … I wanted this weekend to pass quietly.' I felt like whining but wouldn't let myself.

The wallowing lasted about another four seconds.

I guess it's just who I am, but I could not stop my brain from trying to link the things I had seen. Sasha was seen out of bed. Her manager was murdered at the same time. Bobbie's ex-girlfriend was trying to get to see him or stop the wedding or something – I didn't know what her motivation was yet. Sasha's manager was murdered by someone Sasha's size. Gloria was stabbed by someone Sasha's size. The rings were stolen, the cake got smashed, et cetera, et cetera. It all whirled around and around like random atoms, colliding and spinning off until my skull itched and with a jolt, I pushed myself away from Alistair so suddenly it made him jump.

There was one solution that kind of made sense. It was completely nuts, but when I put the pieces together, they all fitted. The concept had some holes, some known unknowns if you will, but I could work them out if I asked the right person the right questions. I knew I could.

Alistair was waiting for me to look up at him. When I did, he asked, 'Is there something you need to do?'

I nodded. 'Can you help me?'

I voiced my question quietly because I wanted no one else to hear. My friends needed to gather themselves and get ready for the wedding. That had to be their priority, but I needed to see if I was right and that meant silently slipping away.

Acting as if Alistair were taking me back to our room for a rest and so I could get ready for the ceremony, we made our excuses.

As if jolted by my announcement, Deepa grabbed Martin's arm, twisting it so she could see the time. She swore. 'I need to start getting ready!' her eyes bugged from her head.

Barbie responded by stepping up to her friend's side. 'I'll help,' she volunteered. 'You're already gorgeous, babes. It won't take long to get you into your dress.'

'We can help too!' cheered Deepa's two younger sisters with excitement. It was a funny moment in an otherwise fraught day. I wanted to slip away but I didn't need to use subterfuge now; everyone was heading to their rooms to change into their wedding day finest.

We hadn't bothered with makeup and hair professionals for the day even though Felicity had offered them. Deepa had long, lustrous jet-black hair that required little effort to look amazing and the guys all had short military style hair. The four lieutenants would all be in uniform as would Alistair, so it was just Deepa and her two bridesmaids to prepare.

I would not be a part of that – I was only here as a friend. I would get my own dress on and settle the dogs – they'd had a busy morning, and then I would ask Bobbie why he hadn't appeared at any point in the hour after his fiancée was almost murdered.

## What's in Bobbie's Closet?

Once back in my room, I changed my mind about putting my wedding outfit on. I'd had one made for the occasion; a complete ensemble from hat down to shoes, but a little voice warned me that I was still chasing down a killer. If I put my new clothes on now, what was the likelihood they would get trashed before the ceremony?

Pretty high, right?

Anna and Georgie had a drink from the water bowl and were both happy to curl up in their bed for a sleep.

I called Felicity. 'Can you meet me at Bobbie's room?' I asked.

'I'm on my way there now, actually,' she replied. 'I need to speak with the bride and groom because they haven't cancelled the ceremony yet. I still have people working on getting everything set up. If I call it off myself, I stand a chance of forfeiting my bill.'

The wedding had not officially been called off yet? Surely it couldn't go ahead. The bride's real BFF had been stabbed. On top of everything else that had happened I didn't think it was plausible for the ceremony to proceed.

With a final check to make sure I had my things, I went for the door, phone wedged between shoulder and ear. I said, 'I'll meet you there,' and went out the door as Alistair opened it.

Once I dropped my phone into my handbag, Alistair asked, 'You asked for my help. Do you wish to enlighten me as to how I might assist you?'

I looped my arm through his. 'I need you to find someone. They won't want to be found, not by anyone other than the person they are here to see, and that's why it has to be someone like you. Someone who isn't anything to do with the Howard-Box wedding party.' As I explained what I thought I knew and where I believed he would find his quarry, he nodded his understanding: it wasn't just me, my theory did make sense.

Nearing the groom's suite, Alistair stopped moving. A tug at my arm swung me around so we were facing, and he kissed me. When it broke a few seconds later, my head was spinning just a little, but in a good way.

'Good luck,' he wished me as he started to back away. 'Where will I find you?'

I wrinkled my nose in thought. I needed somewhere that would house everyone. 'The library, I think.'

He nodded his understanding. 'I will message you when I am ready.' With that he was gone, rounding a corner to begin his search.

Outside of Bobbie's room, one of Vince's guards, one I hadn't seen before, looked relaxed yet ready. I was the only person in the corridor and his eyes were on me as I came toward him.

'Is Bobbie in?' I asked.

The man shook his head. Like the others, he looked to be somewhere in his thirties, trim, strong, and alert. 'Mr Howard-Box is not here.'

The answer prompted a new question. 'Do you know where he is?'

'I am not at liberty to say, ma'am.'

It was a textbook professional security answer.

'Very well. Will you allow me inside his room? I need to collect something for him.'

I got a slight narrowing of his eyes and a quick shake of his head. 'No, ma'am. If Mr Howard-Box needs something, he can request it via another member of the security team. It will be taken to him.'

Okay, well that told me he was somewhere there were guards, but it didn't narrow things down much because they were all over the bride and groom.

I pursed my lips. I needed to look in his room.

Movement to my left revealed Felicity. Buster wasn't with her for once. 'They finally cancelled,' she announced, looking flustered yet relieved at the same time. 'It brings its own set of problems but at least I can tell everyone to relax now.' Arriving next to me, she asked, 'Is he there?'

I shook my head, but the guard answered. 'He's with Mrs Howard-Box in her suite, Mrs Philips.' Apparently, Mrs Philips is on the allowed-to-know-things list.

Felicity started to move away again; she expected me to follow as Angelica could be found in that direction.

'I need to get something from Bobbie's room,' I told her.

I got a curious expression from her, but she came back. 'What is it you need? I have a master key,' she volunteered. 'Carl here will make sure we don't mess with anything, won't you, Carl?'

Carl didn't speak into his cuff; there was no man inside with no principal there to be minded. He swiped the door with his own card instead, nodding to us as we passed.

Going inside, I casually asked, 'Do you have a number for Vince?'

She eyed me suspiciously. 'Why do you ask?'

'Because I'm willing to bet he knows why Angelica hired him and I need him to tell me.'

'Do you think he will?'

I puffed out my cheeks. 'I might have to make him.'

Inside Bobbie's suite there was no trace of what I expected to see, which made my lip curl in disappointment. Until I noticed that the room was spotless, and the bed was made. Room service had been through.

Striding into the bedroom, Felicity trailed after me. 'How are you going to get him to reveal what he knows?

I took a deep breath and lied. 'I intend to coerce him.'

'What are you looking for anyway?' she wanted to know when I opened a wardrobe.

A satisfied smile stole across my face, my grin confusing Felicity even more until I showed her what I found.

'But how?' she asked, unable to comprehend what she was seeing. 'Why? Why would he?'

I could have told her right there and then, but what fun would that be. Also, if I did that, I would have to explain things at least twice which sounded redundant.

'I need a bag,' I announced, looking around. 'This is evidence.'

Felicity didn't argue, but she did ask, 'Yes, but evidence of what?'

## Coercing Vince

I had Felicity call Vince and ask him to meet her. He was in Angelica's room which didn't suit me right now. I would be dealing with her shortly.

He agreed to excuse himself, revealing that Mrs Howard-Box was still trying to bully people into going through with the wedding even though her son Bobbie had already stated quite categorically that it was being postponed. I could imagine how that went over. I also believed I knew why he had put his foot down.

I waited with Felicity in the library. It felt like a good place to have our conversation with Mr Slater, mostly because it was empty.

We didn't have to wait for long; Vince appeared a couple of minutes after us. By that time, we were comfortably sitting in chairs at a long rectangular table and ready for him.

'Ladies?' He gave us both a quizzical look as he pulled a chair from the other side of the table to sit down. We were arranged like this was to be a job interview.

'Who are you working for here?' I asked him.

His cheeks coloured. It was there and it was gone, the mature investigator able to control his reaction but not quite fast enough. It told me what I already believed.

Nevertheless, he said, 'Mrs Howard-Box. You already know that.'

I nodded, pursing my lips and frowning slightly. 'I know that is what you are telling people and certainly Angelica thinks you are working for her. Tell me, Vince,' I shifted the subject deliberately because I knew he didn't wish to stick with the current one, 'why did Mrs Howard-Box employ you?'

He blinked and gave a little chuckle. 'You already know this too, Patricia. She was concerned for the publicity surrounding the event and worried someone might do something to interrupt the ceremony or the events around it. Clearly, she was right. I have to say I feel I have failed this weekend.' He made his face look annoyed and ashamed. 'There was too much ground to cover to prevent the damage to the cake.'

'Yet the dress and the wedding rings were in rooms your guards were protecting.' I pointed out, interrupting him.

Again, his cheeks coloured slightly. 'The guards for those rooms are yet to be found,' he replied, his lips tight with worry. I thought he was doing a good job of acting his role.

I cut to the chase. 'I need to hear why Angelica hired you, Vince. The specific reason, not the nonsense you keep telling me about her being concerned.'

'I don't know what you're talking about, Patricia,' he lied.

Felicity leaned across to whisper in my ear, 'I thought you were going to coerce him?'

Locking eyes with the man across the table, I said, 'If you tell me the truth, Felicity will go out for dinner with you.'

'Yes,' said Felicity. 'I'll ... hold on a moment!' she cried as her brain caught up with what I had said. 'I never agreed to that!'

Across the table, Vince was grinning in a self-satisfied way.

'You didn't,' I agreed with the wedding planner, 'but now you can. It doesn't have to be anything but dinner, and he can pay.'

'No problem,' Vince grinned again.

'We need to know what he was told. I think it is important,' I begged her.

Vince was lapping it up now. 'This is the only way you can possibly hope to unbutton my lips, Felicity.'

Felicity, her mouth gaping, stared at me, then swung her gaze across to Vince who wiggled his eyebrows at her. Then she looked back at me, her mouth still open and I think she was genuinely considering saying 'no'.

With a defeated sigh, she said, 'Oh, okay then. You're taking me somewhere nice though. Somewhere I get to pick.'

'Suits me,' Vince agreed happily. 'Mrs Howard-Box received a handwritten threat telling her Bobbie would be killed if he attempted to marry Sasha Allstar.'

There it was. Angelica thought that necessary to keep secret and I believed I knew why. Vince and his security firm were here because she believed someone might try to hurt her son. She put guards on Sasha's door too and her own, but Bobbie was the target.

Good. Now I had that part confirmed, I could finish the game. I checked my watch. It was almost one thirty. I had ninety minutes to get the interested parties together and to see if I had it all worked out. Less if I wanted to also get dressed for the wedding.

I leaned forward and fixed Vince with a hard stare. 'Now that bit is out of the way. Let's go back to the question about who you are really working for.'

## Assembling the Pieces

With Vince doing something Felicity and I gave him little choice about doing, my next step was to locate Chief Inspector Quinn.

Making our way through the grand rooms of Loxton Hall, I asked Felicity, 'What will this mean for you? The wedding going this badly south, I mean.'

She let a small laugh escape her, the sound of someone who wanted to rant and whine but who also knew no good could come of it and how insignificant of a problem it really was. 'In all honesty, it probably won't have any effect at all. Not in a negative way at least. I would have received a boost from the publicity because it was supposed to be in all the glossy magazines. That's gone, but it's probably a bigger problem for the glossy magazines than for me. I don't have empty pages to fill and I was paid in advance. Of course, my rivals will enjoy hearing that it turned into a disaster, but I doubt I will lose any clients over it. None of the issues here were due to a failing on my part. I guess I break even at worst.'

It was a good philosophy to have, a wise standpoint from which to view the debacle this particular celebrity wedding had become. I hadn't told Felicity much of what I believed yet, just enough to convince her to help me with Vince.

Heading for the back of the building where doors to the garden would lead us to the police mobile headquarters, a set of double doors swung open and a familiar French accent wafted out.

Two tired looking men emerged through the doors walking backward and dragging a wheeled trolley. Upon the table was a giant seven-tiered wedding cake. It looked exactly like the one I saw this morning but this one had fewer axe marks in it. Actually, it had none. Two more men were pushing the trolley with Chef Dominic providing unnecessary guidance.

'Slowly, idiot! I did not spend seven hours crafting this masterpiece just so you could bump it!'

I wasn't sure which of the men he was talking to, but they all looked about ready to kill the short French chef.

'Ah, Madame Philips, aye was 'oping to find you, and 'ere you are. The cake ees finished,' he grinned triumphantly.

Felicity looked at me for help. I shook my head; she was on her own for this one.

Stumbling a little, she manged to say, 'Yes, thank you Chef Dominic. You have produced a miracle as I knew you would.'

He smiled as if her compliments were too kind. 'Where shall I 'ave them take it? I want to make sure it is positioned exactly right. You know my eye for detail, Madame Philips.'

Felicity let her shoulders sag. 'Well, the thing is, Chef Dominic?'

'Oui?' he encouraged her to keep speaking, a frown beginning to form on his brow.

'Well,' Felicity was trying desperately to find a gentle way to break her news. 'The thing is, I rather think the wedding is off.'

Chef Dominic looked stunned for a few seconds. Then he burst out laughing. 'Oh, very good Madame Philips. You almost 'ad me there. A practical joke, no? How droll you British are.'

Felicity choked out another laugh and shook her head. 'No, no joke, Chef Dominic. I guess you have been tucked away in the kitchen all day.

The bride's best friend was stabbed. The bride's manager has been murdered. The best man is in hospital. I really don't think the wedding is going ahead.'

A tick appeared next to the chef's right eye, a small muscle beginning to spasm. He looked at the cake and back at Felicity, to the cake and back at the wedding planner who hired him again. 'No wedding?' he wanted to confirm.

Felicity shook her head. 'No. No wedding. Sorry. You'll still get paid though.'

'Paid!' the little French chef roared. 'I am an artist! What do I care about getting paid?' With that he raised both fists and ran at the cake.

He would have made it too were it not for the swift reactions of the men around the cake. I guess they felt enough effort had gone into it that seeing it destroyed by an annoying Frenchman was too much. The two nearest moved to block him while the other two moved it out of the way.

An idea popped into my head. Taking Felicity's arm and guiding her away from the insult slanging match now taking place, I took a glance to confirm Chef Dominic wasn't going to get to the cake, then asked, 'That thing is in need of a home now, right?'

Instantly understanding the subtext of my question, Felicity grinned at me. 'You know something, Patricia? I keep forgetting I organised two weddings for this weekend. Now that I have no distractions, I think I should focus my efforts on the one that will go ahead.'

We reached the backdoors of the building and went outside. Ahead of us, the police mobile headquarters was still a bustle of activity, and walking up to the officer managing access, I heard Chief Inspector Quinn's voice echoing across the still autumn air.

Beside me, Felicity was making a call; she had some things for her team to do and they needed to do them really, really fast.

I think someone near to the chief inspector spotted us approaching because the senior man turned his head and looked right at me before I needed to say anything.

I got to see him visibly groan, his head sagging as if he'd just been handed a fresh pile of work he neither wanted nor felt he deserved.

'Sorry, ladies,' the officer barring our way held up a hand to stop us. 'Police only beyond this point. Is there something I can help you with?'

My eyes never wavered from watching the chief inspector. I thought he might have the sense, or perhaps decency, to see why I was visiting, but he was attempting to leave the area.

Rudely ignoring the young officer's question while Felicity spoke fast on the phone a yard or two behind me, I raised my arm like I was in class and shouted, 'I know who did it, Chief Inspector. Can you arrest someone for me, please?'

His left foot froze in mid-air. Had I not called to him, I think he would have retreated inside the mobile headquarters and shut the door. I let a smile flicker to life. My itchy skull when I thought about the chess pieces in play and where they now sat on the board reassured me. I was right about all the vital details and the bits I could only guess were trivial enough that it wouldn't matter if I had some small elements wrong.

Chief Inspector Quinn could not afford to ignore me, and I was offering him the arrest on a plate. No one would know he hadn't solved the crime. Well, apart from the officers who just heard me shout. There were a dozen faces staring at me now, all in uniform and no doubt many of them wondering what it was that I thought I knew.

The chief inspector altered his trajectory, walking at a casual pace as if he had better things to do but would spare me a few moments of his time out of respect.

'Hello again, Mrs Fisher,' Chief Inspector Quinn said with a sigh. 'Exactly what is it that you think you know? Which *it* are we talking about?'

I smiled more broadly. 'All of *it*, Chief Inspector.' I felt I ought to caveat my statement by adding that I was fairly certain though not entirely sure I had it all figured out, but to so do would undermine my feigned confidence and I needed that to make him dance to my tune.

'I am listening,' he replied, still acting as if he were humouring me.

I backed away a pace, my smile replaced by a serious expression. 'I need to get all the key players into the library, Chief Inspector. Can you help me with that? I doubt Mrs Howard-Box will come if I invite her.'

A deep frown formed on Quinn's face. 'I am not in the habit of taking orders from amateur sleuths, Mrs Fisher.'

I continued to back away, making it clear I expected him to follow me. 'I have my own private investigation agency, Chief Inspector,' I argued. 'That makes me a professional detective at the very least.' I could have pointed out that he was a police officer and not a detective; the detectives' branch being a different stream of officers, yet I knew to do so would be not only pedantic but also counterproductive. 'Besides, I begged of your help. I did not give you an order.'

He still wasn't moving, so I stopped, facing him fully and shifting to a face that made me look like I was imploring him for help. 'Chief Inspector, thirty minutes from now you can have suspects in custody and this entire mess cleared up. I just need your help to do it smoothly.' When it was clear my argument still hadn't done the trick, I added, 'Or I can just use my friends and make citizens arrests on the guilty parties. I think quite a few members of the press are still here.'

It was the kick in the butt he needed. 'You most certainly will not,' he snapped, striding through the gap in the barrier.

As he glared at me with slits for eyes, I asked, 'You don't want any additional officers?'

My question brought a small snort of amusement from him. 'I think I can handle one or two arrests, Mrs Fisher. I am an old hand at this game.'

I translated his words because what he really meant was he wanted as few people as possible to see it wasn't his powers of deduction that unravelled the mysteries wound around this sham of a celebrity wedding.

I let it go, nodded as if his decisions pleased me. 'Very well, Chief Inspector. Here is who I need to have present ...' I reeled off a list of names from my head, adding one or two for good measure.

As we re-entered Loxton Hall via the same set of back doors, Felicity finished her call and gave me a silent thumbs up – all was in place. A check of my watch showed me I had a little more than an hour to finish this.

## In the Library with a Knife

I had butterflies in my stomach when the first people started drifting into the library. For ten minutes, I'd been running through things in my head. Challenging what I thought I knew and attempting to poke holes in my assumptions had given me even more confidence that I was right. However, the nerves were a natural reaction to placing myself in the limelight and though I didn't welcome them, I did my best to ignore their unsettling presence.

My phone pinged, loud in the quiet of the library. I fished it out, quickly reading the message from Alistair. I knew he would succeed and here was the reassurance I needed.

First to arrive was Cara Fright's boyfriend. I had only learned his name – Simon Phoenix – from Chief Inspector Quinn when I asked him to find Cara Fright's boyfriend. Quinn asked why I wanted him - though of course I refused to say – and pointed out that Phoenix had been interviewed following his girlfriend's death and had an alibi for the time of her death. A solid one since he wasn't yet in the country. His flight in from Canada landed at 0515hrs.

Nevertheless, the chief inspector was good to his word and made sure the man found his way to me.

'Why am I here?' he demanded to know, an edge of anger in his voice. Or was it fear?

I crossed the room, my right arm outstretched to shake his hand. 'Good afternoon, Mr Phoenix. My name is Patricia Fisher.'

He nodded. 'I've seen you in the paper.' He was wearing a different outfit from the one I'd seen him in first thing this morning outside the ladies' restroom though I found it natural that he had changed after a such a long flight. Now attired in jeans and a hooded top, both his hands were tucked inside the pouch at the front until he removed the right to shake mine.

'Yes,' I pushed his comment about my fame or notoriety quickly to one side – the pictures were not flattering. I suspected the press had gone to my house where Charlie willingly supplied them with the worst shots of me he could find. 'I was asked to work out what was happening here today. I am sure you are aware the Howard-Box wedding has just been called off. This morning their cake was destroyed by someone, the bride's dress was reduced to ribbons and the rings were stolen. It would seem they have a rather nasty stalker trying to ensure the wedding would or could not go ahead.'

His eyebrows meeting in the middle with indignation, he snapped, 'Well I hope you don't think it was me!'

'No, no, of course not,' I did my best to reassure and soothe. 'But in the course of my investigation, I believe I identified who it was that killed Cara.' I lowered my tone for the last sentence, saying her name carefully and respectfully as one always must for the recently bereaved.

Rage fluttered behind his eyes at the mention of his girlfriend's killer and I got to see his lip twist as he almost said something and just managed to bite it down. 'Who is it?' he demanded, taking a step forward so he came into my personal space.

He meant to wring the information from me if he needed to. He was shorter than me but would be stronger for sure.

'Ah, here we are,' said Chief Inspector Quinn, sweeping his arm through the door to show people inside. I locked eyes with him for a moment. He'd seen Simon Phoenix standing dangerously close to me and chose to make himself heard rather than intervene directly.

Phoenix stepped back a pace, glaring at me with silent insistence that I give up the name. Thankfully, I guess, it was the main body of the wedding party coming through the door now and that, of course, meant Angelica.

Her roving eyes looked about the room but caught sight of me in the first heartbeat.

It took less than a nanosecond for her to start screeching. 'What! What is the meaning of this? What is she doing here?'

'Please come in, Angelica,' I invited her, my tone, body language, and words polite though what she probably deserved was a set of cuffs and a gag.

'I will not!' she spat, turning on her heel to leave the room again.

The doorway behind her was blocked by other people trying to come inside as the chief inspector requested. Only a member of Vince's security detail had come in ahead of her to check the room, but she had another one right behind her, and Bobbie was on her heels with two of his own.

It sounded to me as if there were yet more outside; questions being asked about what was happening as Angelica tried to force her way back against the human tide.

I got to watch, Angelica's antics entertaining me for once. The smile on my face only fuelled her rage when she spotted it.

'I will not spend any more time in that awful woman's presence! she shouted, shoving a guard in his mid-section to make him move backward.

'Stop!' commanded Chief Inspector Quinn. He was still in the corridor outside. Speaking at a normal volume now that everyone, Angelica included, had fallen silent, he said, 'Everyone will assemble peacefully in the library. There we will listen to what Mrs Fisher has to say. Anyone who does not wish to comply will be taken into custody.'

He didn't ask if his instructions were clear – he knew they were. And he didn't repeat himself. He simply waited for the people outside to start moving in again. Angelica, cowed now by the senior police officer who would tolerate no argument, moved into the room as if it were what she wanted to do all along and selected a seat that faced me.

She was still missing half her makeup and not one of her children or any of the people in the wedding party had seen fit to tell her.

I'd taken a couple of minutes to arrange the chairs, moving tables out of the way so I had a rough horseshoe with me at the open end. Angelica sat at what would be the leading edge of the horse's hoof, her eyes locked on mine as if she could boil me inside my own skin if she focused hard enough.

Bobbie, flanked by his guards, sat on my right, almost as far away from his mother as he could get. His sisters were with him and tellingly, they didn't sit near their mother either. Sasha was next through the door, yet another pair of Vince's security detachment watching over her. She had two members of her entourage with her, both of whom were holding her hands in a show of physical and emotional support. I'd seen them before when I first visited Angelica's room this morning. One was an overtly gay man so skinny I had to wonder if he had an eating disorder, the other a plus sized girl with a willing smile. She was whispering to Sasha the whole time; a constant pep talk to keep her going during a terrible day.

Finally, Vince entered the room, which completed my line up of guests. Chief Inspector Quinn closed the library door, and the room was silent. They were all watching me.

My knees felt weak.

Angelica could see my nervousness and revelled in it. Her quirky, smug little grin had two effects. Firstly, it made me want to pick up the stapler I could see on the librarian's desk. I thought a few staples in her forehead might change her attitude. I didn't do that though because the second effect was that her continual superiority chased away my butterflies.

Feeling renewed with energy, I started to talk.

'Thank you all for coming.'

'Ha!' scoffed Angelica. 'I should hardly say we had a choice.'

I nodded at her point. 'Yes, thank you for raising that, Angelica. You did, in point of fact have a choice. You could have challenged the chief inspector and let him decide if he wanted to take you into custody.' She narrowed her eyes at me. 'That was unpalatable though, was it not? Chiefly, I imagine, because of all the lies you've been telling.'

Her cheeks coloured. 'Lies? What lies?' she opened the door for me.

'There are several, in fact, Angelica, but I'll start with the one about wanting extra security because you thought it would be a good precaution.' This bit was easy because I knew for certain she had no way to argue. 'The truth is that you had a very specific reason to hire private security. Do you wish to tell your son now?'

Her lips quivered.

Bobbie's head swung between me and his mother and back again. 'Mum? What's she talking about?' Angelica didn't answer and never took her hate-filled eyes from mine. 'Mum!' he raised his voice.

I supplied the answer, 'Your mother received a threat against you. The emails, there were several I believe, threatened to kill you if you attempted to marry Sasha Allstar.'

'What?' Bobbie couldn't believe it.

Across the room Sasha choked out a surprised gasp. 'I thought it was for me. I thought someone was after me. The spray-painted warning was in my room this morning,' she pointed out.

I acknowledged her comment. 'We'll circle back to that in a moment, Sasha.' Piercing Angelica with a look that invited her to comment, I said, 'We'll consider that fact then, shall we? However, the threat against Bobbie was investigated by Vince Slater, a private investigator and owner of a private security firm, and he was unable to trace the emails to a source.'

'Unable? Yes, that's about right. I should have hired someone competent,' Angelica spat.

Vince took the insult with a sly smile.

A knock at the door drew everyone's attention. Standing by the exit, or effectively blocking anyone from leaving if you wished to see it that way, Chief Inspector Quinn opened the door.

'Sorry,' said Felicity, slipping inside with an apology on her face. I knew where she had been and what she had been doing.

All the seats were taken apart from the one next to Vince, undoubtedly a deliberate ploy on his part. Quickly, Felicity took her place and I returned to my summation.

'Someone competent,' I repeated Angelica's words. 'You say that because you already believed you knew who the threat came from.' I made it a statement, though it was a guess on my part; one of those things I had no way of truly knowing.

Angelica is predictable though and I had just given her a chance to show off how clever she is. 'Of course I knew,' she chuckled. 'It's a mother's job to protect her children.'

Muttering from Bobbie and his sisters made it clear they felt their mother's protection went way beyond that which was acceptable.

'Okay, so you knew who was sending the threat, but Vince Slater was unable to prove it, right?'

'Right,' replied Angelica as if she were scoring a point.

'Wait,' said Bobbie, feeling perplexed and beginning to get annoyed at being kept in the dark. 'Who are we talking about here?'

'In a moment,' I assured him. Then to Vince, I asked, 'Why could you not prove who the guilty person was when Mrs Howard-Box identified them to you?'

He looked directly at Angelica. 'Because they didn't do it,' he told the room. I'd coached him that he was to remain gender neutral in his answers; the time to reveal that person's identity was not yet upon us.

'Why am I here?' Simon Phoenix wanted to know.

I offered him an apologetic face again. 'I'm sorry, Mr Phoenix. I am getting to the part that will interest you.'

Angelica wanted to argue about Vince's statement, but I got in first. 'Sasha?' I looked her way as I said her name.

Her head had been down, the proceedings not interesting enough to penetrate the thoughts swirling around her head.

When her head snapped up, I said, 'You lied to the police about being out of your bed last night.'

As if I had walked across the room and slapped her face, the room reacted in shock. All except Vince and Felicity that is.

'No, I didn't,' she lied again.

I let that linger in the air for a moment as I backed up a pace to collect something I'd hidden from sight on a bookcase behind me. As I turned back to face the room, there was one set of eyes that flared while everyone else's narrowed in question.

I looked at the wide eyes and asked. 'Do you recognise these?'

Bobbie swallowed hard before saying. 'Yes. Those are a pair of my running shoes.'

I lifted my hand up to show everyone. 'The red mud you see on the bottom of the shoes got there last night when you walked through it.'

It was Angelica's turn to ask a question. 'What were you doing outside, Bobbie?'

He ignored his mother, his jaw muscles twitching nervously. I waited. I waited until he risked a glance at Vince.

'You see Bobbie didn't know about the threat his mother received. He didn't know because she didn't dare tell him.' I shot Angelica a look, daring her to argue. 'He believed the security was massive overkill, so too did Sasha. Between them, they were paying for it anyway. They have paid for everything at this wedding, so having decided it wasn't necessary and after Mr Slater revealed there was no credible threat he knew of, Bobbie paid Vince extra to look the other way while he squirrelled the guards away.'

The colour drained from Bobbie's face and he closed his eyes so he wouldn't have to look at anyone.

I knew who would ask the next question and waited for it.

'Why, Bobbie?' demanded Angelica. 'Why would you want to get rid of the guards?'

I doubted he wanted to answer, so I did it for him. 'For two reasons, Angelica. Actually,' I corrected myself. 'I guess it is three reasons, but I'll get to the third one in a minute. Bobbie bribed a Loxton Hall groundsman,' I saw his eyes flash open, wondering how I could possibly know that and knew my wild guess was on the money. The door was locked when I got to it and that meant someone had a key. To get it, he either stole it, or flashed around his superstar sportsman wages. The latter seemed more likely. 'Then, in agreement with Vince,' I saw the chief inspector glare at the back of Vince's head, 'Bobbie took the guards and hid them out of sight beneath Loxton Hall.'

'Why, Bobbie?' Angelica repeated her question. She didn't want to hear it from me.

'To create a panic,' I stated. 'To make you and others believe there was a credible threat to the wedding.'

At a nod from me, Vince lifted his right arm and spoke into his cuff. The door behind the chief inspector opened and six of Vince's security team came in – the six missing men. They filed silently past the police officer whose men had put countless hours into searching the grounds.

'Where were they?' Chief Inspector Quinn wanted to know. As usual, he posed the question in a studious manner, very little inflection making its way into his voice.

'In the pump room we visited until about ten minutes before we got there. Vince saw me outside with my friends and guessed I'd either worked it out or stumbled across it.' Once Felicity and I started to show we knew most of it, he caved and told us the rest. 'The truth is I saw Bobbie leading two of them there last night. Vince got them out just before you and I arrived with your officers this morning, Chief Inspector. Your men had finished searching Loxton Hall by then, so Vince's guards went back to their rooms.'

Vince was smart enough to look guilty about his part in the subterfuge even though he was guilty of no crime – except perhaps wasting police time. It was down to CI Quinn to decide if he wished to pursue that.

Angelica was still shaking her head. 'I still don't understand why. Why did you want to make people think there was a credible threat to the wedding, Bobbie?'

I answered for him again. 'For the same reason Sasha carved up her own dress and trashed the cake.'

Like watching a tennis match, standing at the head of the horseshoe, I got to watch all the heads swing across to gawp at the internet star.

I hadn't dealt with the lie she told about not being out of her room, but it was time for that now. Like Bobbie, her face was drained of colour, her crimes revealed for all to see. Even her entourage were looking at her in disbelief.

'It wasn't you people saw out of bed last night, was it, Sasha? You sent Gloria to destroy the cake for you. She was the one person you trusted above all others.' Sasha's chest was beginning to rise and fall visibly as she hyperventilated. She was bordering on fainting or slipping into shock, so I hurried. 'You sent her to trash the cake and spray the message on the wall in the kitchen and then you did the same in your room after you carved up your own wedding dress. You should have made sure the same hand sprayed both messages. That they were so different was a big clue.'

Sasha hung her head.

'It was also obvious something was amiss because the Sasha people saw was wearing your famous outfit. Earlier you told me you hated it. Gloria likes dressing up as you though, doesn't she?'

'Why?' begged Angelica, barely able to believe what she was hearing.

'The same reason Bobbie took the wedding rings,' I told her, again guessing but feeling fairly confident now I was on a roll.

'He did not!' insisted Angelica.

I didn't reply, I merely turned my head and watched her son. Slowly, reluctantly, Bobbie fished in the pocket of his trousers and pulled his hand out again. Opening it with his palm face up, we all saw the light catch on two gold rings.

'WHY!' screamed Angelica.

It was time. 'Because you mess with people's lives, Angelica.' I delivered a line that I knew would hurt but which I also knew to be true. 'You think you know what is right for other people and do not trust them to make their own decisions. Worse yet, you are a bully.'

'I am not!' she was horrified by the suggestion.

'Yes, you are, mum,' said Bobbie, refusing to meet her eyes.

I sniffed deeply, filling my lungs with air because I suddenly felt very weary. Weary of running around trying to solve the mystery of the wedding vandal and Cara Fright's murder. Weary of battling Angelica when I would happily just have nothing to do with her.

Bobbie's comment had shut his mother up, her stunned expression stuck in place as she tried to work out what to say next.

I asked her a question. 'What was the name of the person you believed to be behind the threat to Bobbie if he attempted to marry Sasha?'

Angelica shifted uncomfortably in her chair. 'It hardly matters,' she replied, as if that would stop me probing.

'Her name?' I pressed, letting the room know we were talking about a woman.

A question formed in Bobbie's mind, bringing a frown to his face. 'Who was it, mother?'

She mumbled something no one could hear.

'WHO WAS IT?' he bellowed across the room.

She met his eyes, exasperated by his insistence to know something she knew he didn't need to know.

'Teagan Clancy,' she replied at an audible volume.

The room was silent, all eyes on Bobbie as he slumped back into his chair. He was shaking his head unable to believe he'd just heard her name.

'She dumped me two years ago,' he muttered to himself, questioning why she was even a factor.

I moved, taking a step forward and in so doing drawing the eyes in the room back to me.

'This is what I mean about messing with people's lives, Angelica.' She looked at me with a complete lack of comprehension. 'Did Teagan dump Bobbie?' I asked. 'Or did you intervene and pay her to do so because she wasn't good enough for him?'

She didn't answer, but Bobbie surged to his feet. 'You did what?'

Angelica remained calm, looking up at her son as if he were still a child who could not possibly understand the concepts being discussed.

'You are with Sasha now, Bobbie. What does it matter about a girl you broke up with two years ago?'

'Why did you trash the cake?' I interrupted Angelica to pose a question to Sasha. 'It's all out in the open now. You might as well get it all off your chest.'

Embarrassed and ashamed, she shook her head and held it high when she said, 'Because I don't want to get married.' She looked at Bobbie the whole time, sorrow in her eyes for the pain she was causing him. 'I mean, I like you, Bobbie. I really do, we have such fun together, but I'm still young and …'

I interrupted her before she could say more. 'Why did you take the rings, Bobbie?'

His shoulders slumped and his head went down, but when it came up again a second later, he was laughing. 'Because I don't want to get married either. I don't even remember how it happened. How did we end up getting engaged?'

Sasha got to her feet and ran to him, pulling the footballer into a hug. Not the kind that you might see from two lovers, but one that made me think they were good friends more than they were anything else. In the midst of all the woes they suffered this weekend, the biggest clue was how little time I saw them touching each other. They ought to have been holding hands, kissing, hugging. When she was almost murdered at the BFF thing, he didn't bother to seek her out. When they came into the library, they sat on opposite sides of the horseshoe, not together. When they did that, I knew I was right about everything.

Sasha had tears of relief running down her face and an answer to Bobbie's question. 'Your mother bullied you into proposing. That's what happened.'

Angelica said nothing.

Bobbie let go of his friend and stepped back a pace to ask her a question in return. 'Okay, but why did you say yes?'

She bowed her head, the truth hard to articulate.

I did it for her. 'Because her manager was using photographs taken by a former lover to blackmail her into behaving. They had a whole new celebrity show lined up for the pair of you to star in. They didn't care if the marriage worked. Filming the whole thing fall apart would have made good television I expect.'

'Is that true?' Bobbie asked her.

Sasha nodded sadly.

'Why didn't you tell me?'

She raised her head to meet his eyes. 'Why didn't you tell me you didn't want to get married?' He didn't have an answer for her, but she had another question for him. 'Who is this Teagan anyway?'

'Excuse me?' insisted a voice we hadn't heard from for a while. 'I still want to know why I am here.' I turned to look at Simon Phoenix. 'You told me you were going to tell me who killed my Cara,' he reminded me. 'I don't think that is necessary though because I already know.' He glared at Sasha. 'You killed her didn't you!' he roared.

Sasha seemed physically rocked by the accusation, taking a pace back as it hit her.

'No!' she gasped in shock. 'I would never!'

'She had pictures of you. You just admitted it and I know she was using them to make you obey your contract. I've seen them – the disgusting things you were doing. No wonder you didn't want them getting out. You killed her to get your hands on them, didn't you?'

Turning to face Simon placed Chief Inspector Quinn behind me, but I felt him move, nevertheless. We were getting to the parts that were going to interest him. He didn't care about smashed cakes and broken hearts, he wanted to catch a killer.

Facing Simon, I asked him, 'Why are you here?'

He swivelled his head to face me. 'Because you had your pet police officer escort me here,' he snarled in accusation.

'No. I mean, what brings you to Loxton Hall this weekend?'

His brow furrowed. 'I was meeting Cara here. If Sasha hadn't murdered her last night, Cara and I would be heading into London after the wedding.'

I persisted, trying to get to the point I wanted to make. 'Yes, but why are you still here?' Now a look of alarm filled his face. 'Cara was dead before you got here. You arrived to a scene of utter chaos and your girlfriend's body was taken away hours ago. There was no need for you to even put your bags down, let alone remain here.'

'Why are you questioning me?' he screamed, spittle flying from his lips.

'Why is your left hand still inside your pocket, Simon?' I asked him, my voice calm. 'Did you cut it when you stabbed Gloria?'

'She's the killer!' he raged, his anger bubbling over. 'Sasha's the one who strangled my Cara!'

I shook my head. 'Is that why you tried to stab her earlier?'

'She deserves to die!' he yelled again.

It was close enough to a confession to get Chief Inspector Quinn moving. Not fast enough though because the bit I hadn't anticipated was Simon having a knife in his pocket.

He rose from his seat like a sprinter leaving the blocks, thrusting upward and outward to get to Sasha. Still closer to the door than his target, Quinn was never going to get to Simon before Simon got to Sasha.

Sasha froze like a rabbit in a set of oncoming headlights, unable to get a message from her brain to her feet. Bobbie was moving but he was being heroic, throwing his body into Simon's path where he was guaranteed to get stabbed.

All around the room, mouths were forming horrified O's as the knife started its upward trajectory toward the soccer star's heart. Simon's lips were drawn back in a terrible leer, like something from a horror movie and he intended to kill.

Vince punched him in the side of his head.

He was barely out of his chair when he did it, getting his backside far enough off the seat that he was within striking distance. I got to watch the whole thing, unable to believe the force Vince generated with a short jab.

Even though the blow could not have been at full power, Vince is a big man and Simon is more like a jockey. It was bantam weight against heavy weight and one punch was all it took.

Simon crashed to the side as the energy of the blow threw his head to the right. His lights were out before he hit the floor and the knife came loose. It skittered over the polished floorboards to be stopped when Angelica put her foot on it.

Vince sat back down and straightened his tie, playing it seriously cool next to the woman he was trying to impress.

Chief Inspector Quinn stepped around me to get to Simon Phoenix. He paused to check the man still had a pulse, nodded an acknowledgement to Vince because it would have been awkward if Phoenix had killed someone while the chief inspector was in the room, and pulled a set of cuffs into the daylight.

We all heard the cuffs ratchet together, but we were not done yet.

While Chief Inspector Quinn used his radio to summon help, I finished the game.

Looking around the room, I met as many sets of eyes as I could. Bobbie was holding onto Sasha again, for comfort and support after the shock of Simon's crazed attack this time. They backed away to the edge of the horseshoe to give me room.

'We have dealt with how your wedding came to be halted. And we have dealt with how Gloria came to be stabbed in the back this afternoon.'

'It was meant for me,' sobbed Sasha though I think she had always known she was the target.

'Gloria was the only person you told about the photographs, isn't she?' I raised my voice, startling her into meeting my eyes.

'Yes,' she whispered meekly.

'When you heard Cara had been killed, did you confront Gloria?' Sasha said nothing, her eyes widening in panic. 'You knew Gloria knew the truth about Cara blackmailing you. She knew the truth about the wedding too. She had to because you asked her to help you. People thought they saw you out of bed, but it was Gloria. She dressed as you so she could sneak up on Cara and strangle her.'

'I didn't know she was going to do it,' Sasha wailed.

I believed her. 'But you suspected it was her, didn't you?'

The library door opened, and police officers came in. Looking for their boss, they quickly fanned out as he commanded their movements. Two came to get Simon Phoenix, the man on the floor beginning to groan as consciousness seeped back.

My eyes never left Sasha's. 'You couldn't call off the wedding when you discovered Cara had been killed because you knew to do so would swing suspicion your way. Maybe you could have proved it wasn't you, but could you do that without putting Gloria in the frame? Probably not. Even with Cara out of the way and the chance to stop the wedding within grasp, you couldn't dare do so because your best friend would go to jail.' Sasha hung her head. It was all true. 'I'm afraid she will now anyway.' I was guessing the doctors would be able to save her life from the stab wound.

The room was silent save for the sound of the police officers' boots as they removed Simon Phoenix. At Chief Inspector Quinn's instruction, they moved in to take Sasha Allstar too; she was needed for questioning.

'If I might stay you for just one moment, Chief Inspector?' I begged.

He gave me a questioning look. 'You are not finished?'

'Just one last thing,' I promised. 'Alistair?'

All heads swung around as my boyfriend, Captain Alistair Huntley of the Aurelia, appeared in the frame of the open door. He looked to his left at someone standing outside and smiled.

Gasps, most notably from Angelica, filled the room as Teagan Clancy stepped into the room. Gone was the Sashatastic outfit she'd worn to get into the premises and pass unnoticed today. In its place, a simple elegant dress, one of Barbie's I knew because I'd seen my blonde friend wearing it before.

Teagan was beautiful, and the look of hope as she spotted Bobbie was enough to break my heart. I knew the story because Alistair explained it in his text. Teagan took the bribe from Angelica and dumped the man she loved but only after Angelica assured her she would never allow the two of them to marry.

With two police officers flanking her, waiting to take her into custody, Sasha nodded her head at Bobbie and whispered, 'Go to her.'

I could only marvel at the indomitability of love as Teagan and Bobbie ran to each other, meeting in the middle of the horseshoe where they clung to each other like shipwreck survivors on a raft.

Sasha nodded once and let the police lead her from the room.

I smiled at Alistair. His mission to find the woman I felt certain had to be loitering in Loxton Hall somewhere was a success. He'd found her in a stairwell where she was watching Bobbie's room in the hope she might catch him alone at some point and be able to say what she felt she must.

She wasn't behind the threat to Bobbie, Angelica was. At least that's what I believed. Teagan had no number for Bobbie and Angelica made her sign a legal agreement stating she would never attempt to make contact with him. Teagan told Alistair everything when he found her. What she had done was contact Angelica, begging her to take the money back. She loved Bobbie and regretted splitting up with him as soon as she had done it. Angelica hired Vince and his security team to stop her getting to see Bobbie.

It almost worked.

The couple were back together now and there was nothing Angelica would be able to do about it this time.

Suddenly aware of the time, a spasm of fear jolted me. I needed to get moving! I still had to change, check my face, and tidy my hair. I spun around to follow my feet to the door, and almost bumped into Chief Inspector Quinn.

He sniffed deeply, pursing his lips as he studied me. 'There will be a press release shortly, Mrs Fisher,' he told me. 'I'm afraid you will not be mentioned in it.'

'Why ever not?' asked Alistair, overhearing what Quinn said and demanding an explanation. 'Patricia solved the whole thing.'

I waved a hand. 'It's fine, Alistair. I genuinely don't care. I told the chief inspector he could have this one. I just needed it done in time for us to get to Deepa's wedding.' I checked my watch again. 'We really need to get going.'

Quinn stepped out of my way but had a parting comment. 'Well done, Mrs Fisher.' His praise was something I had not heard before. 'I don't often say this,' he added in a tone that made me think it genuinely pained him to force the words out, 'but that was a fine piece of detective work. When I have time, I might like to pick your brains about how you spotted some of the clues I missed.' That he admitted missing things came as a complete shock.

I dipped my head in acknowledgement. 'Thank you, Chief Inspector.'

A rare smile crept onto his face, sliding in from the side as if afraid he might notice it was there. 'The, ah ... the big reveal in the library ... that was a bit much though, don't you think? Honestly, Mrs Fisher, you're not an Agatha Christie character.' With an amused shake of his head, he left the library following the last of his officers out.

It was a typical Chief Inspector Quinn comment.

Bouncing into sight to fill the doorway, Barbie appeared. 'Come on, Patty!' she laughed impatiently. 'We need to go!'

## Surprises

I had pretty pink bows for Anna and Georgie to wear and a brand-new pink leather lead to replace their old one. There could be nothing about my outfit or theirs that looked tired or worn.

Getting dressed and back out of my room was done at a rush, Alistair complaining because his finest dress whites were not the easiest things to get on in a hurry.

He had to hurry though because we still had one thing to do – we had a surprise to deliver. Actually, I guess it was two surprises, but one was an official task as captain of the Aurelia, so it didn't really count.

The groom was in his room looking nervous when we arrived. I let the girls off their leads, letting them wander and explore. Lieutenant Baker's good friend, the tall Austrian, Lieutenant Schneider, was cleaning Martin's dress whites with a sticky roller. Martin was in them and looking handsome ahead of the big event.

On the dressing table he stood before, an empty glass that had once contained port told a story about an unsettled stomach though what he had to worry about I could not guess. He was about to marry a beautiful woman who clearly loved him as much as he loved her.

Pippin had answered the door and let us in, the three men inside all acknowledging their captain as they ought. Alistair whispered to Pippin, sending him back to our room because there was something for him to collect there.

Schneider declared the final dust and lint removal task complete and stood back.

Lieutenant Baker turned around. 'How do I look?' he asked.

'Impeccably smart,' I told him.

Next to me, Alistair frowned. 'I would say you look improperly dressed.' It was an odd statement and delivered with a near-scolding tone. It caught both Baker and Schneider by surprise, both men taken aback as they tried to work out why the captain was picking holes in their appearance today of all days.

'I ... I don't follow, sir,' stammered Lieutenant Baker, colour reaching his cheeks.

Alistair nodded his head, playing the role of wise superior who knows better about everything.

'Improperly dressed, wouldn't you say, Mrs Fisher?' Alistair asked my opinion.

It was a struggle to keep my face straight. 'I should say so, yes.'

Baker and Schneider exchanged a glance. They had no idea what was happening.

Alistair fished in his pocket. 'How can you expect to walk down the aisle to marry that lovely bride when you are wearing the wrong rank, man?'

In his hand when he opened it, was a set of Lieutenant Commander's insignia. Baker looked down, saw what it was and snapped his head up again, a look of absolute shock now claiming his face. He knew what this was but looked as though he didn't dare believe it.

Lieutenant Schneider laughed, a hearty booming chuckle as Alistair stuck out his right hand. 'Congratulations on your promotion Lieutenant Commander Baker. I dare say you will want to get those Lieutenant's pips off now.

Stunned into silence, Lieutenant Commander Baker let the captain pump his arm just as Schneider moved in to fiddle with Baker's epaulettes.

Pippin, who'd been waiting just behind and to the side, stepped forward with a tray he'd collected from our room. On it was an aged bottle of whiskey and four glasses, one for each of the men. My lack of inclusion wasn't a gender thing – I'm not part of the crew yet. I don't much care for whisky anyway.

Alistair explained that he found out a few weeks ago, Purple Star Cruise Lines having reviewed all the recommendations for promotion from around the fleet and selected Baker for advancement. It wasn't supposed to be official for another month, but Alistair knew Baker's wedding day was the right time to promote him and argued for it.

'If you are wondering what this will mean for your position on board the Aurelia, I have further good news,' Alistair revealed. He explained to me earlier that typically people being promoted are moved to a different ship where they are not friends with everyone who is suddenly their subordinate. 'There is a new position opening up.'

This was news to me; Alistair had left this bit out.

'What is it, sir?' Lieutenant Commander Baker asked.

'Well,' Alistair took my hand and lifted it so he could kiss my fingers. 'Purple Star agreed to the concept of a ship's detective.' I felt my legs go wobbly. 'The Aurelia is to be the first ship with one and we will pilot the program to demonstrate how effective such a role can be.'

I had the whirlies. 'Ooh, I need to sit down,' I said, reversing to the bed.

Alistair chuckled at me. 'The ship's detective needs a support team which I was permitted to handpick. I think you can probably guess the three lieutenants and one lieutenant commander I selected for the role.'

I flopped back on to the bed to stare at the ceiling. Alistair was still talking, the four men in the room discussing the new team that would support me. It was really happening. I knew it was what I asked for but until this very moment, it was still a fantasy. Now Purple Star had approved it and I was to be employed. So much was changing, and it felt like the planet was shifting under my feet.

Finally noticing me, Alistair asked, 'Are you all right, Patricia. We really must be heading down now.

I waved a hand limply in the air. 'I might need a glass of that whisky.'

## Getting Married

Buoyed up by the shot of hard alcohol, I got off the bed and all five of us hurried to the ceremony to make sure we got there before the bridal party.

At the bottom of the grand staircase, the groom attempted to turn left and would have done so had I not hooked a hand into his elbow and steered him to the right.

'We need to go this way,' I told him, tugging at the girls' leads to make them go the right way too.

His brow knitted in confusion. 'But we're getting married in the small registry office at the back?' he questioned.

I smiled at him. 'Not any more.' Ahead of me, a pair of twins who looked like bookends, stepped forward to open a pair of ornate doors. 'There have been a few last-minute changes,' I explained.

Loxton Hall's specially constructed main wedding room, the feature that drew many of the rich and famous to use it and one which had graced countless glossy magazine articles, was a stunning masterpiece of matrimonial design.

Bedecked with silver and white, with seating for an orchestra and enough pews to hold five hundred attendees, it was a sight to behold. So that was what we did. Five of us, plus the two dachshunds stood in the entrance beholding the incredible view.

Deepa's family were arranged on one side of the central aisle, Martin's on the other. Both families were smiling at the groom when he found his feet and made his way to the front. Alistair and I slid into a pew behind

Martin's family, bolstering the numbers on that side as he had fewer people attending. From there we watched and waited, taking it all in.

From the side of the room, Felicity caught my eye and gave me a wave. This was, of course, the room reserved for Bobbie and Sasha. It had been decorated for them but a few changes – Felicity's hurried phone call earlier getting her team to move fast – made it personal enough for Martin and Deepa.

The cake had given me the idea, and they were getting that too. It was too fine a work of art to go to waste and there was another surprise yet to come.

Deepa arrived just a couple of minutes late and like Martin, just stood and gawped at the mouth of the room before the music started. Remembering what she was supposed to do, Deepa, looking radiant and wonderful in a fabulous yet simple dress, floated down the aisle with her sisters in her wake. Barbie and Jermaine snuck in behind – I'd employed them to make sure the bride arrived at the right place. They sidled up next to me.

The ceremony wasn't a long one, I don't think they ever are, but it was beautiful, and I felt bewitched to be watching it.

When the music struck up again, bride and groom led a procession down the aisle where Felicity's master of ceremonies was waiting to take them to the ballroom where their reception was to be held.

However, like the ceremony itself, the reception had moved rooms.

If the sheer opulence of their surroundings wasn't enough to etch memories into the heads of everyone present, the cake was. They wheeled it out, the trolley taking four men to control.

A harpist played music while the guests chattered and ... what can I say? It was a magical occasion.

## Concerned Friends

I awoke on Monday morning with a sense of righteous purpose. The meeting with Charlie and his lawyers was just a few hours away now but I felt no desperate sense of dread, just a mild fluttering of nerves. The previous evening, I had been feeling out of sorts. Partly that was because I had a lot riding on the card I was going to play today. Like a game of high-stakes poker, whether I won or not might come down to how well I could bluff. There was also the question about whether Charlie would say something clever or smug and if it would cause me to snap.

There was a real danger I would launch myself at him with a view to gouging his eyes out.

A few gins last night ensured my brain found rest and I slept soundly for many hours. However, though still dark outside when I opened my eyes, it was morning and time I was up.

Barbie had promised to put me through my paces and that was what she did, making me run faster than I wanted to for more miles than I wished to cover. It provided a distraction while making me believe I was doing something that was good for my mind, body, and spirit.

My body wasn't entirely convinced.

Our route through the countryside and around the village took us past Angelica's house where I imagined I could still hear her ranting and cursing my name. Barbie let me walk the last quarter mile to allow my muscles to cool down. Jermaine was at the door waiting to open it upon my arrival and he had a hand towel ready so I could wipe off the sweat and mud and probably dribble before Alistair saw me.

My devilishly gorgeous boyfriend was in the kitchen eating toast and reading a paper. He looked very much at home and relaxed. It made me feel very warm and content. It also made me want to maintain the vision in front of me which could not happen because we were returning to the ship. Even if I defeated Charlie, which I believed I would, Alistair and I retiring to this house to grow old together was a fantasy set in a distant future.

'Your breakfast wishes, madam?' asked Jermaine, standing poised by the refrigerator.

I followed my hard-fought miles of effort with Barbie by requesting a carb and fat loaded bacon sandwich. I wanted the guilty pleasure of it and not only felt I deserved it but believed it would aid me in preparing for the meeting. It was less than two hours away now.

Eating my naughty but nice breakfast and savouring every bite, I became acutely aware that my friends were all acting strange. To start with, I ordered a dirty breakfast and Barbie made no comment at all. Silently observing them for a minute and thinking about what they were not saying as much as what they were, it took me a while to cotton on, but I soon saw what it was.

'Okay,' I said, breaking the near silence in the kitchen. 'Did you think I wouldn't notice you all trying to not talk about it?'

Alistair reached across to place his hand on top of mine. 'We are just concerned for you, darling.'

I met his expression with a sad smile. What else could I do? I wanted to tell him there was no need for him to be concerned but I would have to lie to do that, so I said, 'Thank you. I believe it will be okay. Whatever the outcome, we will all return to the Aurelia soon and that is what I am focused on.'

Barbie came around behind me, placing a hand on my left shoulder. 'We just want you to be happy, Patty.'

Jermaine came around to the right. 'Our own happiness is invested in yours, madam.' I got what he meant. Could I be happy if I knew he was not?

I did my best to reassure them. 'I know you think I have got this all wrong. I know you think I should have spent whatever it might cost to get myself a team of lawyers to fight Charlie's claim over this house and half of all that I have.' I fell silent for a second, collecting my thoughts. 'I am going into that meeting with my head held high and I will come out the same way. It doesn't matter what happens in the meeting because we can walk away from all this,' I gesticulated around the room to show them I meant the house and all that went with it. 'We are what matters. Not these material things.'

The thing is, as I said the words, I knew they were true – the house, the cars, the money ... none of it really mattered. I would give it all up for any one of the people in the kitchen, but they were not on the line. Nothing was.

If I lost, I didn't lose my friends and family, I lost stuff.

However, at the same time, if I lost, what I lost was dignity. I would lose self-respect. I needed to be able to look at myself in the mirror tomorrow and that meant kicking Charlie in the metaphorical balls today.

I finished the last bite of my bacon sandwich and pushed back from the table. No one had said anything for most of a minute and I needed to be out of the *cloying concern for Patricia* I currently felt, or imagined, they were all feeling.

Upstairs, I stared into my wardrobe for a good ten minutes. I could not decide what to wear. I worried Alistair would come back upstairs looking for me, but he proved to be wiser than expected. He gave me distance and respect, something I needed even though I also felt a desire to cling to him.

He made me stronger. I recognised that in an unexpected wave of self-awareness that shook me to my core. Looking back now, I saw that everything in my life changed when I met Alistair. He helped me with the embarrassment in the queue to board the Aurelia the very first time, and he made me feel special. It was something no one else had done in years.

He was just being a cruise ship captain, but at the time it sparked a change in me, and that change was still taking place. He was the catalyst that made me who I am today! The thought was provocative, but no sooner did it surface than another came along to argue with it – it wasn't Alistair who caused the change, it was Jermaine.

Jermaine. I loved him as much as I loved Alistair, that was unquestioned. The affection and the manner in which I displayed it to each man was very different, but if bullets were to fly in our direction and I had the power to stop them, who would I dive to protect? In that gut-reaction moment, I believed a person's most basic instincts took the wheel and I could not predict which way I might go.

I shook my head, breaking the spell, and with my eyes shut, I thrust my arm into the closet and grabbed the first thing my hand found. Opening my eyes again, I breathed a sigh of relief - I was grasping what I considered my power suit.

Okay, it wasn't Joan Collins in her *Dynasty* days, but it told anyone looking at it that the wearer had purpose and wasn't to be taken lightly. At least, I hoped that was the message it sent.

Dressed for the day, I packed a new leather briefcase with a notebook and nothing else – because I had nothing else to pack - and went downstairs.

I paused in front of the large mirror by the front door to check how I looked. To my eyes I looked like a tired woman in her fifties. I knew that was overly harsh and did my best to rationalise my thoughts, yet at the same time, I had to accept I was in my fifties and I could look better.

Barbie, Jermaine, and Alistair were not in sight and I knew my Aston Martin was parked out front waiting for me. I could just walk out the door, deal with Charlie, and return. Would it upset them if I did?

Regardless, I needed to go. Time was not on my side.

I squinted at my reflection, told myself to be strong, and went out the door.

Today was going to be a good day.

## Getting Divorced

The meeting was inside the premises of Charlie's lawyers in Maidstone. It was a large building at the edge of the central business district and imposing. A brass plaque mounted on the wall by the large front door advised callers they were about to enter the offices of Warhurst and Clay Family Law.

They owned the whole building. Charlie really had gone to town to get the best team. He was such a greedy pig. Inside the plush reception area, decorated in a modern style with sleek textiles and neutral colours, a smart young woman in a stylish suit worked behind a desk. She was typing something while conducting a conversation via a headset.

She looked up as I approached. 'Mrs Fisher?' she enquired. It caught me by surprise. I had been about to introduce myself. 'Mr Clay and Mr Warhurst will be along to collect you in just a moment. Please take a seat.'

I chose to stand, fighting my rising butterflies. The owners of the business, or the senior partners, whichever they were, had chosen to collect me themselves. I was beginning to feel like a fish who swam into a shark tank.

True to her word, I heard conversation coming my way less than a minute later. It was partially muffled until they came through a door and into reception.

'Ah, Mrs Fisher. So lovely to finally meet you,' said a man in his sixties. His hair was a thick bush of very dark brown speckled with grey above the ears. His face was a confusion of thin red lines leading to a bulbous nose and he was both tall and thin, a shape that many would call lanky. He extended his hand. 'Geoffrey Clay.'

I shook his hand. 'Pleased to meet you.' I wasn't sure I meant it.

He shifted to his left so the other man could get to me. 'Harold Warhurst,' Clay's partner wanted to shake my hand as well. In contrast to his colleague, Harold was short. Shorter than me by a head which made him five feet and two inches. A glance downward revealed he wore Cuban heels which probably made him less than five feet in his socks. He looked less like a cadaver than Clay and had a healthy tan as if recently returned from a holiday. Also in his sixties, his hair was almost all gone, leaving an inch wide ring above his ears that went around the back of his head. It was almost pure white and matched a trim moustache.

Harold let go of my hand and swept his arm back the way they had come. 'If you are ready, Mrs Fisher, your husband is already here.'

This was it then. I was willingly swimming into the shark tank. Yes, I could refuse to sign anything and still find myself a lawyer or lawyers to fight them on my behalf, but I suspected that would put them on guard and I wanted them to feel in control and unthreatened.

Like a person walking to their execution, I stayed silent and acted meekly as they guided me along the corridor and into a meeting room.

The room was set up to intimidate me. A long table dominated it, with a pair of empty chairs at one end for the two senior men. On the far side in the chair closest to the partners sat Charlie. To his right were six more men in suits – his team of lawyers, including the two I met on the Aurelia: Hobbs and Renshaw.

They all stood up as I came into the room.

As if cued to do so, Charlie said, 'Good morning, Patricia. Thank you for coming.'

I wasted no time in doing that which I planned – I gave him one last chance. 'Are you sure you want to do this, Charlie?' He said nothing in reply. I wondered how much coaching they had given him. 'There is still time to stop this madness and avoid the damage it will do.' I gave him a sincere expression. 'I will even pick up their bill if you walk away now.'

A small snort of amusement escaped him. 'I think not, Patricia.'

Clay and Warhurst took their seats at the head of the table, Clay indicating that I should sit. There was only one chair on my side of the table, and it was directly opposite Charlie.

I placed my briefcase on the floor, shrugged off my lightweight winter coat, and sat. I didn't glare across the table. I didn't grind my teeth and think hateful thoughts. Mostly, I wondered how I had lived with him for so long because there was nothing about his behaviour now that was different from how he had always been.

Mr Clay started the meeting, wasting no time as he selected a pile of paperwork. 'We have assessed your various assets, Mrs Fisher, and those of your husband too. The house in East Malling, formally that of the Maharaja of Zangrabar is currently valued at twenty-seven million pounds. The valuation was conducted by ...' His voice became a drone to which I paid no attention. He was rattling out numbers, talking about the net worth of the cars, proposing to help me in selling the house and other assets so I could produce the half Charlie expected to get.

After what felt like half an hour, he reached the end of the list and his partner took over.

Looking my way, Mr Warhurst was smiling when he said, 'Due to the enormous discrepancy in net worth, and due to a verbal agreement to split your assets in two, we have prepared a binding document for you to sign. Can I assume that your lack of legal representation means you are agreeing to sign the document today?' His expression changed to hopeful.

'Charlie has to sign it as well, yes?' I asked.

Mr Warhurst dipped his head. 'Naturally. The document will be binding for both parties. Mr Clay and I will both act as witnesses. The money that you have been spending recently will not be taken into account. Mr Fisher has generously agreed to divide the assets as they are today.'

'Very generous,' I murmured to myself.

As if I had signalled him, Mr Warhurst shifted a neatly bound document around so it faced me. It had little sticky flags poking out where I would need to sign. There were two copies, each half an inch thick.

Mr Warhurst produced a pen and flicked the first set of paperwork open. There was my name next to a space where I could sign.

I looked up at Charlie. He appeared to be holding his breath.

'If I do this,' I asked the room while staring right into my husband's eyes, 'we split everything we own exactly in half, yes?'

Mr Warhurst fielded the question. 'Well, naturally some assets are not divisible and will either be sold, such as the house, or will be retained by one party or the other.'

'It is all laid out in the document, Mrs Fisher,' added Mr Clay. 'You may take it away and read it. That is your right.'

I looked down at the half inch thick pile of legal gibberish. There was no chance I was even going to read the pages I needed to sign.

I reached for the pen but had one more question. 'Half of what Charlie has is mine then, yes?' My question caused a few confused looks to be exchanged. 'Half of what is in his bank accounts, for example. Half of his shares, half the house we lived in together. I get half of all that?'

Mr Warhurst frowned at me, biting his lips as he fought for words. Then, speaking as if he were addressing someone too stupid to grasp the concept of what was happening, he said, 'Yes, Mrs Fisher, in theory that is correct. However, you do understand that when dividing the assets by half, you are the one who has vastly more than your husband?'

I looked across at my husband. 'I want him to sign first.'

Charlie snatched at the nearest set of paperwork, unable to move his hands fast enough. Mr Clay handed him a pen. No one spoke as Charlie squiggled his name on three separate pages in both sets of documents. He finished the final one with a flourish and all eyes in the room turned to me.

The documents were there, ready for me to sign. Half of everything. My hand shook a little when I picked up the pen.

## Gin and Tonic

'You really signed it?' asked Barbie. She sounded both incredulous and sad at the same time.

I sipped my gin and tonic. It was barely noon and I was in a bar in West Malling High Street. Leaving Clay and Warhurst Family Law, I sent a message to Barbie asking if she could meet me. I needed someone to talk to and felt that a ladies' lunch was in order.

Putting my glass down, I nodded my head. 'I signed it. Charlie and I will split everything in half.'

Barbie's face couldn't work out which emotion to go with. She was disappointed for me, and I thought perhaps she wanted to rant that I shouldn't have signed, but knowing Barbie as I did, I thought it more likely she would just wrap me up in a big hug.

'How soon will you have to move out of the house?' she asked. 'What will this mean for your job on the Aurelia? Will you need to stay here to deal with things and buy a new place so you have a home address?'

'Oh, I'm not going to sell the house,' I told her. I got the quizzical look I deserved. 'I think it's time I told you what happened after I signed the paperwork.'

I took her back to the meeting room at Clay and Warhurst Family Law.

'When I finished signing both sets of paperwork, I confirmed one of them was mine to take away. Mr Clay told me I could take either one. I picked up my briefcase and placed the documents inside. With the lid closed again and the locks snapped into place, I looked at Mr Clay and Mr Warhurst and said, "Legal and binding, yes?" to which they replied it was.'

Barbie was chewing on her bottom lip and pulling a face. 'You did something devious, didn't you, Patty?'

'I'm not sure I would use the word devious,' I replied, picking up my gin and tonic for another taste. 'I let them make all the rules. They wanted me to sign, so I signed.'

'Patty what did you do?' Barbie demanded to know.

'Well, do you remember Mr Worthington?'

Barbie's eyes rolled upward as she scoured her memory. 'Oh, the lawyer? The one who came to the ship when you got off the first time?'

I nodded. 'That's the one. It was his law firm who handled the Maharaja's request to give me the property in East Malling. They handled the transfer of deeds and all of the paperwork that would make the house and everything else mine.'

Barbie couldn't see where I was going or what I might be leading up to. 'I don't get it, Patty. Is Charlie getting the house or not?'

'The thing is I called Mr Worthington a few weeks ago when an idea occurred to me. You see there was something Charlie's lawyers failed to consider.'

'What?' Barbie begged me to tell her.

Mr Worthington's law firm handled the transfer of deeds and set all the paperwork in motion in England. But they have no control over the Zangrabar end of things. They were dealing with a law firm in Zangrabar and ... well, let's just say the paperwork there is yet to be filed.'

My startling revelation hit Barbie like a bucket of ice water to the face. 'You don't own it!' she squealed, drawing the attention of two old gentlemen quietly drinking pints at the bar. 'Oh, my goodness, Patty. You don't own the house, do you?'

'Not yet,' I smiled triumphantly.

Barbie was holding the sides of her face, her eyes as wide as saucers as the gravity of my news sank in.

'I had Mr Worthington check to confirm what stage they were at. I only got the answer yesterday afternoon. If you are wondering why I didn't tell you or anyone else about this before, it's because I didn't know. It was a wild card.'

'Oh, my goodness,' she said again. Gasping when a new thought occurred to her, she blurted, 'Did you tell them?'

I made her wait while I picked up my glass for another drink. And then made her wait a little longer while I took out my phone. Opening the app that stores videos, I placed the phone down so it faced Barbie and pressed play.

I could hear my own voice when I said, 'I did try to stop you, Charlie.'

'Why are you filming me?' he asked.

There was just no way I could keep my smile from showing any longer. 'Because I will want to remember this,' I heard myself reply. 'Charlie there is something rather vital you should know.'

Barbie watched the video with rapt fascination, as I was sure many others would when they found out about it. She howled with laughter at the face he pulled when it finally dawned on him that he'd managed to hoodwink himself. There was money to be shared, but it was his not mine. I had repeatedly offered to let him keep it all and the house, but now I was going to take him for half of everything, just like he wanted.

Listening to the video playback and sipping my gin, I knew there were only a few seconds of film left. I'd been backing toward the door with my briefcase under my arm as I used both hands to keep my phone steady. Listening to Charlie ask his lawyers what they could do now was priceless.

He was begging them to find a loophole, and it was clear he was finally learning that no matter who loses, the lawyer always wins because they present a bill either way. And that was what they did.

Charlie cried, 'But I can't pay that! I don't have the money for it! It was supposed to come out of her half!'

Barbie guffawed, wiping tears from her eyes at the sound of me laughing on the video. The footage was terrible because I hadn't been able to keep my shoulders still from laughing so hard. She watched it through twice, the second time anticipating the best bits and might have gone a third time had our lunches not arrived.

We ate seabass with fennel and bulgar wheat and talked about how soon we would leave England to catch up to the Aurelia. Alistair had plenty of holiday time he could take yet, so there was no rush for either him or me to return. Barbie wanted to get back to Hideki, of course, but I wanted to spend some time at home and see what life was like being with Alistair all day and night. I didn't bring it up, but there was also the terrible fact that when Jermaine returned to the ship, he was going to be in the Windsor Suite as the butler, and I would not be there with him. We would find time to still see each other, but it would be far from the same and it made me sad. Too sad to dwell on it.

Our lunches finished, I paid the bill, and we were about to leave when my phone rang. Expecting it to be Alistair, I was surprised to find Lady Mary's name displayed on my screen.

'Mary?' I answered.

'Patricia? Oh, thank goodness!' she blurted. 'I need your help! It's George. He's gone missing!'

The End

## Author's notes

Hello,

Typing this final note, I am looking through the window of my log cabin at the rain coming down outside. A small heater is beating away the worst of the cold, but I could really use a cup of tea on which to warm my fingers. It is early February in 2021 which means the UK and lots of other places, are in full Covid lockdown. It has been like this for almost a year now.

In this book I talk about dress uniform and being incorrectly dressed. The incorrectly dressed thing is something I heard many times in my army career. It was an in-joke often used when a person had been selected for promotion but, blithely unaware, would still be wearing the previous rank. It happened to me once. I was fortunate enough to be promoted many times, each of them coming as a surprise.

As for dress uniform, it was deigned to look smart once on, but could be devilishly awkward to get on and off. Rather than getting dressed, in some cases it was more like assembling the uniform around your various body parts. I still have one of mine in a suit carrier somewhere in the house. They had to be tailored to the individual and the individual was expected to buy it – a grant was provided. I hadn't thought about it, or the fact that it is still in the house, for several years until I started writing that chapter.

At the start of the book, I touch on the subject of stag parties – Bachelor parties for the American readers – and the association with strippers and general debauchery. I choose this time to admit that the fifty-year-old author with twenty-five-years military experience behind him has never attended a stag party. It's not that I actively avoided them, I just never knew anyone who was getting married. People either were married, or they were single. In theory I have a brother though I have only seen him once in the last two decades (at dad's funeral) and he is ten years my senior which means I was too young to have attended his. It never occurred to me to have a stag party of my own, drinking was never my thing and strippers certainly weren't.

The story of Patricia's inevitable divorce has been whirling around in my head for more than a year. Sometimes my brain works like that, but I had to write the previous nine books to get to this one. The divorce is done, Patricia is with Alistair and they are set to return to the boat shortly. First though, they must unravel what has happened to the husband of Patricia's gin-sloshed friend Lady Mary Bostihill-Swank.

I hope you are ready for some more adventure because there's plenty to come yet.

Take care

Steve Higgs

What's next for Patricia Fisher?

# Dangerous Creatures

A desperate call for help is more than enough to get Patricia and friends in motion, especially when the call is from Patricia's socialite friend and zoo owner, the rather gin-soaked Lady Mary Bostihill Swank.

Her husband, an acclaimed thriller writer has gone missing from her home but there is no ransom note and no sign of foul play. With no crime to investigate, the police are doing nothing and that's not good enough for Patricia.

Amid a backdrop of strange occurrences, which include jewellery stolen from inside Lady Mary's mansion, a note that suggests he might have been kidnapped by Bolivian freedom fighters, and a lady tiger somehow pregnant from immaculate conception, the team must wade through a confusion of clues to find the truth.

Will they be too late? Is George dead or alive? Will Lady Mary run out of gin?

With Patricia's ability to attract trouble working overtime, every hour counts, but as Patricia begins to close the net, the dangerous creatures that surround them reveal a far more deadly crime is taking place ...

**Solving mysteries can be murder.**

## A FREE Rex and Albert Story

There is no catch. There is no cost. You won't even be asked for an email address. I have a FREE Rex and Albert short story for you to read simply because I think it is fun and you deserve a cherry on top. If you have not yet already indulged, please click the picture below and read the fun short story about Rex and Albert, a ring, and a Hellcat.

When a former police dog knows the cat is guilty, what must he do to prove his case to the human he lives with?

His human is missing a ring. The dog knows the cat is guilty. Is the cat smarter than the pair of them?

A home invader. A thief. A cat. Is that one being or three? The dog knows but can he make his human listen?

More Cozy Mystery by Steve Higgs

**Baking. It can get a guy killed.**

When a retired detective superintendent chooses to take a culinary tour of the British Isles, he hopes to find tasty treats and delicious bakes …

… what he finds is a clue to a crime in the ingredients for his pork pie.

His dog, Rex Harrison, an ex-police dog fired for having a bad attitude, cannot understand why the humans are struggling to solve the mystery. He can already smell the answer – it's right before their noses.

He'll pitch in to help his human and the shop owner's teenage daughter as the trio set out to save the shop from closure. Is the rival pork pie shop across the street to blame? Or is there something far more sinister going on?

One thing is for sure, what started out as a bit of fun, is getting deadlier by the hour, and they'd better work out what the dog knows soon, or it could be curtains for them all.

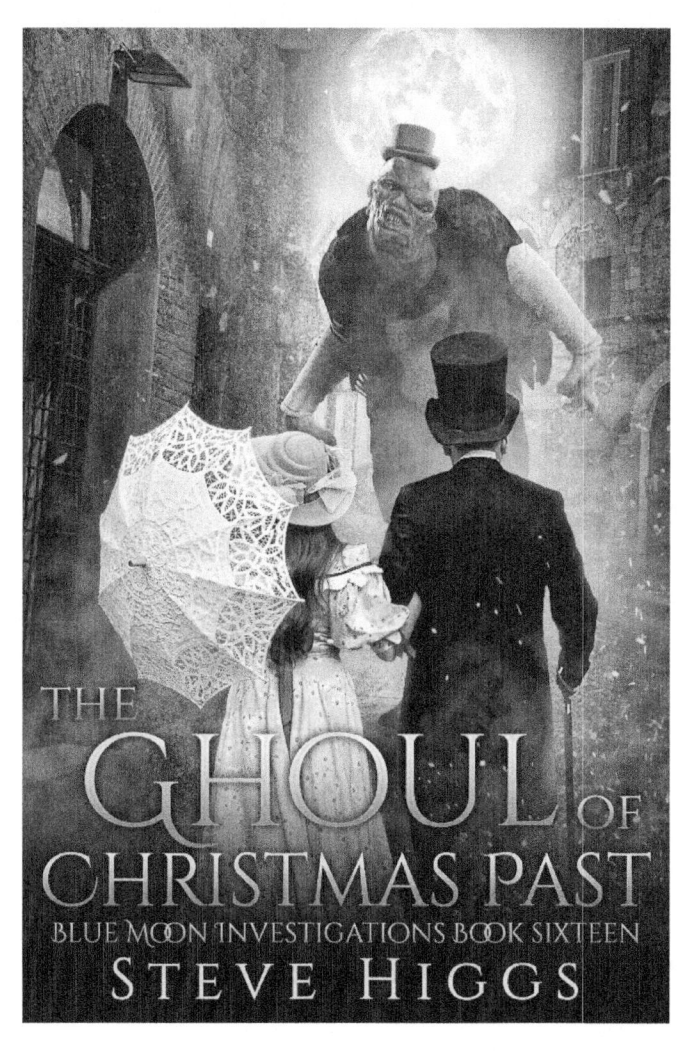

# THE GHOUL OF CHRISTMAS PAST
## BLUE MOON INVESTIGATIONS BOOK SIXTEEN
### STEVE HIGGS

Twas the day before Christmas and Michael Michaels is about to upset his wife.

Recent adventures with his son, Tempest, have piqued his need for a little more action in his life …

… but when he finds himself facing off against a giant ghoul a few hours later, he begins to think he should have listened to Mary and stayed at home.

In trouble with the police, in trouble with his wife, and generally just in trouble, Michael Michaels knows he has uncovered a mystery, but just what the heck is going on? A theft from a museum, a missing man, and a scary figure lurking in the shadows … what do they add up to?

Michael has no idea, but he's going to find out.

With a little help from a certain bookshop owner and his assistants, Tempest's dad has only a few hours to solve this case. But when the chips are down, does he have what it takes to come up with a cool line at the right time? Or is he just another pensioner trying to do more than his old bones will allow?

**The paranormal? It's all nonsense, but proving it might just get them all killed**

# More Books by Steve Higgs

## Blue Moon Investigations
Paranormal Nonsense
The Phantom of Barker Mill
Amanda Harper Paranormal Detective
The Klowns of Kent
Dead Pirates of Cawsand
In the Doodoo With Voodoo
The Witches of East Malling
Crop Circles, Cows and Crazy Aliens
Whispers in the Rigging
Bloodlust Blonde – a short story
Paws of the Yeti
Under a Blue Moon – A Paranormal Detective Origin Story
Night Work
Lord Hale's Monster
The Herne Bay Howlers
Undead Incorporated
The Ghoul of Christmas Past

## Patricia Fisher Cruise Mysteries
The Missing Sapphire of Zangrabar
The Kidnapped Bride
The Director's Cut
The Couple in Cabin 2124
Doctor Death
Murder on the Dancefloor
Mission for the Maharaja
A Sleuth and her Dachshund in Athens
The Maltese Parrot
No Place Like Home

**Patricia Fisher Mystery Adventures**

What Sam Knew

Solstice Goat

Recipe for Murder

A Banshee and a Bookshop

Diamonds, Dinner Jackets, and Death

Frozen Vengeance

Mug Shot

The Godmother

Murder is an Artform

Wonderful Weddings and Deadly Divorces

Dangerous Creatures

**Albert Smith Culinary Capers**

Pork Pie Pandemonium

Bakewell Tart Bludgeoning

Stilton Slaughter

Bedfordshire Clanger Calamity

Death of a Yorkshire Pudding

Cumberland Sausage Shocker

Arbroath Smokie Slaying

Dundee Cake Dispatch

**Felicity Philips Investigates**

To Love and to Perish

**Real of False Gods**

Untethered magic

Unleashed Magic

Early Shift

Damaged but Powerful

Demon Bound

Familiar Territory

The Armour of God

Free Books and More

Get sneak peaks, exclusive giveaways, behind the scenes content, and more. Plus, you'll be notified of Fan Pricing events when they occur and get exclusive offers from other authors because all UF writers are automatically friends.

Not only that, but you'll receive an exclusive FREE story staring Otto and Zachary and two free stories from the author's Blue Moon Investigations series.

## Yes, please! Sign me up for lots of FREE stuff and bargains!

Want to follow me and keep up with what I am doing?

Facebook

Printed in Great Britain
by Amazon